# ANOMALY

DAVID KAZZIE

GRUB CLUB PUBLISHING

ISBN-13: 978-1-7331341-3-2

ISBN-10: 1-7331341-3-1

❀ Created with Vellum

*For J & M*

# ACKNOWLEDGMENTS

To Alan Ashby, Margaret Baker, David Buckley, Kathryn Funk, K.C. Funk, Rosie Jonker, Helen Leis, Wes Walker, and Scott Weinstein for their thoughtful notes and advice on early drafts of the manuscript.

To Steven Novak for his wonderful cover design.

All errors are mine alone.

# 1

Claire Hamilton stared at the time on her phone, wondering how only four minutes had elapsed since her twins' soccer game had kicked off. She had held off checking the clock for as long as she could, certain that she could make it, if not all the way to halftime, then pretty close to it before checking. And when she had finally looked, when it felt like hours had gone by, that the referee would be reaching for her whistle at any moment, Claire's stomach flipped. Nope. Four minutes, each second elongated by the stiff wind and cold drizzle pelting down on her and the other parents jamming the sideline of Field No. 9 at the Seattle Strikers soccer facility.

The clock stared back at her unflinchingly, not caring at all.

Time did not lie.

A mere four minutes had passed.

She did the math in her head. Eight minutes left in the first half, plus the full twelve of the second, plus that wind coming in hard off the Elliott Bay that had her teeth chattering. She was glad she'd worn so many layers; she'd been burned too many times on that score. Today she wore flannel long johns underneath her jeans, two long-sleeve shirts, a sweatshirt, and a heavy coat. A wool University of Washington cap kept her head warm. This wasn't her first rodeo.

It wasn't that she didn't enjoy watching her six-year-olds, Hugo and Miranda, play soccer. She did, really and truly. She loved how they looked in their little black shorts and turquoise jerseys and tiny little shin guards and how they tried so hard, well, Miranda a little harder than Hugo. And typically, she wouldn't have it any other way. There would always be time to sip coffee and read the paper. Watching her kids just be kids filled her with a kind of joy she once believed would not be possible for her. But watching a bunch of first graders clump around a ball like malignant cells on a raw Saturday morning in October was not as appealing as, say, lying in bed with those kids and reading the *Seattle Post-Intelligencer* as the rain pattered against their roof and windows.

And when she'd called the weather hotline that morning, hopeful that the game would be canceled, her heart sank a little as the recorded voice had pleasantly informed her that all fields were open. Even the kids had been disappointed when she told them to hurry up, they needed to go. Time waited for no man or child. Their team, the Hurricanes, would be taking on the Tornadoes precisely at eight, rain or no rain.

Her phone buzzed in her hand. A text from her husband Jack. Like many of the other parents, she kept one eye on the field and the other on her screen.

*How's the game?*

She typed a reply.

*Cold.*

*What's the score?*

*No clue LOL*

She glanced up at the sideline, where her daughter was getting ready to throw the ball in. It never stopped being adorable, her tiny Miranda holding that ball over her head as she scanned the field while fielding suggestions from her coach and about twenty well-meaning but misguided parents. The tip of Miranda's tongue protruded from her mouth just so, as it often did when she was deep in concentration. With all her might, she flung the ball into play; it traveled about four feet and landed right at the shoe of an opposing player, who proceeded to kick it right back out of bounds. Circle of life.

Claire's phone buzzed again.

*This coffee is good.*

Her eyes narrowed. She had forgotten her travel mug on the counter in their rush out the door.

*You better save me some.*

She received the winking-eye emoji in return.

He would save her some, no doubt about that. Jack, a headmaster at an all-boys' private school just outside Seattle, was the husband who got up and made the coffee, brought it to her in bed every morning because she was not a morning person and the aroma of the fancy shit he brewed was enough to get her stirring. He brewed it, dressed it up just the way she liked, two sugars and a splash of creamer, brought it to their bedroom. How lovely it would be to sit up in bed and lazily enjoy her coffee, but he drove a hard bargain. The deal was that she couldn't have a sip until both her feet were on the floor. It wasn't a bad deal.

It was, in fact, an excellent deal she had ended up with, and so it always flummoxed her to become hyper-aware of the locket hanging from her neck at the very moment she counted her blessings and good fortune. Even now, her hand had drifted to the hollow of her throat, tracing the outline of the necklace held snugly in place by her sweatshirt. The locket had a funny way of doing that. She could take it off and close that door forever, but that didn't seem right.

"Big game tonight," she heard someone say.

She glanced to her right; another parent - *maybe Clementine's father? She could never keep all the names straight* - was pointing at the cap on her head. They were already six weeks into the season, but she had barely gotten to know any of the other parents. They seemed nice enough. But there was just never enough time to establish a real connection with these people, so why bother. It was a little depressing, to be honest, to know you were at that stage of life where you didn't want to meet anyone new. There just wasn't enough time.

"Oh, right, the game," Claire said.

The University of Washington was playing host to its rival, the Oregon Ducks, that night under the lights. Claire didn't care for football, but Jack was a die-hard Ducks fan, having earned his bachelor's and master's degrees there.

"If we can win this one, we're in the driver's seat for the Pac-12 title," said the man.

"I'm sorry, what was your name again?" Claire said.

"Jason," he said. "I'm Clementine's dad."

"Claire," she replied. "The twins."

"Nice to meet you. Miranda is quite the spitfire."

"Thank you," Claire said.

"So what year did you graduate?"

"Actually, I'm a professor there," Claire said.

"Oh. What do you teach?"

"Astrobiology," she said.

"What's that?"

"It's the study of the origin and evolution of life, both here on Earth and elsewhere," she said, awaiting the inevitable reaction to her canned response. People meant well when they learned what her field of study was, and there really was intellectual curiosity percolating. All good things. But it always came back to the same thing.

"You mean like aliens?"

She smiled.

"Haven't found any yet."

"You think there are?"

"I do," she said, and she meant it. "The universe is simply too big for us to be the only life form. We've just started to scratch the surface of what there is to know."

"Wow," came the reply.

"That being said, I think there's a good chance we never find it."

"Why?"

"Same reason. Because the universe is so big."

"Then why study it?"

"Someone needs to set the table," she said. "Future scientists will make breakthroughs, but they need something to build on."

"Be pretty cool if we did," he said.

"Yeah," Claire said, with an eye toward agreeability. She still wasn't sure she ever wanted to make contact. She didn't know if the Jasons of the world could handle it because she wasn't even sure that the Claires of the world could handle it.

"Well, good luck," Jason said, as though she had signed up to run a half-marathon rather than devote her life to perhaps the most important scientific work in human history.

"Thanks," she said, and the conversation fizzled out.

A ripple of depression. Interest in her work, in the sciences generally, in what made it all go was often shallow, unless, of course, the alien thing came up. She did believe there was life out there, somewhere, because it simply did not make sense otherwise. The firm belief always amused her, this faith she had, a woman of science and logic and reason. Claire had left the church long ago and struggled when talk turned to God and blessings and prayers and all of it. She could not, for the life of her, understand how people took on faith alone the existence of an all-powerful, all-knowing deity; yet, she believed just as heartily in the existence of life beyond her home planet.

On the plus side, this little conversation had eaten up a good bit of time. Just as her fingers had stiffened into frozen rictus and her cheeks burned with wind, the referee blew her whistle to signal the end of the game. While another mom handed out snacks, Claire began packing away her chair, noticing that it was probably time to replace it. The mesh had torn and the metal rods were orange with rust. It seemed like they had just bought these chairs, but that's the way time worked. Everything in her life always seemed like it had just happened. Momentous and mundane, events raced into the past while the memory of them burned brightly in your mind. Time was the enemy of all things.

It was a bit of a struggle to feed the folded-up chair into the fraying bag, leaving her to wonder why they didn't make the opening for the bag just a few inches bigger in diameter. The cinch rope always got hung up on a chair leg and it took forever to get it just right. As she slung the chair bag over her shoulder, her twins, Miranda and Hugo, came bounding toward her, their sweet faces warm and pink in the cold. Steam curled off their sweaty heads.

"Mommy, did you see me?" each of them said, almost simultaneously.

"I did, guys, you were both so awesome."

"Did we win?" Miranda asked. "I bet we won."

"You played like a team," replied Claire, not having the first damn clue who won the game. They didn't even keep score at this age. Well, not officially at least. There was one dad who kept score religiously and yelled at his son after each game. As the old saying went, *if you don't know who the asshole is, it's you.* Always getting on his kid about his positioning, about his hustle, and the kid would stand there, his face holding together like porcelain that may or may not shatter. More often than not, it held. She didn't know where the kid found the fortitude not to break down crying, but he did. He would either become a billionaire or a serial killer. Only time would tell.

"You always say that," Miranda cut in. "Can we have our snack now?"

"No," Claire said. She never understood the purpose of post-game snacks. Burn two hundred calories during the game and then inhale four hundred calories worth of fruit gummies. "You guys ate before we left."

"Aww," whined Hugo.

"Let's go, guys."

They fell in line behind her as they made their way to the car. It was Saturday, and they had nothing else scheduled for the day, which was both a curse and a blessing. At six, the twins were right at that age where they could entertain themselves for a bit, but just for a bit. They got along well enough, but rarely a day went by without some pitched battle being waged between them.

It had started drizzling, and rain was forecast through tonight, which meant that it would be an indoor type day.

They could bundle up, drink hot chocolate, do that *hygge* thing they did in Norway. Curl up with blankets and books and movies. Feed them chicken nuggets and then order Chinese for her and Jack while they watched the game. Hugo loved watching football with his daddy.

"Everyone strapped in?" she asked after she had loaded the chair in the back of the Toyota Highlander.

"Yes, Mommy," they replied, again almost in unison.

Both were able to buckle themselves into their car seats, which turned out to be a more significant milestone than she had ever imagined. When they were small, it had taken a good ten minutes to get them strapped in; it had been one of those things that ate up far more time than you realized, little temporal vampires. That's what they didn't tell you about parenting, how long even the littlest things took. Oh, your kid is dressed? Bravo. How about another ten minutes fighting about shoes and then another twenty when your son decides to change his shirt for the third time?

Every drive with the twins was different; sometimes they bickered, and sometimes they got along. Hugo was the cut-up of the pair and every once in a while he would have his sister laughing so hard she was crying. Claire stole a peek in the rearview mirror and saw Hugo making weird scrunched-up faces at Miranda, who was trying very hard to ignore him.

About halfway home, her phone rang.

"It's Daddy!" cried out Hugo, leaning forward to catch a glimpse at the Caller ID on the vehicle's information screen.

She clicked open the line using the button on the steering wheel.

"You save some of that coffee for me?" she asked.

"Where are you?" he asked, ignoring her question.

The tone of his voice chilled her more than the blustery

conditions at the field had. If she hadn't had the kids in the car with her, she would've thought he was calling to tell her something had happened to one of them, that Hugo had vanished from the park, that Miranda had choked on a piece of hot dog and she'd better get to the hospital as soon as she could. It was the worst thing about being a parent, the constant worry that gnawed at you like the ocean eating away at the beach. Anytime the phone rang and she wasn't with them, her heart froze, her mind racing to the worst-case scenario. It felt like she was falling, her stomach pushed up against her rib cage until she confirmed otherwise.

"What's wrong?"

"When will you be home?"

"Ten minutes," she said, noticing a slight tremor in her voice. "What happened?"

"You've got visitors."

Her heart fluttered.

"Who?"

"NASA."

Claire struggled to keep her focus on the road. It had been a long time since she'd spoken to anyone from NASA. More than a decade.

"What do they want?" she asked.

"They said it's about Peter."

*Peter.*

Peter Abbott.

Claire's first husband.

Gone twelve years now. Almost thirteen.

His body. They had finally found his body.

She needed to pull over.

Claire swung over to the right lane, forgetting to check her blind spot and earning a sharp horn blast from the car coming up quickly on her rear bumper. The other driver, an older gentleman with a bald head, slipped over into the passing lane; Claire glanced over in time to catch him giving her a middle-fingered salute that she probably deserved. She gave him a sheepish wave as he sped away.

She merged over once more, into the breakdown lane, and brought the vehicle to a stop. The kids said nothing, instinctively knowing something was amiss. She ran her hands through her light brown hair and took a deep breath. The car was quiet but for the soft purr of the engine and metronomic ticking of the hazard lights she had activated.

"Babe, you still there?"

Jack was still on the line.

"Did they say what it's about?"

"They won't tell me."

"OK. We'll be home soon."

She wondered what her voice sounded like to Jack. The pitch, the tone, the tremor. Was there a way she should sound? She should care a little bit, of course, but if she sounded like she cared too much, it would make things weird.

"OK," he said. "Love you."

He clicked off before she had a chance to reply, maybe unsure whether she would say it back to him. What could be worse than that, after all, telling someone you loved them and not hearing it in return? She did love him, deeply so, but part of her was glad he'd hung up quickly because then she wouldn't have to worry about how she sounded when she said it. Now it was all she could think of, how her voice sounded to Jack.

"Mommy, why did we stop?" Miranda asked.

Claire glanced at them in the rearview mirror. Hugo was chewing the inside of his cheek; Miranda twirled a lock of her hair. Both sets of eyes were locked in on her rearview mirror.

"I was just talking with Daddy about something important."

"What?" Miranda asked.

The more inquisitive child, she was never mollified by the watered-down explanations and non-answers that parents loved feeding their children. She questioned, she probed, she hated not knowing things, even when those things would not make sense to her six-year-old mind. In a way, she reminded her of Peter. It was a little weird. They had never met, of course, they would never meet. It wasn't that she looked like Peter or that they shared any similar mannerisms. But maybe the part of Peter that had spilled into Claire long ago had cascaded into her little girl, like one of those multi-level fountains.

"There are some people I used to work with waiting at the house," she said. "I just need to talk to them for a bit."

"About what?"

"I'm not really sure," Claire replied, checking her side view mirror as she began rolling down the breakdown lane again.

"Who's Peter?" Miranda asked.

"Is he your boyfriend?" Hugo asked, which drew an embarrassed giggle from his sister.

Claire smiled and felt tears well up in her eyes.

"I'll explain everything later," she said, merging back into traffic. "I promise."

TEN MINUTES LATER, she turned into Langtree Farms, their vanilla-named subdivision, her heart rate inversely proportional to the distance from her house. By the time their street came into view, her pulse was throbbing in her ears, her chest so tight she could barely breathe. Their house, a forty-year-old colonial with a big country porch, stood at the bottom of a cul de sac, flanked by half a dozen other homes of similar construction. They had lived here for six years, closing on the place a couple of months before the twins were born. It was a quiet neighborhood where they got along with their neighbors and the kids could play outside until it got dark.

Hard to believe it had already been six years. It was a good place, a warm place that felt like home. When she was inside that structure, nothing but brick and beams and drywall and wooden floor joists, there was no place else she wanted to be. It was where they marked the kids' heights on the door jamb of the laundry room, where the kitchen smelled like garlic more often than it didn't, where she wanted to be when the rain was pouring down.

But as she neared her home, with a big black Suburban parked awkwardly against the curb curling around the front yard, it seemed different, smaller, like it belonged to someone else, like it had never been home at all. A strong sense of déjà vu washed over her. Easing down the street, that Suburban parked right there, the kids in the back seat, the gunmetal sky spitting down cold rain. It reminded her of the day they had come to tell her about Peter, even though it had been sunny that day, even though she hadn't lived here then, even though she wouldn't meet Jack for another two years.

"Oooh, look at that truck, Mommy," Hugo said.

She smiled nervously as she eased down the driveway, parking next to Jack's Jeep. The kid loved trucks. Hugo was much more laid back than his sister. He was a bright kid, but he didn't need to know everything right then and there. He lived in the moment. He feared nothing because he didn't like to think that far ahead. If you didn't think about what came next, there was nothing to be afraid of.

While the kids unbuckled their seatbelts and collected their gear, Claire took a few moments to collect her thoughts, settle herself. After all, this was a day she had long hoped for. Until Peter vanished, she had never understood people who talked about needing a body for closure, even when that person had been gone for years. But she got it now, yes, indeed, she did. Death was painful, she had learned that from her mother's passing, but a disappearance was a hole that was never filled, a phantom limb that continued to itch.

They went in through the side door, Claire directing the kids to the laundry room to unload their soccer gear, smelly shin guards and muddy cleats. She could hear muted voices in the family room on the other side of the corridor in which she now stood. When they were done, she sent them upstairs to the playroom with instructions to start a movie while she and Daddy met with their guests.

"I don't want to hear any arguing," she said. "Do you understand?"

"Yes, ma'am."

She pulled them close and kissed the tops of their heads, holding them tightly, feeling uneasy as she did so. The day that she would have to tell them about her past had always been coming, but now that it was here, she wasn't ready for it. She wasn't ready to tell them that for them to exist, she'd had to lose the great love of her life, she'd had to walk through the darkest of valleys that could be expected of someone who was barely thirty years old.

They disappeared up the stairs and she stood alone in the dim kitchen for a moment, trying to find her bearings as her two worlds, separated by a research mission gone terribly wrong, collided.

$$\sim$$

CLAIRE FIRST MET Peter Abbott fifteen years ago at Penn State, where both were working on their doctorates – Peter in Geosciences and Astrobiology, and Claire in Biology and Astrobiology. The Astrobiology program was small, only a few dozen students in total. Claire was deep into her dissertation, a treatise on abiotic sources of organic life. Medical school had been the original plan, but her fascination with the stars and the galaxies had long held a tight grip on her, always pushing her toward the heavens. She'd harbored hope of being selected as an astronaut someday, but the odds of that were incredibly low.

It was early March, State College under the blanket of a late-season snowfall. Claire was a month or so away from finishing the first draft of her dissertation, full of doubt and self-loathing. She'd spent the afternoon reviewing the week's work, wondering how anyone would take her seriously. Her work felt old, tired, derivative. Her friend Simone Farrow, another grad student, swung by around seven with a bottle of Pinot, undeterred by the snowfall rapidly piling up outside.

It was probably a night to stay in and drink by the fire, but Claire been cooped up for two straight days; she desperately needed to blow off some steam and a single bottle of wine between them wasn't going to cut it. And when they were sitting at the bar, each into a pint of Guinness, she decided it had been worth the effort to pull on the snow pants and the heavy coat and the boots to sit there in the noisy squall of young people laughing and flirting and setting the stage for bad decisions to be made later.

Peter showed up during the second pint; he and Simone knew each other from undergrad at Ohio State. Claire liked him right away; he was soft-spoken but funny, possessed of a dry wit. Simone confessed that they'd had a brief fling when they were in college; the DNA of a shared past was stamped all over their interactions.

Then, as fate would have it, Simone called it an early night, suddenly feeling unwell. Initially, Claire had thought it a ploy to leave her alone with Peter, a bit of matchmaking at play, but as it turned out, Simone had spiked a fever just in the couple hours since she had darkened Claire's door. Claire touched her hand to Simone's forehead, and yes, indeed, she was burning up. Simone had come down with the flu, knocking her out of commission for a week, a turn of events that they all joked about at their wedding a year later.

Their relationship blossomed slowly at first and then exploded all at once. Claire hadn't really been looking for anything serious, but truth be told, single men and single women didn't become friends for the sole sake of being friends. She once thought they could, but friendships spanning the sexes always proved to be fertile ground for something more. And at thirty-one, she was in a place where she was fine being by herself; nevertheless, she found herself wanting to be around Peter when he wasn't around, being disappointed when their time together came to an end.

Two months later, she invited him over for dinner, serving scallops and risotto, wearing the jeans and camisole top she thought she looked the best in, plying him with wine, the whole nine yards. The risotto, which she had made herself, had come out a tad crunchy, something he had jokingly remarked on. His comment had annoyed her a bit, but otherwise, it had been a lovely evening. She went out of her way to make it so awkwardly obvious that there would be no question about her interest, touching him on his elbow, even squeezing his hip a couple of times. She wanted to be with him, and not just in a fist-bumping kind of way. It wasn't like any other feeling she'd had about a man, where she'd waste time wondering if this guy a friend had set her up with was *the one* or maybe that one she'd met at a faculty mixer had been *the one*.

She saw the folly of that now; if you had to wonder, then he wasn't. Now she just knew. And if he didn't feel the same way, although she believed that he did, she wanted to know that too. She didn't want to become one of those women who lived in fear of rejection.

Finally, somewhere around the second glass of wine, he had gotten the message. They were sitting at her small kitchen table, the bowls empty, chatting about this or that, she couldn't even remember anymore.

"This is a date," he said suddenly, the glass suspended between his lips and the table.

It was so disarming, so lovely, that her heart felt like it would burst from her chest.

"I want it to be," she said.

He set the glass of wine down, holding his hand out to her. She took it, sliding her other hand around the back of his neck, pulling him closer until their lips touched and from there, it was the most natural thing in the world. It didn't feel awkward; it felt like it was the thing that they should have been doing since the very beginning. She broke the kiss and led him to the bedroom, where they loudly and joyously drove a stake through the heart of their platonic friendship. She hadn't been with many men in her life – three before Peter, to be exact – but it had never been like that with anyone else.

A cough from the next room broke her out of her daydream, and she was back in the hallway, just outside the mudroom, the air rank with the tangy aroma of the kids' sweaty soccer clothes. A wave of guilt washed over her, her mind focused on Peter's body, the way he'd made her feel, while Jack and these other men waited for her.

"Babe?"

Jack's head poked around the corner. His handsome face was tight with worry. He looked like he'd aged a decade since she'd kissed him goodbye this morning. Before today, the life and death of Peter Abbott had just been a story, a history lesson from his wife's past. Now it had come crashing into his life, into his home, like a hurricane, and there was no way to know what kind of damage it was going to do.

"Hey," she said, trying to sound calm. If she remained calm, then he would too. "Just taking care of the kids' soccer stuff."

*See how fucking calm I am? So calm I can deal with mud-caked cleats while men from NASA cool their jets in my house!*

She followed Jack into the family room. Two men - one black, one white – stood up as she entered the room. The black guy, the younger of the two, was clean-shaven and bald. He was quite tall and barely fit on the loveseat. His partner, a heavy-set redhead, Claire remembered from before. Eugene Murphy. Director of the ORCHID mission. He'd been the one to break the news to her a dozen years ago. He looked about the same as he did that day he'd sat in the living room of the small house she'd shared with Peter, albeit with a few more lines on his face.

"Ms. Hamilton," he said, still cleaving to the honorific as he had back then. He was a Boston native, but the accent had softened a bit in the intervening years.

"Gene," she replied. "It's been a long time."

"It has."

"What brings you by?" she asked, her voice small. The effect their presence had had on her was profound. It was like the iceberg that had doomed Titanic, rupturing something inside her; seeing that Suburban outside, seeing Gene in her living room had brought it all back, all swirling back to her. All the grief and sadness rushed in like the ice-cold seawater of the North Atlantic.

"We need you to come with us," Murphy said.

"His body," she said. "You found his body."

Murphy cut his gaze to Jack for a second before looking back at Claire.

"Not exactly."

"Then what?"

"We need to do this privately," he repeated.

"Just say it," she snapped, a hint of smoke in her voice.

"Look," Jack said, "you tell her why you're here, or she's not going anywhere."

He took a step toward the men. Jack wasn't a big guy, but he was fiercely strong and knew how to use it. He'd been an Army Ranger who'd done two tours in Iran before a compound leg fracture suffered in a Humvee accident earned him an honorable discharge.

Murphy held up a hand, glanced at his partner.

The man nodded.

"Very few people know what I'm about to tell you," Murphy said.

"OK."

A thought took hold of Claire and refused to let go. It took her breath away, and she wanted to be wrong, she prayed she was wrong because if she were right, her life as she knew it was over.

"You should sit," Murphy said.

Her legs had been trembling underneath her and she was glad for the opportunity to sit down. Murphy came over and sat next to her. He leaned forward, put his elbows on his knees, tapped his fingertips together lightly. He coughed lightly into his hand.

"Look, there's no easy way to tell you this," he said. "Peter's still alive."

## 3

Still alive.

Peter was still alive.

Claire gripped the armrest tightly, as though she might fall over otherwise. She glanced around the room, first pausing on Murphy's face and then on his partner's; both men were watching her with something like detached curiosity. She didn't look at Jack yet, not ready to make eye contact with him; she wasn't sure she wanted to see his face, and she sure as hell didn't want him to see her face. Not just yet. She became conscious of herself sitting here, of her very existence, that all she was or would ever be was contained in this five-foot-eight package of meat and bones. Did anyone ever stop and think just how weird it was to simply exist, to be conscious of one's existence?

She parted her lips, as though getting ready to say something but nothing came out; the only sound she heard was that of her dry lips peeling apart. She took a deep breath and tried again.

"Wait," she said, lightly covering her eyes with her hands. "Wait a minute. Let me just think."

She heard herself saying these words but did not understand why she was saying them.

"Claire?"

It was Jack's voice. She looked at him finally, but his face was a cipher.

"Yes?"

"Are you okay?"

She slung her arm around Murphy and pulled him tightly against her. Just a couple of old friends hugging it out. All they needed was an iPhone so they could take a selfie and post it on Facebook.

"Did you hear what he said?" she said, not really to anyone in particular.

Jack ran his fingers through his hair, a nervous tic of his.

"He's still alive," she whispered. "Still alive."

"I know this is hard," Murphy said, gently easing his way out of her embrace.

"Where is he?" she asked. "We had a funeral, you know. You were there."

"I know."

She looked up at Jack.

"It was beautiful," she said. "Peter didn't believe in God, but his mom did, and she insisted on a deluxe Methodist service. Flowers and the organ and it just had everything."

She turned her attention back to Murphy.

"Remember the funeral?"

He nodded.

"It was very nice," he replied.

"So where is he?" she asked.

Time to get down to brass tacks, as they said.

"Still on the island."

Still on the island. On that little sliver of rock a thousand miles from anywhere, where he'd planned to spend two weeks and ended up spending the rest of his life, or at least the part that mattered.

"Oh good, because for a moment, I thought you were going to tell me he was waiting in the back seat of that Suburban out there."

"No," Murphy said, chuckling softly, the way someone did when they weren't sure if they were supposed to laugh but maybe they were a little bit.

"You told me he was dead," Claire said. "You told me they were all dead."

"I know."

"You came to our house and sat in our living room, and you told me he was dead."

She looked at Jack again.

"They told me he was dead," she repeated, a bloom of panic coloring her voice.

She felt like she had to defend herself to Jack. As though she had known all along that Peter was still alive and had kept it hidden from him.

*It's this thing I do. I wait until my husband goes on a research mission and then I marry some other guy!*

A ridiculous notion, but she still felt guilty.

"Babe, I know."

She turned back to Murphy.

"He's been on that island for twelve years? Twelve fucking years?"

"It appears so."

"How is that even possible? How did you not know?"

Murphy glanced at his partner, whose face betrayed no emotion. It was like stone.

"That's all we can really talk about here," he said.

"Are you going to get him?"

"Again, I can't disclose anything else here."

"Well, where can you disclose it?" she snapped.

"Back at Special Projects," said Murphy's partner, breaking his silence for the first time. "At Ames."

He was talking about the Ames Research Center in Moffett Field, about forty miles south of San Francisco, the heart of Silicon Valley. Ames was one of NASA's ten field centers, focusing on aeronautics, space exploration, and, as Murphy's partner alluded to, special projects.

She stood up quickly and immediately felt lightheaded. She sat back down.

"Is he okay?" she asked.

Again, she was mindful of her tone, and she hated herself for it. She hated Murphy and his partner for putting her through this, she even hated Jack a little bit right now, and she didn't even know why. A man Jack had never met had just dropped an atomic bomb in the middle of his marriage and she was mad at him? She could only imagine what was going on in that head of his, but she put that out of her mind for now. She would have to deal with that later.

"We think so."

"I don't know what I'm supposed to say," she said. "What am I supposed to say?"

The three men remained silent.

"I mean, Jesus, somebody say something helpful."

"Ms. Hamilton," said Murphy's partner.

"You," she said, interrupting him. "Who are you? What's your name?"

"Agent Berry."

"You with NASA?"

"No."

"Who are you with?"

"Defense Intelligence Agency," he replied. "As I was

trying to say, I think it would be in your best interest to go with us to Ames. You'll be back tomorrow."

Claire's breathing was uneven and she felt hot. A bead of sweat traced a line down her back. She felt herself salivating.

"Excuse me," she said, clapping a hand over her mouth as she ran for the powder room. She made it just in time, bending over the toilet bowl as her breakfast came up, her coffee, maybe even dinner from the night before. When she was cleaned out, she wiped her mouth with a section of toilet paper and flushed it all away. They'd had tacos for dinner, the kids' favorite. It was a whole production, setting out the taco bar, the shells and the toppings and Miranda accusing Hugo of using too much sour cream. The very last dinner before this sudden detonation of their lives. She sighed, letting out a shaky breath. Her skin felt cold and clammy but her stomach had settled down.

Slowly, she made her way back to her feet. Jack stood at the doorway, his arms crossed at his chest.

So many questions.

"Hey," he said.

"I'm sorry," she said, even though she didn't know what she was sorry for.

"We'll figure this out."

She took a deep breath and let it out slowly.

"OK," she said.

He held a hand out to her. She took it and slowly climbed to her feet. She looked into his brown eyes, trying to distill something from them. Some forgiveness, some peace, some understanding from him that he knew deep down that this would change nothing between them. She didn't know if that were the case, but it was important that someone hold it together. Couldn't have both pilot and co-pilot freaking out as they hit some turbulence.

"Do you want to go with them?"

"Don't you think I should?"

She saw him working it out in his head. Of course she should go, but that didn't mean he wanted her to go. She would walk out that door with Murphy and Agent Berry and there would be no way to know what version of Claire Hamilton would come back to him. Would it be the one who'd awakened next to him that morning, the one who'd woken up feeling a bit frisky, climbing on top of him, taking him inside her for a Saturday morning quickie just before the twins had woken up? Or would it be the Claire of thirteen years ago, a stranger once more, a woman he never would have met but for this terrible thing cleaving her life in two?

He nodded his head, his jaw clenched, his lips tightened into a thin pink slash.

"You need to go."

"What about the kids?"

"I can handle them," he said. "I am their dad, you know."

"I know," she said with a bit more pop than she had intended. She looked away, toward the sink, hoping he would let it pass. He remained quiet.

The kids. How would this affect them?

The news, less than ten minutes old, was hitting her on so many fronts now, too many for her to keep up with.

"Let me have a minute to clean up," she said. "I'll be right out."

"OK."

He rejoined their guests in the family room, leaving her alone in the bathroom. She checked herself in the mirror; small petechiae had erupted on her face from the force of her emesis. She was pale and her eyes were puffy. She had not cried. She didn't know if she was supposed to.

A wave of panic washed through her. She didn't know what to do. There was no playbook for this. This was supposed to be over and done with. Checkmarks next to each of the five stages of grief.

Denial.

*He can't be dead. He's on a research mission. He's thirty-four years old and we've been married for two years. They'll find him. He's just lost. He'll turn up.*

Anger.

*Why did he fucking go? Didn't he have some intuition that the whole thing was going to go bad? Why wasn't he more careful? Whose fault was it? She was going to sue NASA, she was going to sue her Congressman, she was going to sue the federal government, she was going to sue the company that built the helicopter, she was going to sue everyone.*

Bargaining.

*If they could just find his body, it would help so much. She could cremate him as he'd wanted, scatter his ashes at Moab in Utah, where he loved to visit. If they could just find his body, she could say goodbye and she could move on.*

Depression.

*Won't be getting out of bed today. Nope. The amount of effort needed to get out of bed and go do this life thing, nope and thank you, I'll sit here in bed, eat pizza rolls and flip through these old magazines, the massively thick ones dedicated to getting your life in order, 10 Quick Tips to Get Your Recipes Organized.*

Acceptance.

*He was gone.*

This had been the hardest stage because without a body, your mind refused to close the door all the way. You always left it a little cracked, just enough to let it in hope, false hope, of course, but still a tiny bit of hope. No matter how many times she leaned into that door, it would not close, as though the foundation had shifted and nothing fit like it was supposed to. But the door was closed enough that she could move on, open enough that a bit of hope and nostalgia still seeped through it from time to time like a cold draft.

What was this now? *Psych!* The little known sixth stage of grief?

*LOL JUST KIDDING HE WAS NEVER REALLY DEAD!*

The worst kind of surprise. Yes. This was even worse than finding out he had died. You always worried about losing your loved ones, but once it happened, that was it. At least you could take comfort in its finality. Peter was dead. He was never coming back. Certainly, the fact they had never found his body had kept the door of hope open a bit longer. But a month went by, then six, then a year and no trace. It wasn't like he'd gone out for cigarettes and never come back and maybe he had restarted his life somewhere. He had died in that helicopter crash.

Still though, for years, she imagined seeing him in public, at the grocery store, in traffic, even at the restaurant Jack had taken her to for their first wedding anniversary. That experience had left her sweaty and nauseated, her pork tenderloin half-eaten on the plate. Always out of the corner of her eye, a flash, a shimmer of familiarity, and her throat would close up as she moved in, knowing it wasn't him, but needing to be sure. And of course, it never was.

She ran some water into a cupped hand to rinse out her mouth. Then she splashed some water on her face and smoothed out her hair with a brush she left under the sink. When she felt presentable again, she went back out to the living room, telling herself she still didn't know what she was going to do but knowing that was just a big fat lie.

The men stood when she entered the room.

"I can be ready in half an hour," she said.

"We'll wait in the car," Berry said.

## 4

Claire rode shotgun while Agent Berry drove.

She said nothing as they pulled away from the house, her kids' sweet faces pressed up against the windows. Miranda's face betrayed no emotion at the news their mother was leaving for an overnight trip; Hugo's eyes had filled with tears as she packed. She'd been away from them for a night or two in the past, but never on such short notice. Usually there was time to prep them, to write little notes for them to find each day, to tell them she loved them more than the moon and the stars and all the planets, like the ones depicted in the tattoo on her ankle, to tell them that they would have so much fun with Daddy and they'd better brush their teeth after all that dessert.

"That's a nice family you've got there," Murphy said about twenty minutes into the drive.

She ignored him and no one spoke again during the ride. Murphy fiddled with his iPhone and would sigh occasionally, almost as though he were sulking. Berry was all business, hands at ten and two, back straight, eyes always scanning the road, checking the mirrors. He never once exceeded the speed limit. Traffic was light on this Saturday morning and they made good time. Under the clouds and the rain, the city flowing by looked different than she remembered. It hit her all at once how much the city had changed since she'd moved here a decade ago. New residential developments, new green space, enough new restaurants for virtually every man, woman, and child in the greater Seattle area. You didn't notice things when they changed a little bit at a time; you adapted quickly to little changes even if they added up to very big changes. You only focused on the big moments, which were much rarer.

They made it to Seattle-Tacoma International Airport a little before eleven in the morning. Berry followed the signs for General Aviation, where she presumed a charter plane awaited them. She flew out of Sea-Tac on business a few times a year, but like the city they'd just traversed to get here, the airport looked brand new to her once again. To her north, a jetliner streaked down the runway before climbing hard and then banking south. Flight never ceased to amaze her; in the minute it took to travel a mile down the long service road, the Oceanic Airlines MD-300 had rocketed into the distance, shrinking into a speck.

Berry slowed and turned onto a smaller access road serving a trio of hangars. He drove past the first two and made a hard left into the open third hangar. Inside awaited a sleek Gulfstream jet, its staircase extended to the tarmac.

"You go with him," Berry said. "I'll bring your bag."

She found a seat and strapped herself in. Within moments of Berry joining them onboard, the jet was rolling out of the hangar and taxiing toward the queue. It paused briefly, waiting for clearance, before screaming down the runway. She had never been on a small jet like this; its power and speed surprised her. As the aircraft broke free of gravity's pull, her stomach dropped, and she took a deep breath. The pilot banked hard to the left and brought them on a southerly heading. She could just make out the Pacific, cloaked with mist and fog at lower altitudes; it made for a bit of a bumpy ride. Then they were above the weather; the jet settled into a smooth rhythm. It was mostly clear at this altitude, roughly eight miles above the ground. Murphy read a book; Berry, in the seat facing her, worked on a laptop. He seemed to sense her looking at him and returned her gaze. His intense eyes were very dark brown, almost black. She wondered if he had known Peter, if they had met during that supposedly routine mission to explore a large meteor on an uncharted island in the South Pacific, about a thousand miles east of Australia.

Two hours later, the Gulfstream began its descent into San Francisco, where the weather mirrored that back home. A bit of chop made her stomach flip again as they dropped through the clouds and wouldn't that be something to die in a plane crash before she found out anything and with Peter outliving her rather than the other way around. Her ears popped uncomfortably as they descended under the cloud cover.

But the plane landed without incident, and within minutes of touching down, they were in another black Suburban, en route to Ames. On the way, Berry stopped at a sub shop and bought sandwiches for the group. Claire wasn't particularly hungry, but her stomach had settled since this morning. So she ate, knowing she would need her strength. The coming days and weeks were going to be rough on her, on Jack, on the whole family, and she would need to be on top of her game. Skipping meals would be a fool's errand.

She wondered about Jack and the kids; maybe they were

eating lunch right now, maybe they were sitting at the breakfast nook dunking chicken nuggets into ranch dressing while Daddy tried to focus on them. Again she was reminded of the brutal unfairness of it all. At least she was in a position to get some answers, away from the chaos of parenthood. Jack was alone, cut off, his mind in two places at once.

She finished her lunch as they arrived at the outskirts of the Ames Research Center. NASA Ames was a huge installation, home to more than two thousand research personnel and an annual budget of nearly one billion dollars. Claire had been here many times, as Ames was NASA's primary campus for work in astrobiology, the search for habitable planets, and robotic lunar exploration. Although not a NASA flight center, Ames had directed NASA's Pioneer programs in the 1960s and 1970s.

The rain picked up as they approached the main checkpoint, a small outbuilding with an orange roof. To their right was an asphalt lot, in the middle of which sat an odd-looking oval-shaped building resembling a large egg. An electronic display reading *Complete Stop for I.D. Checks* blinked disinterestedly in front of the booth. They waited while a security team inspected the vehicle with dogs and mirrors. Berry flashed his identification to the guard, who lifted the security gate and waved them through.

"Gene?" Claire said as they wound through the outskirts of the campus.

"Yeah?"

"How long have you known?"

"A week."

Then a more frightening question occurred to her.

"Did you have any reason to believe he was alive?"

This query scared her because the answer could mean

they let her live her life without telling her the whole story. There was a big difference between *he's dead*, and *well, we're pretty sure he's dead, don't swear us to that.*

Berry glanced at Murphy through the rearview mirror.

"No."

A few minutes later, they entered a large traffic circle, ringed by a dozen buildings of roughly equal size. This was the heart of Ames. Since it was the weekend, there weren't many people or cars, but there were a few milling about. Berry parked at the far side of the circle, in front of a two-story glass and steel building with mirrored windows, and the trio alighted from the vehicle. The building bore no markings. As they neared the building entrance, a woman exited and approached them. She was short, dressed in a beige pantsuit.

"Hope Martindale," she said, extending a hand to Claire. "Nice to see you, Ms. Hamilton."

Claire shook the woman's hand, trying to recall if they'd met before. She could not remember.

Martindale acknowledged Berry and Murphy with a subtle nod of her head.

"If you'll follow me," she said, "they're waiting for you."

Claire followed Hope inside the uncomfortably chilly building; she was glad to have her fleece pullover.

"Did you have a nice trip down?" Martindale asked during the elevator ride to the third floor.

"It was fine," Murphy answered after a long awkward silence.

The elevator doors swooshed open on a short corridor flanked by small offices. Most were dark, but lights burned in a few of them. At the far end of the floor was a conference room that was abuzz with activity.

As they made their way down the hallway, Claire's legs

felt like liquid; she resisted the urge to use the wall for support, as she did not want to seem weak. She felt like a condemned inmate walking to the death chamber. In a way, she was. One life had ended when Peter had disappeared; a second one was now ending with his return.

The room went silent as they entered. Murphy directed her to the end of the large table, where she was relieved to sit down. She sat quietly, not making eye contact with anyone, not ready to do so yet. Several faces were familiar to her, folks Peter had worked with, people who had come to the funeral.

Someone handed a thin manila folder to Murphy, who then set it in front of Claire.

"This is a non-disclosure agreement you'll need to sign," he said, flipping through the documents.

"My security clearance expired," Claire said.

"We, uh, reactivated it when we found out."

She glanced up at him.

"What are you not telling me?"

He gave her a thin smile.

"Sign these, and you'll see."

## 5

Peter Abbott first told Claire about the research mission over dinner on a rainy night in March. Claire had made a vegetable lasagna and some garlic bread; Peter had opened a bottle of Pinot he'd picked up on the way home. It was her favorite kind of night, gloomy and cold, a bit of fog limning the edges of their street, nowhere to go. After dinner, they would binge-watch their favorite shows until they fell asleep. They had been married eighteen months by then, and she was a little surprised by how nice it had been. Sure, they had their little differences, little personality differences that bumped up against each other like rogue tectonic plates, but for the most part, it had felt natural, smooth, like a key fitting into a lock.

Earlier that day, NASA had approached Peter, who was working for a private foundation at the time, to gauge his interest in a research mission. An intrepid sailor named Thomas Chang had stumbled on a large meteor, about the size of a city bus, on an uninhabited island about one thousand miles east of Australia. Chang posted a photograph of it on his blog, which caught the attention of an astronomer friend. The astronomer thought the meteor looked highly unusual and forwarded the picture to a colleague; eventually it made its way to the Near Earth Objects Division at NASA.

Experts theorized that the meteor's shape and a shallow angle of entry into the atmosphere had caused it to skip along the surface and come to rest exposed rather than burying itself deep in the ground. Examination of the sailor's other photographs revealed the destruction of the forest as the rock had come barreling through, leaving an open glade where the meteor had come to rest.

"So what do you think?" Peter had asked, dunking a hunk of warm bread in a small plate of olive oil and balsamic vinegar.

"It sounds great," Claire had said, balancing a series of spinning plates of envy, curiosity, and fear. She hoped she sounded excited for him because she was. Still, part of her couldn't help but be annoyed that they hadn't called her. This was much closer to her wheelhouse than Peter's; after all, her dissertation had been about life surviving in extreme environments like meteors. In fact, it comprised much of her current work with Penumbra Labs outside San Francisco. Not only that, she was more accomplished, more well known in the field, and Peter knew it. This had eaten at him a bit, but he did a good job keeping it in check. She knew exactly why they hadn't called her. The space sciences were still a boys' club, men outpacing women in doctorates by a five to one margin. The gap was narrowing and would continue to do so, but they weren't there yet.

Besides, it was done. Letting the green-eyed monster

rear its ugly head wouldn't accomplish anything. It wasn't Peter's fault they hadn't asked her, although it kind of was, a little bit, his fault and the fault of all the other men that protected their corner on the market. That said, you could count on two hands the number of people in the world qualified to investigate the meteor – and Peter undoubtedly was on that list. So she was going to pull on her big-girl panties and be happy for her husband. She would always fight for women scientists, for grants, for equal pay, for seats at the table or on the helicopter, but today, she would simply be happy for the person she loved more than anything else on the planet.

"When would you leave?" she asked.

"Monday."

"Wow."

"I know it's short notice, but this is a pretty big find."

"Oh, yeah, no doubt," she said, bristling with annoyance.

She didn't need him to tell her it was a big find. She was a fancy scientist with about a dozen different credentials after her name. Yeah, a giant meteor landing on Earth intact was indeed a big find, thank you very much, Mister Scientist Man.

"You think you can manage for two weeks without me?"

"I'll get by," she said, winking. "I'll watch all the shows you don't like."

That Monday dawned cool and cloudy. She didn't sleep well, as Peter had been up late packing, and had tossed and turned most of the night. He was incredibly jazzed about this trip, as excited as a first-grader on his way to Disney World. They didn't speak much during the drive to the airport, Claire focusing on her coffee and nursing a fatigue-induced headache.

It was during the drive to the airport that her jealousy had bubbled to the surface.

"Oh, crap," he said as they took the exit for the airport.

"What?"

"I forgot to pull the trash to the curb."

"Dammit, Peter," she snapped, "now it'll be full for a week."

"Sorry," he said, "I forgot."

"I asked you to do one thing."

"Sorry," he repeated.

That was the last they'd spoken of it.

She dropped him off at the Delta gate. She didn't know much about his itinerary, only that they were headed to Sydney via Los Angeles for the first leg of the long trip that would deliver them to the island. She kissed him hard, but the residue of her browbeating him about the trashcan hung in the air like burnt cooking grease. She considered apologizing but decided against it. This would be her one dumb trophy from this battle of the sexes, one that Peter probably didn't realize was being waged.

Or maybe he did know, and he was just smart enough to keep his mouth shut about it.

SHE HANDED the forms back to Murphy, who slid them back into the manila folder. He handed that to Berry, who spent a few minutes examining each page, ensuring that all the *i*'s were dotted, all the *t*'s crossed. When he was done, the folder disappeared into his briefcase. Murphy cleared his throat, and the group, which had splintered into smaller pockets of conversation, assembled back around the large glass conference table.

"Good afternoon," Murphy said. "As many of you know, this is Claire Hamilton, who was previously married to Peter Abbott."

He turned to face her.

"Claire, these are the members of the ORCHID project, which was the code name assigned to the meteor."

She nodded toward the group. No further pleasantries were exchanged.

"It might be helpful if you shared with us what Peter told you about the mission before he left," Murphy said.

"Not really much to tell," she replied. "He was off to this island to explore a large meteor. He was supposed to be gone for two weeks."

"That meteor on the island?" Murphy said.

"Yeah?"

"It wasn't discovered by a globetrotting sailor."

"OK."

"And it wasn't a meteor."

"What was it?"

"We don't know."

"How do you know it wasn't a meteor?"

He glanced back at the rest of the team.

"Because it slowed down before landing."

She locked eyes with Murphy, who nodded firmly once.

Yes, she had it right.

"Holy shit," Claire said softly.

She looked around the table, looking at the faces of those who'd already been entrusted with this terrible knowledge. Twelve years they'd known the truth, living their lives, buying houses, drinking gin and tonics, making love, wasting time on Facebook, yawning through their kids' fourth-grade recorder concerts. Terrible because of its burden. Because of what it meant for humanity, for war, for nationalism, for religion, for science, for the very future of the species. For everything. Everything.

And now she knew too.

They were not alone.

"Who else knows?" she asked. She was stunned they had kept it under wraps for so long. It was the most monumental discovery in human history.

"Counting you, ninety-six people know the truth," Murphy replied. "It was ninety-eight, but two have died since first contact."

"How did it get here?"

"So one thing most people don't know," Murphy said, "is that we have very little ability to track inbound objects, especially one as small as the anomaly. It's only about the size of a minivan. We got very lucky. No one even noticed it until a routine audit of radar data from the area about ten days after it arrived. The thing that drew our attention was that it came in at a very high rate of speed and then slowed down considerably. Eventually, it came to an almost complete stop, hovering for seventeen seconds before landing on the island."

"How do we know it wasn't a spy plane," Claire asked, "something that we hadn't seen before?"

"It was traveling too quickly," he replied. "No one has that type of speed yet. Like I said, we got very lucky that we saw it at all. And again, no one came to the island to retrieve it. We've been watching that island for twelve years, and no one has come within five miles of it."

"Really?"

"You'd be surprised how much diplomacy you can accomplish simply by keeping your shit together."

"So you're telling me that we're the only ones who know there's an alien spacecraft on the planet?"

"Not too shabby, huh?"

The news was coming in so quickly Claire could barely keep up.

"Does anyone have a cigarette?" she asked.

## 6

S even minutes for every cigarette. She'd read that somewhere. Every cigarette you smoked shortened your lifespan by seven minutes. She didn't know if that were true, and she preferred not to know.

"You OK?" Murphy asked.

"It's a lot for a girl to take in," she replied, focusing on the nicotine hitting her bloodstream. Her head swam as she expelled a cloud of smoke.

"I know," he said.

She took a long drag and tapped off a cord of ash into a half-empty fast-food drink cup, the liquid a light auburn color from the swirl of melted ice and leftover soda.

"How sure are you?" she asked.

"Pretty sure."

"Pretty sure. Now is that a scientific term?"

"We've gone over that radar data six million ways to Sunday," Murphy said. "It, whatever it is, decelerated rapidly. Then, at exactly one thousand feet, it came to a stop, hovered, and then eased its way to the ground."

"Not the sort of behavior you see in meteors, I guess."

"Got any questions?"

She gaped at him, the cigarette suspended a few inches from her lips.

He held out his hands in mock surrender.

"I mean, I know you have questions."

"I don't even know where to begin."

"Why don't you finish that off?" he said, pointing to her cigarette, "and then come on back. We have more to discuss."

Murphy exited the room, leaving Claire alone.

After a last puff, she snuffed out the cigarette in the cup; she'd left nothing but the filter, which hissed loudly as she extinguished the little bit of heat still burning in the core. This had been worth the seven minutes of life, probably more than any other cigarette in her life. It had given her time to get her thoughts together. It was a lot to swallow. Big, bitter bites of an unbelievable pie. Each of today's revelations would be life-shattering by itself, and here they were expecting her to roll with two like it was no big thing.

Two amazing revelations. Twin revelations, fraternal twins. Similar but different.

Like her kids, back home with Jack, the three of them blissfully unaware that the course of human history was not what anyone thought it was. The entire population of the world, less ninety-six people, completely oblivious. How could she process two mushroom clouds in her life at the same time?

Because she was a twin mom, that was how. She had handled two colicky little ones who didn't sleep through the night until they were nearly a year old; this couldn't be any worse than that, right? People often asked her how she'd managed to handle two babies at once, wasn't it just *impossible*? The truth was that she didn't know any different. She had never been a mother to a single child, so all she knew was taking care of two at a time.

Maybe mothers who'd had a single before or after twins would be able to tell, but for Claire and Jack, double duty was the natural way of things. Two of everything. Double car seats, feedings, diaper changes, baths, stories (OK, maybe they read one story to both kids every night), meals, sippy cups, stomach bugs (without fail, when one got it, the other was not far behind). And she didn't know what it was like to live in a world where she had to deal with only one of these revelations. Nope, the universe had dropped both of these on her at the same time, so she would have to deal with them at the same time.

She checked her reflection in the office's darkened computer screen. Satisfied, she made her way back to the conference room and took her seat back at the head of the table. As she waited for everyone to settle back in, she quickly scratched out a series of questions on the notepad in front of her.

"What now?" she asked Murphy, sitting to her left.

"We get you up to speed," he said, his booming voice cutting short the idle chit-chat in the background.

"Can we start with Peter?" she asked.

She wanted desperately to know more about this object that they'd sent Peter to investigate, the existence of which carried with it staggering ramifications for her, for her family, for everyone on Earth now and in the future. But until a few hours ago, she had just been a grieving widow. That was part of who she was. Even if Peter came back to the world, part of her would forever be a grieving widow. It wasn't just Peter who had died; her entire life, the single seamless unit they had created together had died. It had all been buried with Peter.

"Of course," Murphy said.

"How do you even know he's still alive?"

"I can handle this one," said one man at the far end of the table.

"This is Jerome Layton," Murphy said. "He was Director of Mission Personnel."

"Each team member had a biomonitor implanted at the base of their neck," Layton said. "Pulse, blood pressure, respiration, that kind of thing. We know that at T-plus-twelve minutes, just as they crossed into the island's airspace, we lost the signals for everyone on the team."

Someone darkened the room and a large screen descended from the ceiling to Claire's right. A screencast recording began to play, bathing the room in a soft light. It showed each team member's photograph in three rows of four – and it had been a good one of Peter, handsome, his face tan, a bit of grey at the temples. Next to each photograph was a real-time display of biometric information. She didn't recognize the other eleven team members; before today, she had never even known their names. Seven men and four women. She wondered if any of the other eleven were still alive.

On a second screen was a livestream from inside the helicopter, someone's body camera, streaming back to the ship that had delivered them to the island. It was a jumbled, herky-jerky mess, never quite in focus, never quite out. In the corner of the screen, the words *Live Feed* flashed metronomically. Every few seconds, a glimpse of Peter onscreen took her breath away. This was the first time she'd seen any footage of him from the trip. She'd seen that look on his face, when he was deep in his work, the kind of contentment you hoped for in your vocation. He looked happy but determined.

"Hey, Abbott," someone on the video called out. "Looking pretty green there."

A stitch of laughter from the cabin as the camera panned back up toward him.

The room was dead silent as Claire watched the footage of her husband during what she had thought were his last few seconds on Earth.

"Fuck off, Apone," he said.

The cabin exploded with laughter.

So far, everything was in line with what Murphy had told Claire all those years ago. The helicopter carrying Peter and his team had gone down shortly after entering the airspace above the island. There had been no distress signal and no call for help. One minute, the mission was proceeding normally, and the next, they were gone.

She watched the mission clock at the bottom of the screen as it approached the moment of doom, the aforementioned T-plus-0:12:23.

"Did anyone else survive?" she asked softly, her eyes locked on the screen.

"Not that we're aware of," Murphy replied.

Fifteen seconds to go, and Claire wondered about those fifteen seconds of Peter's life, what she had believed were the *last* fifteen seconds of his life. Had there been any indication, any marker, any warning that things were about to go terribly wrong? Her heart caved in at the thought of how excited he'd been, his knee probably bouncing up and down as the helicopter neared shore. All these years, she had hoped he hadn't been afraid, that it was over quickly.

"Ninety seconds from the landing site," said a tinny voice.

Ten seconds. Five, four, three, two, one.

Then: disaster.

Claire's heart skipped a beat as the Orchid mission met its fate.

All twelve team members' vital signs crashed to zero, all at once. The second screen had gone dark as well, stealing from Claire those last precious moments with Peter.

No pulse. No respiration. No video. No nothing.

The screencast ran for another two minutes before the video operator paused the display. Claire sat back in her chair, suddenly aware of a pain in her lip; she had been pinching it so hard that she had drawn blood. Her heart was racing and her head hurt.

"As you can see," Murphy said, "the mission experienced some kind of catastrophic failure, the cause of which we have not been able to identify."

Claire's gaze remained fixated on the team's vital signs. Next to each biomarker was the signifier N/A. Not Available.

It occurred to Claire how little she knew about the actual circumstances of the mission failure. She didn't know if there had been a rescue attempt because she had been operating under the assumption that one had never been needed. She hadn't asked enough questions, she hadn't badgered them enough. They had told her that the helicopter had crashed, that all twelve passengers had died and she had bought it.

"Was there satellite imagery of the island?" Claire asked.

"There was," someone answered. She looked up to see a tall woman with red hair speaking.

"But..." she began, pausing for a moment. She looked at Berry, who nodded.

"For reasons we cannot explain, there is no sign of the crash site."

"What does that mean?"

"The helicopter just vanished."

"Well that's pretty weird," Claire said. She turned to Murphy. "Wouldn't you agree?"

"There are a lot of weird things at play here."

The room was full of scientific whiz kids and the best they could come up with was *weird*.

She considered the story they had told her a dozen years ago. Yes, there had been an accident. Yes, it had been reasonable to conclude that Peter and his team had died. It was clear, however, that there was more to the story.

"Was there a rescue attempt?" she asked. "I mean, I just had assumed that everyone had died in the crash. But watching this, I don't think that's a guaranteed assumption."

Her question was met with silence.

A whisper from Murphy.

"What was that?"

"Three."

"Three rescue attempts?"

"Yes."

"And?"

"We lost them all."

"How many?"

"Thirty."

"Thirty?"

"Thirty people."

"How could you lose three rescue teams?"

"We believe it's related to the anomaly."

*Christ on a pony. The fucking alien thing. She'd been so caught up in finding out what happened to Peter, she had forgotten about it. There was a fucking alien artifact sitting on the planet and it was possibly the second-most stunning thing she had learned today.*

She took a deep breath and let it out. It was hard to keep track of everything. Around her, she noticed jaws tightening, backs stiffening, as they got back to the guts of the thing. The discussion of the human losses was just to provide context. The real story was the anomaly. Recovering the object was easily worth two dozen lives. It was worth two million lives if you wanted to get down to it.

Which meant she wasn't looking at the big picture yet.

"These weren't rescue attempts," she said. "Not really."

Murphy smiled a thin smile. To her right, she could see Berry nodding, as though he approved of her analysis.

"No. Not really."

"And you still have no intel on the anomaly."

"We don't know any more about it today than we did the day it landed," he said. "Every attempt to reach the island has failed."

She could only imagine the handwringing and hair-pulling over the last dozen years. Not in her wildest dreams did she imagine humanity's first contact would unfold in this manner. She had resigned herself to the idea that at best, someday, they would detect a signal that was clearly from a technologically advanced civilization but that they would be too far away for it to matter in any practical sense. No doubt, a confirmed signal would have been a staggering discovery; it would upend everything about politics, religion, and science. When it became clear, however, that nothing on Earth would change, at least not for a very long time - if it ever did - life would quickly return to normal except among the academics and the talking heads.

Instead, this. Right there and not, so close they could

taste it, but still maddeningly out of reach. She pinched her lip as she tried to process it all.

"When was the last attempt?" she asked.

"Eighteen months ago," he said.

"Why so few attempts?"

"We didn't want to risk drawing too much attention to the island," he replied. "Eventually, someone would have noticed."

"I take it no other anomalies have appeared," she said. "This is the only one."

"Correct," Murphy replied. "And the kids over at SETI have detected nothing."

SETI was the acronym for the Search for Extraterrestrial Intelligence, a nonprofit organization dedicated in part to the search for E.T. They used optical and radio telescope systems in their continuing mission to identify a signal from an alien civilization.

"I bet their funding is up."

"You could say that," Murphy replied, chuckling. "The top brass at the Sagan Center know about the anomaly."

"They hold your nuts to the fire."

"They do," he said. "But we do it quietly. We route the money through a hundred shell companies and open and close new ones all the time. We stay one step ahead of them. And somehow there are still conspiracy theorists out there who've nailed it. Goddamn internet."

"Were there any other scientists?"

An awkward silence filled the room.

"Yes."

"Who?"

He rattled off three names that were vaguely familiar to Claire. None were astrobiologists. All were men. From the corner of her eye, Claire saw one of the female team members shaking her head in obvious disgust.

"Jesus, Gene."

"I know," he said. "Looking back, that was a mistake. We should've told you already."

"How do you know Peter's alive?"

Murphy motioned to the person working the laptop controlling the video screen. Claire watched as the screen flickered, the time frame zipping ahead by leaps and bounds.

"A week ago, this happened," Murphy said. "Watch carefully."

She leaned forward in her chair again, holding her breath, her hands tented at her lips, almost in prayer. She zeroed in on Peter's photograph, on the biometric markers.

A sudden flicker. A pulse.

Claire leaped out of her chair.

Seventy-nine beats per minute.

Then all the other vitals came online.

Respiration. Eighteen breaths a minute.

Blood pressure. One-thirty-one over seventy.

This continued for another three minutes, the vitals fluctuating a bit but remaining within normal limits for a man Peter's age. Claire watched transfixed, digital proof that the man she had buried was still alive. In her mind's eye, she could see him now, alone, fighting, finding a way to get through every new day, through the four thousand sunrises he'd seen on that island. No way to know how many more he would see. For all he knew, all the sunrises he would ever see would be from that island. She pictured his skin brown and leathery from the sun, his hair long and grey and bedraggled.

After two minutes, the signal died again, and his vitals crashed to zero. She gasped.

"What happened?" she asked. "Where did it go?"

"We're not sure."

It had been one thing for Murphy to tell her that Peter was alive; it was like a ghost story, an urban legend, an unverified report. Fake news. This was something different. This wasn't the smoke; it was the fire.

"My God."

She ran her hands through her hair.

"You guys are just going to have to give me a minute here," she said. "I mean, I know you've all had time to get used to this, but I am way off the reservation right now."

"Take your time," Murphy said. "I know this isn't easy to accept. I haven't had a decent night's sleep in twelve years."

"Why are you telling me?"

"Why are we telling you what?"

"Any of it."

"Well, he was your husband, and we thought you had a right to know."

She was shaking her head even before he had finished speaking.

"You're lying," she said. "My husband is-"

She caught herself, a swirl of emotion building up inside her. Already, a crack was forming in the hard shell she and Jack had built for themselves. That's what marriage was. Your own little bunker from which to slay the dragons of life. Impenetrable by outside forces if you did it right. And within a matter of hours, a fault line had appeared.

"Peter is expendable," she said. "All of them were. This thing is far more important than any one person. You even said the rescue missions weren't really rescue missions. Don't bullshit me."

Murphy didn't argue with her this time; instead, he made a clicking sound with his tongue and tapped his fingertips together.

"So, why are you telling me?" she asked again. "I know there's a price for all this knowledge you're giving."

"We're making another run at the island," he said. "And we want you to go."

## 7

Afer one hundred hard laps in the hotel's deserted pool, Claire called it a night. It felt good to be in the water again, the metronomic back-and-forth between the ropes, washing away the stress of the last twelve hours. She had swum competitively in college, never a standout, but good enough to earn a spot on one of the nation's top programs. In the years since, the water had been her refuge, especially during the darkest times.

The hotel was quiet as she made her way back to her room. She sat in a chair, her legs spent, her body still warm from the workout. She chose not to call home, opting instead for a quick text message.

*Long day. Hitting the sack. See you tomorrow. Love you guys.*

Jack's reply had been equally terse.

*OK. Kids are good. Hugo misses you.*

She took a long hot shower and ordered a sandwich and a glass of wine from room service, hoping the workout and the meal would lull her to sleep. But Murphy's words echoed in her ears, scaring away any hope of sleep like a frightened puppy, and so she lay in bed, watching television as the hour grew later and later, past midnight and winding toward daybreak, which found Claire awake as the gloomy dawn approached.

Murphy's words echoed in her ears on the flight home. And they echoed in her ears during the ride home from the airport (no fancy black Suburban this time), even as her driver had made small talk with her about UW's loss the previous night to the Ducks. As though Jack hadn't had a shitty enough day, what with finding out his wife's late husband wasn't dead after all, his beloved Huskies had blown a seventeen-point lead in the fourth quarter last night.

And when the car had pulled up to the curb outside her home a little past six, roughly thirty-three hours after her hurried and surreal exit from the day before, she had been so nervous walking through the door, unsure how things would unfold with Jack. She decided to wait to tell him about the offer to join the mission; she wasn't even sure whether to tell him about it at all. Because she wasn't going. She wasn't going to leave her family, risk everything she'd worked hard to build and re-build for a mission that may well cost her her life, right?

Murphy had given her a week to think it over; he insisted that she use the full seven days before making her final decision. They really wanted her to go. Now that they knew the island wasn't going to give up her secrets without a fight, they needed the world's preeminent astrobiologist to help them in their darkest hour. He had actually said that. That she was the world's preeminent astrobiologist. As if appeals to her pride would be the thing to convince her to go.

She wasn't going.

"Mommy!"

Hugo barreled around the corner from the living room, crashing into her full speed. He knocked her off balance, and they toppled to the floor. She bit back a harsh word as she climbed back to her feet. How could you yell at a kid that was this happy to see his mommy?

"Hugo!" Miranda yelled.

She did not approve of his big-hearted storminess. She loved cuddling as much as anyone, although she wouldn't admit it; she didn't see the need to make a big deal out of it. It embarrassed her.

"Hey there," Jack said. He was standing at the kitchen island, sliding his wallet and keys into his pockets. He looked a little ragged, the way he looked when he hadn't slept well. His eyes were red and he hadn't shaved. This day-old stubble normally looked quite sexy on him, but today it had a different vibe to it. It was the look of a man who cared a little bit less today than he had yesterday.

"Hey yourself," she replied. "Where you off to?"

"Going to pick up China Dragon," he said, leaning in for a quick peck on the lips. "Since our plans last night got interrupted."

They ordered Chinese about once a week; ordinarily, they had it delivered, but she didn't press the issue. If he wasn't quite ready to be in the same room with her, so be it.

"Sorry about that," she said. "And sorry about the game."

"What can you do?" he said. "If we beat Wazu, we still can win the Pac-12."

Wazu was short for Washington State University, one of UW's other rivals, and goddammit if things didn't already feel a little weird between them.

"You know what I want?"

"Moo-shu pork, extra spicy, one spring roll."

"Can't wait."

"Daddy, can I go?" Miranda asked.

"Sure," he said. "Get your jacket."

She watched through the window as they loaded up and backed out of the driveway. In the falling gloom, the street glowed with the rear taillights of Jack's Audi before he eased out of out of view.

Hugo trailed behind her as she went upstairs to unpack. It was one of her habits, one of the things that made Claire Claire, to always unpack the moment she got home. She had done it since she'd left El Paso for her freshman year at UT-Austin so many years ago. It was the best way to tie off the loose ends, close the door on what had come before and focus on the next thing. When you let that suitcase sit on the bedroom floor, empty but for one still-clean change of clothes and a plastic bag of dirty underwear, then every-thing swirled together, leaving you with one foot in the past and one in the present. It was no good.

"I missed you, Mommy," Hugo said, as she emptied the plastic bag of soiled laundry into the hamper. His eyes were puffy and red, a sure sign he'd been crying quite a bit in her absence.

"I missed you too, buddy," she replied. "Want to help Mommy out?"

He nodded as his eyes lit up with joy.

"Roll this suitcase over there by the closet, okay?"

He did as she requested, dragging it across the carpet and setting it just so by the closet.

"Thank you," she said.

"Welcome," he replied. "Wanna cuddle?"

Her eyes watered at this.

"Sure, let's go downstairs and wait for them."

So they sat on the couch and waited as the day bled away, as the twilight deepened and turned into night. She told him about a big truck she had seen, a story that enthralled him. Jack and Miranda returned thirty minutes later with two large plastic bags, packed with the familiar white boxes that always comforted Claire. Whenever she had moved to a new city, the first thing she did was find good Chinese takeout. No matter how awful things were, Chinese food made everything a little better. When her mother had died, when she was trying to get over a bad breakup, when she was stuck on her dissertation, there in the background had been an egg roll, some brown rice and an order of moo-shu pork.

"Can we watch a movie while we eat?" Hugo asked.

"Yeah, can we?" Miranda echoed.

It wasn't often they agreed on anything, but a movie with dinner was something they both loved, a little guilty pleasure for all of them. Most nights they ate dinner at the kitchen table, where it was difficult to get a moment's peace. Hugo often gave them a detailed play-by-play as to how the day went; Miranda then would cut in and tell Claire and Jack how wrong her brother was, even though they weren't in the same class. When Hugo called her out, Miranda would say one of her friends, who was in Hugo's class, had told her on the bus or the playground and then Claire would have to tell them to shut it because they were arguing about the dumbest goddamn thing ever.

Claire's return from an overnight trip felt like a special occasion so she and Jack agreed to the request, and they took their dinner in the family room, setting out the trays and boxes on the coffee table and eating sweet-and-sour chicken and moo-shu pork and chicken wings and egg rolls. Claire nursed a Chinese beer called Tsingtao that always went down smooth with spicy Asian food. The kids watched *Toy Story*, which all four of them loved. They did not speak about her trip, a difficult conversation that would come later, even if she never mentioned the offer to join the rescue attempt.

When the kids were in bed, when teeth had been brushed and stories had been told and foreheads had been kissed, she and Jack retired to the Florida room on the back of the house. It had been a screened-in porch when they first bought the house, useful only a couple months out of the year; they'd plunked down a few grand the previous year to have it enclosed. It overlooked their small yard, bracketed to the west by a small brook and woods to the north. Her favorite time of day was the rare occasion she woke up first and sat out here with her a cup of coffee.

She opened a second beer; Jack poured himself a bourbon, and he was none too shy with the pour. Even with just a single cube of ice, the tumbler was almost full. A serious drink for a serious conversation that he was seriously not looking forward to. They sat in silence for a few minutes as their eyes adjusted to the darkness. He sat on the rattan loveseat; she joined him and held his hand. He didn't pull his hand away, but he made no move to clasp her hand in his own. His fingers lay there like sausages.

"So," Jack said. "How was the trip?"

Murphy had been very clear. The only thing she could reveal was that Peter was still alive and that she had been invited to join a rescue attempt.

*"What if he asks why you need me?" she'd asked Murphy.*

*"I don't care what you tell him. As long as it's not the truth."*

So there it was. She would have to lie to her husband about the most significant challenge they were ever likely to face. They'd already been through a cancer scare a few years earlier, not long after the twins were born, when Jack had been diagnosed with lymphoma. That was awful, a circle-the-wagons kind of thing, a crucible in which cancer had burnished the bond between them. Luckily, it had been caught early by a doctor with a healthy paranoid streak and Jack had responded well to the treatments. He had been in remission for nearly six years, past the mythical five-year mark at which cancer patients were declared cured.

"I'm sorry about all this."

"How do they know he's alive?" he asked, ignoring her statement.

"His biomonitor started broadcasting again."

"They're sure it's not a glitch?"

"Well, there's no way to be sure, but the readings they're getting are consistent with Peter's normal vital signs."

"Why now?"

"Why now what?"

"The signal. Why did it start broadcasting again after all this time?"

"They're not sure."

He took a long sip of his bourbon and sat quietly. In the distance, the hoot of an owl broke the awkward silence.

"Anything could've caused those readings," Jack said. "Power fluctuation, lightning strike, power surge."

"I suppose," Claire said. It was something to say.

"And I assume they're going to mount a rescue operation."

A flutter of nerves butterflied in her stomach. Now the lying would start. It wasn't even a rescue. Sure, if they found Peter and could get him back, great, super, fucking fantastic, that would be a welcome byproduct of the mission, the way pan drippings for gravy were a nice bonus to roasting a turkey on Thanksgiving. But of the top ten priorities for the next team to go the island, the object was numbers one through nine.

"They are," she said.

"Seems like a waste of time to me."

"Would you rather he be dead?" she snapped without thinking. She regretted it before she had finished asking the question.

"That's not what I meant," Jack replied.

"Don't you think he's worth a rescue attempt?"

"Dammit, that's not what I said," Jack said, a bourbon-tinged heft in his voice. "I just don't think it's fair for them to drop this on us unless they were one hundred percent sure. Not fair to you. Not fair to anyone."

There was no one else to be unfair to other than Claire. Peter had been an only child. His father, a high school science teacher who had resented his son's brilliance, had died of a stroke four years ago. His mother Doris was deep in the clutches of dementia; she had already begun the slide into a mental fog when Peter had disappeared. She lived now in a nursing home in Ohio, where she spent her days in perpetual twilight. Claire had gone to visit her once years ago, but the woman did not remember Peter, let alone Claire. Claire had not been back to see her.

"Doesn't Peter deserve a chance?" she asked.

"If he were still alive, sure. But that's the thing. I'm sure it's a glitch or equipment malfunction. Hell, maybe an animal got its hands on it. Who knows?"

Irritation scratched at Claire.

"And even if he comes back, what kind of life will he have?"

This was a good question, even if it wasn't for anyone but Peter to answer. Twelve years of his life, gone like a puff of smoke on the wind. *Tabula rasa.* He would have to start over in a world that bore little resemblance to the one he had left.

"Not for us to decide."

Jack nodded his agreement, if somewhat reluctantly. He demolished the rest of his bourbon.

"What about you?" he asked.

"What about me?"

"How do you feel about all this?"

"If he's still alive, then I'm glad," she replied. She squeezed his hand, which she was still holding. "But that doesn't change anything between us. I love you, I love our life, I love those little stinkers upstairs."

"Okay," he said.

"You know," she said, stroking Jack's arm with her fingertips, looking out over the darkened backyard. "For a couple years after he disappeared, I held out hope for a miracle. That somehow, he would turn up and we'd have this amazing reunion. Rationally, I knew how silly that was, that it was just me unable to let him go. But it still had this huge pull on me, this idea. Then one day, it was gone. It was like a bad cut that had finally healed, the last scab's fallen off and there's healthy new skin underneath. That scab is where the pain lives. I mean, he'll always be part of me, who I am. This doesn't change anything. That new skin underneath is strong. You, the kids, you're all part of that skin. And it's tough skin."

"Will you want to see him?" he asked softly.

The pain and worry in Jack's voice were evident, and it was easy to understand why. It was difficult to fathom, an actual face-to-face reunion with Peter.

"I think I owe that to him."

She could see the profile of his head nodding in the gloom.

"What if the door doesn't swing both ways?"

"Meaning?"

"What if he hasn't been able to let you go?"

She hadn't considered this yet. Peter was a scientist, a profoundly rational and analytical man. He would know the score; when he saw her on the island *(whoa, whoa, where did that come from?)*, she meant when he saw the rescue team, he would understand as a clinical matter that the man who'd put boots down on the island and the man leaving it were two entirely different people.

"That's going to be on him."

Jack sighed, and she wasn't sure if he bought into her reasoning. If he didn't, he kept quiet about it for now. This was starting to feel like the opening round of a very complex negotiation that would take a long time, perhaps the rest of their lives. Because if Peter was indeed alive, that would permanently alter the dynamic between them, even if she never did see him again. After all, her separation from Peter hadn't been a divorce.

"So when is this rescue attempt?"

"In a couple weeks, I think."

He glanced at her, then did a quick double take. She closed her eyes, her chin tilting downward. Jack knew. When she re-opened them, he was looking at her sternly, his jaw set tightly.

"They asked you to go, didn't they?"

When she didn't answer right away, he wagged his finger at her.

"Yeah, they asked you to go," he continued. "That's why they had you go down to Ames. They could've just told you that he was still alive and then been on their way. Hell, they could've just waited until they got him back so they didn't give you any false hope."

"Jack, listen."

"Jesus, how did I not realize this before?"

He yanked his hand clear of hers, stood up, began pacing.

"They certainly didn't have to tell you, and they sure as hell didn't have to tell me."

"It's only fair that you know."

"Fair?" he snapped. "Since when do they give a shit about fair? Fair would've been making sure he was dead before they told you he was dead. Fair would've been not asking you to do this."

This was getting out of hand. They would fix nothing tonight, she saw that now, but plenty of damage, damage they wouldn't be able to undo, could be done if they didn't call it a night. Even now, knowing that Jack had every right to feel however he was feeling, she could feel bile rising in her throat, her hackles up, ready to argue. She choked it back; now was not the time for that. So she said the only thing she could think of, even though, right now, it was a lie.

"Jack, I told them no."

She hadn't told Murphy she wasn't going yet.

She would tell him that she wasn't going.

She would.

laire was up early. Or put another way, she was still awake after another sleepless night. She had turned in early, hoping for a good night's sleep. When sleep wouldn't come, she tried reading that month's book club selection, but the novel had sat open in her lap and she hadn't turned a page. And that was how the night had wound on. Beside her, Jack slept.

The house was quiet but for the hiss of the heat blowing through the vents, the metronomic ticking of the kitchen clock downstairs. After checking the time on her phone – *yikes, barely four* – she crept out of bed and padded down the hallway to the kids' bedrooms. She checked on Hugo first. He had spun around one-hundred-and-eighty degrees since she'd tucked him in eight hours earlier; his head was at the foot of the bed, his feet up on his pillow. Stuffed animals lay askew across the bed and on the floor as if some giant had come in and wrecked their peaceful little village.

Next, she tip-toed over to Miranda's room, where the girl was stretched out on the floor in her sleeping bag. Miranda was in a camping phase. Jack convinced Claire to let it go.

She didn't fight her bedtime; in fact, she was excited about it, and oh, sister, a child who happily went to bed was like finding a unicorn that pooped dark chocolate and pissed wine at the end of the rainbow.

Their golden retriever, Titan, was snoozing by the front door at the bottom of the stairs. Titan was getting up in age and preferred sleeping on the hardwood floors of the first floor. She was still pretty spry for ten years old, a wily old dog. She clambered to her feet and followed Claire to the kitchen for her breakfast. After dumping a cup of kibble in Titan's bowl, Claire made instant coffee and stepped out into the Florida room. It wasn't nearly as good as the joe that Jack made, but that involved a wildly complicated process she knew nothing about.

It had been four days since her return from Ames. Somehow it felt like both an eternity and just an instant had passed since Murphy had broken the news about Peter. Her life, which had been following the first law of motion just fine and dandy, had come to a screeching halt; everything inside had been tossed asunder. She had not called Murphy back to officially decline his invitation. Several times, she had drawn up his number on her iPhone, but she hadn't been able to execute the call. She had even sketched out a text message to him, but again, her finger had hovered impotently over that little arrow that would send her regrets.

She didn't know why.

Did she want to go?

Did she want to leave her family behind, risk her life, risk everything? Because it wasn't just Peter's life at stake. Everything she'd worked for, all her research, her study, her ideas, her inferences, her logic, her leaps of faith, distilled into that thing sitting on that island. The holy grail.

A noise startled her. Titan nosed her way through the doggy door and climbed up onto the rattan loveseat next to her. She pawed at the cushion for a moment before twirling downward into a ball next to Claire; she lifted her snout, sniffed, rested her chin on Claire's knee. Dogs. Peter had hated dogs; he found them dumb and dirty, which had always befuddled Claire. Even videos of cute puppies held no sway over him. But moments like this were what dogs were best at. Dogs had no interest in the affairs of men. They did not worry or fret. Titan would sit here and be happy with a scratch behind the ears, and if none was forthcoming, then with the simple warmth of her master's body. She bet Peter would have loved having a dog on that island with him, the best of companions who would never turn on you, never betray you, who would always have your back.

A gentle lightening in the sky drew her thoughts to the day ahead. She was teaching an undergraduate seminar in evolutionary biology that met at one o'clock. It was her favorite class to teach, twelve very bright and motivated students. Not that she didn't like teaching freshman biology, but wrangling three hundred kids who didn't take kindly to her no cell phone policy sometimes got on her very last nerve. Then she needed to edit an article for a scientific journal. PUBLISH OR PERISH - that was the warrior's code around here. She hoped to make it to the gym for a swim at lunchtime, but maybe she could come up with a decent excuse for herself to skip it and get a cheeseburger instead. She would probably be feeling forlorn about *all this* at lunchtime.

She finished off her coffee and decided to get an early start to the day. With any luck, she could be showered and dressed before Jack woke up. They had not revisited the matter since their uncomfortable discussion on this very couch a few nights ago. They had not gotten up together in the mornings, they had not turned in at the same time. They had not had sex, which was unusual for them. The tension was high.

Yesterday, she had yelled at him for not rolling the garbage can to the curb. Just like she had yelled at Peter on the day he left.

Time had come to a stop, their lives frozen in place as they dealt with the Peter Situation.

She showered quickly in the guest bathroom and dressed while Jack slept. She put on dark pants, a white shirt and a heavy maroon sweater to fight off the morning chill. She paused on her way out of the bedroom, pondering whether to kiss Jack on the head, but she decided against it. Maybe he was asleep, or maybe he was lying there awake, afraid to stir the pot, afraid to interact because of where that might lead. Suddenly everything between them felt forced, phony. Time. It would take time. He would understand. She did plant kisses on each of her kids' cheeks. Both were zonked out; Miranda stirred slightly, but only just so. Before leaving, she took Titan out to do her business. As she brought the dog back inside, the stink of poop hit her nostrils. She checked her shoe to find a wedge of doo on the edge of the heel.

"Dammit," she muttered.

Ten minutes later, the soiled shoes had been exchanged for a clean pair and left on the porch. She would clean them later. As she backed out of the driveway, the low-fuel icon blinked at her.

"Dammit," she said again, her supply of patience for the day running low already and it wasn't even dawn.

It normally took Claire thirty minutes to drive to work, but this early, she expected it would take half that. In the morning gloom, she eased out of her quiet neighborhood, following the city streets before swinging onto the freeway. But instead of finding clear sailing, she was met with a kaleidoscope of lights ahead – red brake and police blue. A wave of irritation washed through her as she braked to a stop. Ahead, a tractor-trailer had tipped on its side, blocking three of the freeway's four lanes. Because of course there was. She inched her way along as the traffic narrowed down to a single lane.

She gave the steering wheel a solid thump with her fist.

"Oh for fuck's sake!"

As she approached the bottleneck, she saw that she'd need to merge over. To her right, the traffic had thickened like artery-clogging plaque, the cars lined up in a very tight queue, and no one was in a particularly generous mood that morning. Claire slowed to a crawl, her blinker on, her head rotated, looking for any gap, any help from a fellow motorist. Eventually, she reached the sawhorse, its lights blinking, and she had to stop. Still no opening to slide into the flow.

Behind her, a horn blew, then another, then a third. Sweat beaded on her body and her skin prickled with heat. She extended her arm through the window and waved at the other cars, but they ignored her. One after another slid around the police barricade while she remained stuck.

"Screw it," she whispered.

She mashed the pedal to the floor, sending her rear wheels into a screeching spin, and punched out the moment she saw a sliver of an opening. As she did, the approaching vehicle screeched to a halt, close enough to seal off her access to the open lane. Claire had moved forward enough to block the other car's egress from the bottleneck as well.

She leaned on the horn, which earned a blast from the other vehicle.

They both leaned on their horns for a good fifteen seconds, neither driver giving any quarter. Claire held the horn down hard. The hell with the other driver. She wasn't moving until someone let her through. End of story. She switched on the satellite radio and found Janis Joplin belting it out on the 60s station, so she cranked up the volume and sang right along with her.

The stalemate continued through the end of the song and the beginning of *All Along the Watchtower*, the Hendrix version, and Claire was ready to wait for as long as it took. So what if it took a little time? It was four-forty-six in the morning and didn't have to be at work for hours. She had nothing but time!

Halfway through the song, the other car's horn went silent, and Claire reveled in her victory. But her glee was short-lived; the horn had stopped because the driver had gotten out of the car. Claire's blood was boiling now and she was out of her car seconds later, stomping toward her traffic nemesis. Her capacity for bullshit was now at zero.

"What the hell is wrong with you?" barked the other driver, a heavier-set woman a bit younger than Claire. In the glow of the headlights, Claire could see the woman's arms were inked from elbow to wrist.

"You couldn't let me in?" Claire bellowed.

"I don't owe you nothing."

"How about some common fucking decency?"

Now they were face to face, their noses inches apart. Her adversary was roughly the same height but more powerfully built. Still, Claire did not back down.

"You don't know me, you little bitch," the woman

warned. Her face quivered with fury. "Get back in your fancy SUV and wait your fucking turn."

She shoved Claire hard, right in the sternum, which took Claire's breath away. She stumbled and tripped onto her seat, the wetness from the roadway dampening her clothes and chilling her skin. The woman took another step toward Claire, her fist clenched. Claire bounced from her bottom to all fours and drove upward, her shoulder connecting with the woman's ample midsection. She swung wildly, her left fist clocking against the side of the woman's head. The woman grunted in surprise, apparently in disbelief that the well-dressed professional woman she had just floored had fought back.

The woman retaliated, catching Claire with an open hand on the side of her face. Claire's cheek burned with pain but she didn't care. She hadn't been in a fight since a skirmish in her high school locker room three decades ago and she'd forgotten how good it felt to hit someone. She readied a second blow but did not get a chance; a pair of powerful arms encircled her waist and dragged her backward. Two other drivers had neutralized her adversary.

"Calm down, lady," the voice behind her said.

She barely heard him as she unleashed a string of obscenities at the woman, thrashing and kicking to get one more shot at that vial of human plague; later, Claire would reflect on the incident and remember that she had called the woman a cunt, she had actually used the c-word, the grandmomma of all curse words.

Eventually, her flailings subsided; the man restraining her was stronger than she was and had her tight. The explosion of adrenaline faded, and she sighed as her body sagged. Slowly, the scene around her came into focus, the fine mist spitting from the sky, the other cars, the other drivers standing in the rain, the lights and horns flooding her senses. What had she done? Behind them, traffic was choked off, backed up at least a mile. Two men were holding her adversary by the arms. A police officer approached from the left, coming up along the shoulder.

"What's going on here, folks?" said the officer, a tall, rail-thin man.

Claire's captor released his grip and she stepped clear of him, smoothing her clothes, running her fingers through her hair.

"These two," said the man. "They just went after each other."

"Any physical contact?"

"They were whaling on each other," said one of the men restraining Claire's opponent.

The flashing lights of a second police car caught Claire's eye as the witnesses relayed the details of the bizarre road rage incident. The officer from the second car joined the discussion, coming up on the first officer's left side. She unhooked her cuffs and made her way toward the other woman. That's when it hit her. They were arresting her.

The first officer turned his attention to Claire.

"Hands behind your back, ma'am," he said.

## 9

Claire's knees buckled as she complied with the officer's request. She shut her eyes tight, willing herself to wake up on the off chance this was all a terrible dream, that she was still lying in bed, buried deep under the comforter, close enough that she could feel Jack's warmth, smell that clean hint of aftershave that lingered from the previous morning. But when she opened her eyes again, she was still standing there, the steel cuffs tugging on her arms. No one ever said how heavy they were. Her wrists were already aching and she'd had them on for barely a minute.

The officer escorted her up the highway, past the bottleneck, past the accident scene that other officers were still tending to; the truck driver was chatting with the cops, a bloody handkerchief pressed up against a nasty gash on his forehead. A bit farther ahead, a cruiser idled on the shoulder, its lights flashing ominously in the predawn gloom. Claire's heart pounded against her ribcage like it was going to burst free from her chest and force these officers to chase it down with hound dogs.

"First time in cuffs?" asked the officer, whose nameplate identified him as Clevenger.

She glanced up and gave a quick nod of the head.

"Can always spot the first-timers," he said, chuckling, as though it was a skill to be proud of. "Can always spot them."

They walked the rest of the way in silence; a female officer was waiting for them when they made it to the police cruiser.

"I'm gonna search you now," she said. "You got anything in your pockets or jacket that might poke or injure me? A needle, anything like that?"

She shook her head, and the officer searched her; then she helped Claire into the back of the cruiser, telling her the best way to sit to minimize the discomfort of the handcuffs. An air freshener hanging from the rearview mirror post struggled to cover the stench of dried sweat and old urine. The radio squawked with police chatter.

*Oh Jesus, oh Jesus, this was really happening.*

As Claire adjusted her seat, the door slammed shut with a terrifying finality. That was the end of her day, almost certainly the end of her pursuit of tenure, maybe her job, and who the hell knew, maybe even the end of her marriage. Fear that Jack's reservoir of patience, deep as it was, wouldn't go this deep buzzed through her like electricity.

"What's your name, sweetheart?" he asked.

"Claire Hamilton," she said, ignoring his patriarchal sexism. "My car?"

"I'm Officer Clevenger," he said. "Your car's gonna be towed, the contents inventoried. You'll get it all back. It ain't cheap, I'm afraid."

She didn't reply.

"Wanna tell me what happened back there?"

She shook her head.

"Fair enough," he said, looking at her through the rearview mirror. "You change your mind, you let me know."

She nodded.

Her cheek had begun to throb where the woman had slapped her. A drop of blood traced down her cheek and curled toward the corner of her mouth, flooding her taste buds with the sharp tang of warm metal. The woman had hit her hard enough to split the skin. Great.

As they cruised the rainy streets of Seattle, dawn rapidly approaching, Claire replayed the incident in her head, the anger at the woman still simmering. How could she have let things get away from her like that? How? She would've found an opening a minute later, five minutes later, hell, half an hour later. Time would have dissolved it; traffic moved. Instead, here she was, reacting like a third-world dictator who didn't get his way. And sitting here, she was still pissed off.

What was she supposed to do now?

Call a lawyer? Her father was a retired judge, a former prosecutor, and the very thought of telling him about this sent a shiver up her spine. She'd spend the rest of her life behind bars before she told her father that she'd let her temper get the best of her.

Call Jack?

No, not him either. Not unless she had to.

There was a lawyer she'd used when Peter had disappeared, one of these high-dollar types from a California mega-firm called Willett & Hall. Neil Rushing had helped her navigate the tricky shoals of dealing with a spouse who was probably but not definitely dead. His specialty was trusts and estates, not criminal law, but she could not think of another lawyer she knew. And she hadn't spoken to him in years, not since he had filed the paperwork to have Peter

declared legally dead, seven years to the day after his disappearance. He was a good guy, a bit dry, a straight shooter.
He'd explained that he never sugar-coated things for his
clients because it was a smart hedge against the future going
bad on you.

"Because it always does," Rushing had said in that dry
way of his. "Eventually, it all goes bad."

And he had been right. Even the thing that had gone
bad, Peter's disappearance, had itself gone bad. She could
just picture herself calling Neil and explaining that well,
hell, wouldn't you know it, Peter's still alive, and yet, she
could picture Neil sitting in his office with his perfectly
knotted tie and crisp white shirt, telling her matter of factly
that he had planned for this contingency as well. That he
had filed some document or affidavit filed in the City of San
Francisco Superior Court protecting his client in the event
that Peter magically reappeared someday.

"Something funny, miss?"

The officer's question broke her out of her daydream.
She had laughed out loud at the idea that Neil had planned
for this eventuality because deep down, she was almost
positive that he had. She wondered if he would help her, but
then she remembered he was a California lawyer and California was a long damn way away. But even if he wasn't
licensed in Washington, she figured he could recommend
someone.

"No."

"Do you want to talk about it?"

"I want a lawyer."

"Suit yourself."

∽

THE KING COUNTY Correctional Facility occupied a series of gleaming white buildings that resembled a Tetris pattern. As it came into view, Claire's heart caught in her throat and she had to remind herself to breathe. The officer turned into a short alleyway off 5th Street and crept toward the sally port, an entry point for incoming inmates.

Two female deputies stood ready for her arrival at the doors. Clevenger shifted the vehicle into park and came around to offload his prisoner.

"Howdy, Clev," said one of the deputies.

"Morning, Sharon," said the officer. "Assault and battery."

"Name?"

"Claire Hamilton," he replied, handing her purse over to Sharon.

Clevenger took Claire by the arm and escorted her to her jailers.

"You be nice to these lovely ladies," he said, "and they'll be nice right back at you."

Claire had no intention of doing anything otherwise.

"That's right, honey," Sharon said. She was about Claire's age, looking crisp and neat in her brown deputy's uniform. "You do what we say, and we'll make sure it's as pleasant as can be. I mean, it ain't a Holiday Inn, you know, but we try. Ain't that right, Deputy Boone?"

Boone cackled as though it was the funniest thing ever uttered in human history and Holiday Inn was the end-all-be-all of hotel accommodations.

"You're not gonna give us a hard time, right, honey?" Sharon asked. "Because we had a long-ass night, isn't that right, Deputy Boone?"

"A long-ass night," came the reply from her partner, the emphasis on the word *long*.

"No, ma'am," said Claire, her eyes locked on the maw of the jailhouse doors. The hard floors, the whitish-yellow fluorescent lights buzzing overhead. It was all very ordinary, very jail chic, and it was fixing to make Claire pass out.

"No, ma'am," Sharon said, echoing Claire's reply. "I do like that, I do like that, yes, sir."

They started her perp walk, the two deputies escorting Claire up through the swinging double doors. Once they were inside the building, the sally port's security door slammed home. Claire kept her head partly down, cutting her eyes from side to side to absorb her surroundings.

They led her to a desk staffed by a sleepy-looking deputy and deposited her into an uncomfortable wooden chair. He went through the booking process, checking her identification, taking her fingerprints, taking her mug shot, the other mechanics of processing her into the City of Seattle's criminal justice system. She answered the questions they asked, her mind laser-focused on the jail cell that awaited her.

Neil.

She'd have to call Neil.

"When can I call my lawyer?"

"Soon as we're done here," replied the deputy, whose name was Blumstein.

As Blumstein worked his terminal, she glanced at the clock on the far wall. It was only five-twenty; scarcely an hour had passed since she'd been drinking her coffee in the Florida room. Jack would be asleep for another forty minutes, the kids for another thirty after that, assuming they didn't wake up early and toddle down the hallway for a few minutes of Mommy snuggle time. And here she was, getting ready to cool her jets in a jail cell. God, what had she done? They could never find out about this. They could never know Mommy had gone to jail, real jail. All those times they had joked about the police coming for them if they hadn't done their chores loomed large in her mind.

A ruckus behind her caught her attention. The other woman from the traffic jam was being escorted into the station, cursing up a storm. They locked eyes briefly but Claire looked away. Just seeing the woman made her feel sick. A pair of officers held the woman back as they waited for Blumstein to finish processing Claire. Then they were done, and it was time to call her lawyer. The deputy scrolled through the contacts on Claire's cell phone and punched up Neil's number. She left a voicemail for him and followed it up with a text message, but no reply was immediately forthcoming.

"You'll appear before the judge after lunch for arraignment and bond."

Panic bloomed in her belly. Nothing remained between her and her date with the cell, where she would spend at least the next several hours. The deputy motioned for her to stand up and follow him, and he escorted her to an empty holding cell on the far side of the booking area.

"Unlock AA-23," said the deputy into the communicator fastened to his shoulder.

There were no bars on this cell, just a heavy door with a small window. The lock disengaged and the electronic door retracted slowly, like a giant beast awaiting its meal. It was small, about eight by eight square, a bedroll on one side and a small toilet and sink on the other. It reeked of decaying body odor and urine. She gagged once as the deputy ushered her inside, just as the aroma's intensity peaked in her nostrils.

"What about my lawyer?" she asked after she choked down her dry heave.

"If they call back, we'll let you know."

He exited the room and the door cranked shut, leaving Claire alone in the cell, leaving her almost unable to breathe. She stood in the center of the cell, her hands clenched tightly by her side, frozen, unable to move a muscle. This was it. She was in jail. Law-abiding citizen, brilliant scientist, doting mother, beloved wife, now just an inmate.

She wouldn't be here long, right? She had no record and her crime was a minor one. They'd release her on her own recognizance or on a small bond and she would come back a month or two down the road for her trial. Maybe she could plead out on a disorderly conduct charge and that would be it. Maybe. A lot of maybes.

She stood at the door for a while, looking through the small port window, watching the booking area come alive with activity as the day shift arrived for work. Time crept along slowly. She could feel it slow down around her, knowing that the next few hours would be among the longest of her life, right up there with those first hours after they told her Peter had disappeared. They had confiscated her wristwatch and she couldn't see the clock on the wall, so there was no way to know whether five minutes or five hours elapsed. She reminded herself to assume that less time had gone by than she believed. If it felt like an hour, it probably had been ten minutes. This would help keep her sane.

Eventually, she bored of window-shopping and she sat down on the cold floor with her back to the door. She drew her knees into her body and wrapped her arms around them, trying to keep her head clear, trying to think about anything but the awful mess she was in. The kids' faces lit up her mind, their happy smiles from a skiing trip they'd taken the previous year to Park City. Both took to it pretty well; Miranda was much more cautious and took her time coming down the slope. No hill was too steep or too fast for her brother, however.

After some interminable period, it felt like four days but probably had been twenty minutes, a knock on the window startled her. She scurried away from the door and climbed up to her feet, one of which had fallen asleep. A second later, the electronic door groaned on its track as it slid open. Standing in the doorway was Deputy Blumstein.

Behind him was Agent Berry, the DIA agent who'd accompanied Murphy to her house.

"Time to go," he said.

## 10

"Let's go, Miss," Blumstein said. "Looks like some bigger fish have their eye on you."

He cuffed her and escorted her back to the booking desk. Next to his keyboard sat a document with a header reading *Transfer to Federal Custody*. Claire had questions, so many questions, but she was too afraid to ask them. Agent Berry stood ramrod straight, silent, while Blumstein tapped away at his keyboard.

"All right, Agent Berry," said the deputy, "looks like everything is in order. She's your prisoner now."

"Remove the cuffs."

"You have your own?"

Berry did not reply.

Blumstein eyed him for a moment, caught in that battle between insisting on protocol and not wanting to deal with any hassle. Then he motioned for Claire to turn around and unlocked her cuffs.

"What about my hearing?" she asked.

"It's been canceled," Berry said, not waiting for Blumstein to answer. "Let's go."

Without another word to the deputy, Berry took Claire gently by the arm and they made their way out of booking, through the main door to the reception area. The lobby was mostly empty, but a few sad-looking folks sat slumped in uncomfortable-looking chairs, sipping bad coffee from small white Styrofoam cups. Outside, the day had broken cloudy and drizzly, annoying if you were outside too long but not worth opening an umbrella for. The air smelled fresh and cold and she could not remember the last time it felt this good to be outside.

"Is it over?"

"Your car is in the parking deck," he said. "Top level. Yes, it's over."

"Thank you for this."

He reached into his pocket and handed over her car keys.

"How did you know I was here?" she asked.

"We've been keeping an eye on you," he said. "The mission is too important to throw away on a silly catfight."

Claire nodded as her cheeks flushed with shame. Putting aside the sexist undertones of the word *catfight*, he was right. This was an important thing she was dealing with, and not very well, as it turned out. Quite possibly the most important discovery in human history, and they had entrusted her with the knowledge. All of a sudden, she felt exhausted, as though her very last bit of energy had drained out of her.

"Yeah," she said softly. "I know."

"Make sure you keep that in mind."

"What about all this?" she said, nodding toward the jail building.

"Like it never happened. The arrest will be expunged. Look, right now, you have very powerful friends in your corner. More powerful than you realize. But their patience is not limitless. They want you to go on this mission. This was, quite literally, your get-out-of-jail-free card. Now you can make your decision with a clear head, without any other complications weighing on you."

"I can still say no, though, right?"

"Murphy actually wanted to hold your feet to the fire on this," Berry replied. "He was furious. If it had been up to him, you'd have to agree to go in exchange for making all this go away."

"So why isn't up to him?"

"I talked him out of it," he said. "I don't think you will say no. And I think the mission will be stronger for it."

"And if you're wrong? If I say no?"

"Then I owe Eugene a very expensive bottle of whiskey."

Claire smiled.

The precipitation picked up, transitioning from a drizzle to a steady shower.

"I think that's our cue to bring this to a close," he said.

"Thank you again," she replied, covering her head with a hand.

"My car is right here," he said, pointing to a black sedan with blue government plates slotted in a spot marked Government Use Only. "Want a ride to your car?"

She shook her head.

"You've done enough," she said, holding out her hand.

They shook.

"I'll be seeing you, Ms. Hamilton."

"You're awfully sure of yourself."

He winked and left her standing in the rain. She watched as he got into his car, started the engine, pulled out of the parking lot. Just like that, he was gone, vanished into the morning mist.

She made her way toward the parking deck, indifferent toward the intensifying rain. Several people ran by her, anxious to get out of it; she found herself not caring as her clothes became cold and damp against her skin.

She took the steps instead of the elevator, replaying the events of the morning in her mind; already the memory of the stuffy cell was receding like a bad dream. Left in its place was the problem at hand, intractable, unsolvable, merciless. Getting out of jail hadn't made her problem go away any more than getting thrown in jail had.

By the time she was back in her car, the heater on full blast, she was as miserable as ever. She lit a cigarette from a pack she'd stowed in the center console earlier in the week; she had bought them from a convenience store the night she spent at Ames. The car would reek of smoke and Jack would be pissed off something fierce but she didn't care. While she smoked, she tuned the satellite radio to the Bruce Springsteen station. She hadn't given it any thought; one moment, the car was silent, and the next, she was listening to the Boss. They were replaying a live show from Philadelphia, back from the year she had met Peter. Of course it was.

Jesus.

*Positive, girl, you've got to think positive.*

*Okay, okay, okay.*

If Berry wasn't bullshitting her, and she had no reason to think he was, this little incident would soon be wiped from existence, if it hadn't been already. There. A positive. Regardless of what had caused it, the incident had the potential to ruin her. But the joy of her quick release and the dismissal of the charges dissipated quickly, the way the quick rush of that office donut faded as the reality of your diet, of your job, of that workout you skipped, came in on you hard.

Every time she tried to pull herself out of this funk, it always came back around to Peter and the island. And the truth – *being honest here, girl, just you, me, this menthol and the Boss growling at you from Philadelphia twelve years ago?* It wasn't that extraterrestrial object she was thinking about. It was Peter. Her mind was like a rambunctious toddler, misbehaving, definitely not listening, not focusing on the really important thing.

Her day. The day ahead.

She glanced at the dashboard clock. It was almost ten-thirty. She had that undergraduate class to teach at one o'clock, which she could do in her sleep. The rest of the day was clear for research and writing. She would lock herself in her office and get some words down on the page. If she was going to be miserable and frustrated, she might as well redirect that bad energy toward something productive.

IT WORKED. Kind of. The lecture class went off without a hitch and no one seemed to suspect that she'd spent part of the morning in the slammer. As the afternoon wore on, she reviewed some new data her research assistants had collected and churned out a few paragraphs on a new journal article. Granted, she would probably toss most of them when revision time came around, but the day was not a total loss. No one called her, no deputies showed up at her door to tell her that there'd been a big mistake and she really was going back in the slammer, and *oh yeah, here's a felony escape charge to boot*.

As she saved her work and decluttered her desk, her phone buzzed.

A text from Jack.

*When will you be home?*

Reality, man. Reality.

She wasn't in any particular rush to get home. What an awful thing to think. She hadn't seen her kids awake in almost twenty-four hours and she was trying to stretch that out even more. But she was worthless right now. Wasn't it quality over quantity? What good did it do them if she was a sack of meat and bones sitting on the couch, wound up tight, liable to blow at the first minor transgression?

*Soon. Maybe an hour.*

The blinking dots of Jack typing a reply.

*Hugo's running a fever.*

She sighed, the guilt cutting her hard, as palpably as an errant knife slipping into soft flesh while she cut vegetables.

*Will be home in thirty.*

Assuming she didn't get arrested again.

She laughed. You had to laugh sometimes.

SHE MADE it home in a little under thirty minutes, even managed to avoid getting into a brawl or hauled off to the slammer. The house was dark but for a light shining in Hugo's room. Her heart sank at the idea of her sick little guy; as crazy as he drove her, seeing him under the weather, when all the energy had drained out of him and he was a miserable little lump, was a million times worse. As much as she enjoyed peace and quiet, she didn't like it when he was down. And when he kicked whatever bug had laid him low, when he ramped back up to full strength, it was terrifying and wonderful at the same time.

After gathering her things, she locked the car and let herself in the house. She dropped her briefcase by the door and hung her jacket on the coat tree. The smell of something garlicky wafting through the house reminded her that she hadn't eaten all day. Maybe she would have a bowl of cereal or maybe she would say the hell with it and dive into a pint of ice cream. Maybe she and Jack could sit and eat and watch television and forget this day ever happened.

She came around the corner and flipped on the light.

Then fifty people standing in her living room shouted in unison:

"Surprise!"

## 11

It was her birthday.

Her forty-fifth birthday.

She had forgotten. The chaos of the last week had swept over everything in her life, including the imminent anniversary of her birth. She didn't have a strong opinion about birthdays one way or another. She didn't love the idea of getting older, but she loved the alternative – not getting the chance to get older – even less. The kids were at the right age to make the most adorable deal of it, crafting homemade birthday cards on thick slabs of construction paper.

She stood at the threshold the family room, her mouth agape, her eyes frozen open, as her friends and neighbors raised plastic flutes of champagne. Jack emerged from the crowd with a pair of drinks and kissed her, but she was too stunned to kiss him back.

"I guess you're surprised," he whispered into her ear.

She nodded firmly as he handed her a flute.

"Sorry, I planned this weeks ago, before they came, and it seemed weird to cancel."

The fruitiness of the champagne did a poor job covering the whiskey he'd obviously been drinking. His words were running together a bit, a sure sign that he'd been imbibing for a while.

"It's okay," she replied. She took a long sip, draining the champagne in one pull.

"I guess Hugo doesn't have a fever."

"Nope."

He kissed her cheek again.

This was turning out to be the weirdest day.

"Someone's ready to party!" came a shout from the crowd.

She raised her empty flute to the crowd and everybody cheered. An off-kilter symphony of *Happy Birthdays* followed, and she made her way into the crowd to greet her guests. Hugging and cheek-kissing one after another, she felt dizzy, like she was riding a roller coaster that was a bit more than she had bargained for. Here were Chad and Kevin Richardson, the couple next door, and Florence Coffey, her friend from the PTA board, and the girls from book club, and Jefferson Keith, her department chair at UW who would never know how dumb Claire thought he was and on and on. As she finished her trip through the receiving line, she spotted the kids, both of them dressed to kill. Miranda wore a lovely blue dress and Hugo looked dashing in khakis and a crisp blue Oxford button-down. They looked so cute that her troubles simply faded away.

She knelt and motioned for them; they ran into her arms at full speed, probably owing more to their competitive nature to get to her first than to their desire to shower Mommy with love, but what the hell, she would take it.

"Happy birthday, Mommy!" they both crooned.

"Were you surprised?" asked Miranda.

"Yes, very," she said. "You guys did a great job keeping the surprise."

Miranda frowned.

"What's wrong?"

"Daddy didn't tell us about it until everyone got here."

Then she folded her arms and harrumphed quite loudly.

Of course. The best way for Hugo to keep a secret was to make sure he didn't know about it in the first place.

"Come see all the food, Mommy," Hugo said, pulling her by the hand.

Claire remembered how hungry she was as she accompanied her son to the catered spread in the dining room. The table was loaded down with carved prime rib, crab dip, fruits and vegetable trays, cheese plates, little quiches, bruschetta. A bar with a real bartender stood in the corner. He handed her a gin and tonic, her favorite cocktail. The kids worked together to fix her a plate, and she sipped her drink while they argued about whether she would want four cubes of cheese and two sliders or four sliders and two cubes of cheese. Eventually, they settled on a compromise and proudly handed her the plate. Somehow, they'd managed to work together without descending into anarchy.

Florence sidled up next to her and chatted her up about the school calendar, the handful of events left on the schedule before Winter Break; as Florence droned on, Claire found her thoughts slipping away to the island. The winter concert suddenly seemed trivial. She wondered how the others who knew about the anomaly had adjusted. How did they go on in light of this massive paradigm shift?

"So what do you think about that idea?" Florence asked.

Dammit. Florence had asked her a question and Claire had stopped listening two minutes ago.

"I'm sorry," Claire said. "I'm just a little overwhelmed by everyone being here. Thank you for coming."

She leaned in and gave Florence a half-hearted hug and quickly moved on to the next guest. They talked about this, that and the other and with each successive conversation, Claire felt herself drifting farther and farther away from her own party. She drank too much and ate not enough and soon, the swimminess of intoxication had seeped in. She felt like she was watching someone else's party unfold, she wanted to yell and scream that none of this mattered, not the fancy sandwiches or the full bar or the ten-dollar gag gifts, that she had been ejected from her own life. It wasn't fair being ejected from your life at forty-five because you had worked pretty hard just to make it to forty-five, to that point in your life when you were not afraid anymore, to learn the painful lesson that most of your mistakes, the ones that mattered anyway, could be attributed to fear. Fear of what might happen. The funny thing was that by the time you got your shit together, it was often too late for it to matter.

But she was afraid all over again.

Forty-five years old. In the second half of her life. That was a hard thing to wrap your head around. And Peter, poor Peter, still on that island, half his adult life blown away like it had been nothing at all.

Another drink would help.

She staggered to the bar, the ground increasingly uneven beneath her feet, but telling herself she was still good to go. Her body could probably handle another two drinks, maybe even three, especially with another plate of food to soak up the booze. Gin and tonic, she had stuck to the same drink all night because she was nobody's fool, she was old enough to know she shouldn't mix liquor with beer or wine.

The tinny twang of a fork on crystal drew her attention, quieting the guests down. She followed the sound to their galley kitchen, where the crowd was gathering. On the island counter was a large sheet cake from Westhampton, her favorite bakery in the city. She toddled up next to Jack, and he put his arm around her shoulder, gently squeezing it. It felt nice. Sure. It felt nice to be loved. How did Peter feel not to be loved on that island? He must have felt pretty fucking unloved, wasting away on that island, wondering why they had abandoned him.

"Everyone, everyone, I want to thank you all for coming," Jack said. "I know it's a school night, but I think it helped save the surprise, as Wednesday is usually Claire's writing day. You know her, she's squirreled away in that office, hunched over her desk, her reading glasses sliding down that pretty nose-"

This elicited a few laughs and more than a few *awwws*.

She smiled amid the fake shutter click of a dozen camera phones, and in the back of her mind, she suspected she was going to look a lot drunker than she felt standing here.

"She's the most amazing person I've ever known," Jack was saying. "A wonderful mother, an amazing scientist, a great friend and the love of my life. Cheers to you, sweetie. I love you. To a hundred more birthdays!"

A hundred more birthdays. Why did people say that? That was dumb. She didn't want a hundred more birthdays. She would rather just stay in her forties, but since that wasn't possible, she'd take another few decades with her mind and body intact and then boom, a massive stroke to take her out before she knew what hit her. God knew she didn't want to end up bedridden in one of these long-term care facilities, wearing a diaper, not knowing her own name, where they had to roll you every two hours to prevent bedsores. No, that was no way to go.

A hundred more birthdays. Please.

She raised her glass, cleared her throat, prepared to say a few words.

"Thank you all for coming," she said to a group of people who were unaware that they were not alone in the universe.

"You're all so important to me," she continued, speaking to forty-three individuals who were also blissfully ignorant of the fact that the woman they'd come to celebrate was now married to two different men.

Everyone was an iceberg. Just the tip exposed, the part that other people saw and upon which they based their judgments. But that wasn't fair. Later, some of her guests would talk about how many G&T's she had put away, how standoffish she was, how distant, didn't she appreciate the wonderful party Jack had put together for her, maybe even an *I don't know how he puts up with her* thrown in for good measure. The screaming unfairness of it all.

"I'm lucky to have so many wonderful friends," she went on, ready to wrap it up. "Thank you again, this is a day I will never forget."

At least that part was true.

From a jail cell to the guest of honor. It truly had been a remarkable day.

"Cheers to all of you."

She shakily raised her tumbler, splashing some of her drink onto the kitchen floor.

"Someone cut her off!"

Laughs.

Jack leaned in and kissed her.

The party wound down rapidly after that, another round of insincere hugs and cheek kisses as the guests streamed out into the chilly night. By eleven, the house was empty but for the echoes of the party gone by. Jack told her to relax and he picked his way through the house with a trash bag, collecting bottles and cups and plates.

Both kids were asleep on the couch, the dog curled up in between them. It was pretty goddamn cute and maybe it was the booze talking here, but it felt her heart might explode right out of her chest. And a terrible thought zoomed right through her mind, that it would have been better if Peter had died on that island because she had earned this little bit of happiness here in her middle age, and it seemed terribly unfair for it to be ripped away from her. Not as terrible as the thought itself, though. What a terrible thing to think, and she hated herself a little for thinking it. Peter had done a brave thing by going to that island and this was the thanks he was getting from his wife, the love of his life?

As she watched her kiddos, she tried to gauge how drunk she was. A good solid buzz, but fortunately, she'd stopped drinking before the room started spinning, a tell-tale sign that one was headed for a date with the toilet. That was the worst, that feeling you'd let things get away from you. She didn't need to throw up to feel like that; wasn't her life already getting away from her?

"How are you feeling?" Jack asked, making his way into the living room.

"Good," she said. "Pretty good. You're cute."

He laughed.

"You're smart when you're drunk."

"You're funny, too. The whole package. The whole enchi-lada. Think I'll keep you."

She heard herself saying these things and wondered if they sounded as silly to Jack as they did to her. She wondered if she had started repeating herself, another one of her habits when she'd had too much to drink. If she had, Jack didn't mention it. He didn't point out your foibles when you were vulnerable. As he cleaned, as the kids snoozed with their dog, a warm feeling of contentment washed through her. Her eyelids drooped. She was tired, and she felt like she could sleep for the first time in days.

It was a good thing that Peter was alive.

She chuckled out loud to herself.

"A good thing."

"What, babe?" Jack asked.

"Just talking to myself, nothing," she said. "Today was a crazy day!"

"Did you have fun at the party?"

"Yes, so much fun. Thank you. So much fun. I love you."

"I love you too."

"Know how much I love you?"

"How much?"

"Shh," she said, tapping a finger against her lips. "Shh. I'm gonna tell them no."

"Tell who no?"

"Them. Murphy. I'm not gonna go on that trip. It's fine. I'm glad he's okay."

Jack froze as he was reaching for the last cup on the mantle, and now she felt very drunk all at once. She had said something bad but it was already out of her head. She couldn't remember. What she needed was a court reporter to read back the transcript. That would have been helpful.

"I thought you already told them no," he said.

"I mean, yeah, I was going to."

"You told me you turned them down."

She slept.

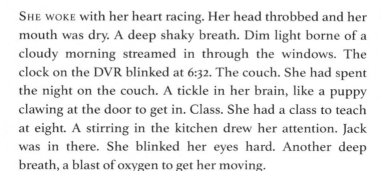

SHE WOKE with her heart racing. Her head throbbed and her mouth was dry. A deep shaky breath. Dim light borne of a cloudy morning streamed in through the windows. The clock on the DVR blinked at 6:32. The couch. She had spent the night on the couch. A tickle in her brain, like a puppy clawing at the door to get in. Class. She had a class to teach at eight. A stirring in the kitchen drew her attention. Jack was in there. She blinked her eyes hard. Another deep breath, a blast of oxygen to get her moving.

She made her way to the kitchen, where Jack was pouring coffee into a travel mug.

"Morning," she said.

"That it is," he said, not looking at her.

The chill in the kitchen was evident.

After preparing his coffee, a splash of creamer, he grabbed his wallet and his keys and made his way for the door.

"Is something wrong?" Claire asked.

He paused at the door, his hand on the knob. He did not turn back to look at her.

"You said you had turned them down."

Claire stood at the counter frozen, memories of the night returning in bits and pieces like luggage on an airport baggage claim carousel. She could see herself now, slumped on the couch, saying the words.

*I'm gonna tell them no.*

*I'm gonna tell them no.*

He exited the house without another word, slamming the door behind him hard enough to shake the house.

## 12

Claire taught her eight o'clock class by rote and then locked herself in her office with a bathtub-sized cup of coffee from the café in the commons building. Her article was open on her laptop, but this morning it held little interest for her; instead, she was scrolling through her photos on her iPhone, photos of the kids, of Jack, even a hidden album dedicated to Peter. The Peter album was stored locally on the phone and did not sync with the family's other devices. She didn't really hide it its existence, but she didn't advertise it either. It just didn't seem right to let it mix in with the others.

The number of photos they had taken over the years was stunning, more than thirty thousand floating in her digital cloud, a comprehensive visual play-by-play of the kids' lives, from the moment of their births to the breakfast they'd eaten that morning. Hilarious when you thought about it, especially compared to the number of photos of her own childhood in El Paso. During a recent trip to visit her father, a retired judge, she had found a manila folder containing less than twenty photographs, covering the period from the day she was born through her high school graduation. Her parents had never been the sentimental type; to her father, and, by extension, her mother, there was nothing remarkable about simply being.

But this endless stream of pictures, a virtually uninterrupted stop-motion movie of their lives, let her travel through time. Here was their summer vacation trip to San Diego. There was Hugo petting the giraffe at the zoo. Here was Miranda reading a book in the hotel. A picture of Jack's particularly sublime filet mignon. Memories faded, but seeing their day-to-day lives unfold was like opening a door and poking your head into a world that was so vivid and comprehensive it felt like it was still happening, whooshing by you like a subway train.

She scrolled through a couple months' worth before she reached her limit. There was something exquisitely painful about looking at pictures now because they were from before. Before she had learned about Peter. Her life, cleaved into two pieces now.

*Prepare for the worst.*

That was a lesson her father had drilled into her head. It was his life's motto, largely because life had thrown him the worst. Bradford Hamilton was a bright man. After law school, he went to work as an assistant district attorney and developed a reputation as a fearless trial lawyer. He moved up to the U.S. Attorney's office and made a name for himself taking down violent drug gangs operating on the U.S.-Mexico border. That service earned him an appointment to the U.S. District Court for the Western District of Texas at the tender age of thirty-four, where he served with distinction for three decades. However, he had his sights set higher, on the U.S. Court of Appeals, a call that never came. He was socially awkward, intimidating, and just never made the right kinds of friends that would go to bat for him when an appellate seat opened up.

And there was always the matter of Alicia Hamilton, perpetually indisposed. You couldn't take her anywhere, which meant even if he hadn't been socially awkward, he couldn't take her to cocktail parties and state bar functions. Hell, maybe that was why he was socially awkward. Twenty years of marriage before the stroke took Alicia while she worked in the garden one glorious April afternoon and the man had never been able to relax, not once.

The progeny of a long line of alcoholics, Alicia had started drinking as a teenager, a full-blown drunk before she even became pregnant, and it took everything her dad, then a young district attorney, had to keep his wife sober for the nine months she carried Claire. It was a brutal battle, day in and day out, necessitating constant eyes on Alicia. Neighbors watched, her picture was up at the liquor store, he even hired a lady to sit with her during the day just to keep her dry; still, there were one or two times she managed to get her hands on a bottle of hooch and get plastered. The judge barely slept, powered mostly by high-octane terror that his wife was going to drown their unborn child in whiskey. Claire was born on a brutally hot day in late July, and, despite her father's best efforts, had come out with the shakes. Claire had been a bit behind on the developmental milestones, but she caught up quickly, by the grace of God, as her father liked to say.

She wondered what he would think of all this. He had been rather fond of Peter, respecting the man's brilliance and his work ethic. Peter had grown up poor, another trait that her father admired in folks who became successful. They didn't speak much on the rare occasions they had spent time together; when she and Peter had visited the

Judge in El Paso, they would sit on his screened-in porch with cigars and good scotch. Claire often joined them, enjoying scotch as much as the next girl because she was nothing if not her father's daughter. It had been important to him that she appreciated scotch, introducing her to it when she was eighteen. Another one of his lessons.

He had taught her the world was a boys' club that would try to hold her down and the best way to beat them was to join them. He taught her the tricks they would use to marginalize her (that he knew these tricks because he had used them himself only occurred to her many years later), he taught her what made men respect women, especially in the macho world of rural south Texas, where life was mostly football and guns. The playing field would never be level, and so she would have to game the system in her favor.

"Women are too nice to men and too mean to each other," Judge Hamilton had told her one night a few weeks before she left for college.

When she looked up from her phone again, it was nearly eleven o'clock. The hangover had largely faded, thanks to some ibuprofen and the gallon of coffee in her belly. She had a conference call at eleven-thirty with some folks at Penn State and Arizona State about this article she was working on and boy, were those guys going to be making some bad assumptions about the current state of the space sciences, as it were.

She still felt mentally off, unsettled, as though she no longer fit into her own life. And it was because there were truths about herself that she did not want to be true. Her last conversation with Agent Berry replayed in her head. He barely knew her, and yet somehow he had been confident that he wouldn't need to hold her feet to the fire. Was it intuition or his training at work? He believed that she would leave her family behind, her two small children, to go on a possible suicide mission.

That had never been said, of course, not to her, and maybe they didn't even think that, despite the evidence to the contrary. They would succeed this time, that was how these NASA guys thought. And quite frankly, it wasn't like they had any choice in the matter. They would have to keep trying because regardless of whether Peter was dead or alive, they had to get to this object; she would be surprised if they hadn't had a plan in the works even before they found out about Peter. But no matter how lofty the goal, the danger to Claire was real and, in fact, likely. If nothing else, if this mission ended in failure as well, they could cross off this version of the plan. They could be unsuccessful as many times as they needed to be; you only needed to succeed once.

A growing certainty in her mind.

Sure, she could say no. They would still go, and they might rescue Peter and finally put their hands on the object. After all, they had sent other teams in with her none the wiser. No one would judge her; no one would condemn her. Murphy and Berry would understand. Hell, despite having her by the balls, they still had given her a way out. Because they knew her, perhaps as well as she knew herself.

She could say no, but she wasn't going to.

She had lied to Jack, which was bad enough, and now she was going to pour gasoline on that fire by giving him the very news he had feared in the first place. After years on the periphery, in the smoke and the fog of the past, the ghost ship that was Peter Abbott was coming home to port now, bringing with it ethereal cargo of jealousy and suspicion, casting a shadow over everything they had built. It wasn't fair to Jack, of course it wasn't fair, any more than it was fair for the past to wrap its skeletal arms around Claire.

*How could she do this to the kids,* he would ask, *forget about me, what do you think Hugo will say when you tell him you'll be leaving for God knows how long?*

The idea that she was abdicating her responsibility as a mother for a man who was not her children's father weighed heavily on her mind. Abdicating it for a job that other people could do, other people with less to lose than she did. But that was a shitty thing to say, especially in light of all those who had died trying to get to the island. Weren't they sons and daughters, husbands and wives, mothers and fathers to someone? Was she better than they were?

And that brought her to the kicker, really the only thing that mattered.

The others who might be tasked to go would do so out of a sense of duty or obligation or adventure or pride, a desire to be the ones to make first contact. But for Claire, it was much simpler than that. It had nothing to do with the object. She had made a promise to Peter many years ago, a promise that expired only upon death. Until Saturday morning, she had reasonably believed that promise had expired. But circumstances had changed. How could she look her children in the face and tell them that it was okay to turn your back on your family (and that's what Peter was, he was family, regardless of whether they ever saw each other again) because that was the convenient thing to do? How could she ever expect them to do the right thing if she wasn't willing to do it herself?

After all, she was the right person to send. She was one of the world's preeminent astrobiologists, and they needed people who knew what they were doing. Even if she didn't know exactly what she was doing, she would be less clueless about it than almost anyone else on Earth. Someday, her kids would understand. They would grow up and tell their own kids that their mother had done a great and important thing. That whatever step they had taken as a species was, in part, because of a decision she had made right here (*pride goeth before the fall*), sitting in this chair on this chilly fall morning in Seattle.

It all sounded pretty convincing.

She wondered if Jack would buy it.

She wondered if *she* bought it.

She had to go because she couldn't stay.

She couldn't say no any more than she could stop breathing. Ever since Murphy had set the offer at her feet, she had been making excuses for why she couldn't go. But she had learned a long time ago, and this was hard-won knowledge, that when you had to talk yourself into doing something or, in this case, not doing something, it was usually a very bad idea – jobs, relationships – if you had to convince yourself of an idea's merit, well, that was just asking for trouble.

And here she was.

The phone was in her trembling hand.

She scrolled through her contacts until she landed on *Murphy, Eugene.*

Her thumb hovered over the touchscreen as her sanity pleaded its case one final time.

*Please, Claire, don't do this. It's not your battle, not your mission. Maybe once upon a time it had been, but no more. Think about Hugo. He will hate you. He will cry every night that you're gone, a period of time that might add up to forever, and you won't be able to soothe him.*

She should say no, stay here and do her duty as a wife and mother and be filled with regret and shame. That was what she should do. That was her mandate now. But even as she was thinking about Hugo's sweet face and his chipmunk cheeks, her thumb had tapped the screen and the call was cycling through, the signal bouncing off the cell tower atop the biology building, looking for Murphy's phone out in the ether.

The phone rang once before he answered.

"Murphy."

"It's me."

"Claire."

"I'll go."

She hung up quickly, as though such a dramatic display precluded her from changing her mind before she actually embarked on the mission. But in a way, it had. She had said the words that five days ago, she believed she would never say. She had set it in motion, the series of events that would ultimately determine her fate, Peter's fate, that of her family, of her marriage. Once things got moving, it was very hard to stop them again.

She did not know what would happen.

She sat in the chair looking at the darkened screen of her phone for a long time.

# 13

The kids were at Jack's mother's house for the night. Hugo had raised a bit of a fuss, but he quickly remembered that his Nana let him get away with murder, plying him with treats and unlimited screen time whenever he came to visit. Judy, who had been on her own since the death of Jack's father fifteen years ago, wasn't Claire's favorite person in the world, but they got along well enough. And for the parents of young children, there was nothing more valuable than a free babysitter who would take the kids for an afternoon, an evening, even overnight on virtually no notice.

Claire usually relished the rare moments when she and Jack could get away for a bit, where they could have an adult discussion about this or that, or even just sit and enjoy the goddamned quiet without having to deal with the ultimate parental paradox – that somehow the kids simultaneously believed that their parents knew nothing about anything but also the location of every object they had ever owned.

But tonight was different. It was Friday night, the end of the work week. She'd been dreading this moment since she had called Murphy from her office the day before. Jack would be back from dropping off the kids and picking up dinner any minute now; she had already poured him a large drink.

She considered pouring one for herself, but seeing his wife hitting the bourbon would tell Jack that something was very wrong. Bad enough that she had built this night on yet another lie. She had told him she wanted a quiet night together, that they deserved it after such a long week. Sure, the party had been fun, but they had barely spent any time together as she flitted from one guest to the next. And she wanted a chance to explain the drunken lie he'd caught her in.

And he was going to get an explanation. It just wasn't going to be the one he wanted.

The unfairness of it all shook her. As massive and over-whelming as her love for Peter had been, it had been easy to lock it away in a deep crevice of her heart and move forward with Jack. But now. Now. She didn't know what she felt or what she was supposed to feel. There was no playbook, no support group for this. She had even done an internet search for *my husband was found alive years later*, but the only results she got were cable television movies, a few novels, a bizarre conspiracy-rich blog post, and a link to some guy's unproduced screenplay. And the worst part was that she couldn't even tell him the truth about why she was going. It was the most important thing she would ever do in her career, probably in her life, and she couldn't tell Jack. If there was a plan to share the discovery with the general public, she was not aware of it.

Headlights splashed the windows as Jack eased down the driveway. Her heart raced as the moment approached, as the most significant discussion of their lives brushed up against her like a hurricane threatening landfall. Only time would tell the damage it would inflict; only time would heal the wound she was about to slash into their lives.

By the time he came inside, heavy rain that was expected to last all night roaring outside, she could barely breathe. As soon as she told him, she would be pouring that bourbon after all. She quietly set up the food on the table as he hung up his jacket and took a seat. As she spooned some brown rice onto his plate, he brought the whole evening to a head in one fell swoop.

"You're going, right?"

She froze, the spoon suspended between the white takeout box and Jack's plate.

"That's what this is all about."

She nestled the spoon in the remaining rice and sat down in the chair closest to him. He turned his attention to the bourbon, ignoring the food for the moment.

"I'm sorry I lied to you," she said.

He swirled the tumbler around the table in tiny circles, careful not to spill a drop of the precious liquid. She could feel the anger and the hurt emanating from him. But she didn't know what else she could do. She had to go because she couldn't not go.

"That's the least of my concerns right now."

He took a long sip of his drink.

"Okay," she said. An opening. Something to work with. "What are your concerns?"

He guffawed derisively.

"I'm serious. I want to talk this out."

"What good is that? Is it going to change your mind?"

"No," she said. "I don't know. No."

"I see you commit to NASA about as well as you did to me."

His words made her stomach flip.

"That's not fair," she said. "What am I supposed to do?"

"You are supposed to stay here with your family," he said. "Your husband and those two kids."

He got up from his chair and stomped into the family room; a moment later he returned carrying a framed photograph of the four of them, holding it by the kickstand like it was a shield. Perhaps it was a shield tonight. This memory of them from a trip to Coronado two years ago, the Pacific a dazzling blue behind them. It was one of her favorite photos, the first time it looked like the kids were real kids, not babies, not even toddlers anymore. He set the photograph on the table and pointed at Hugo and Miranda.

"These two here," he said. "You remember them? They come first. Before you. Before me. Definitely way before Peter."

"I am putting them first!" she shouted, loud enough that Jack recoiled. She couldn't remember the last time she had raised her voice like that at him. She wasn't sure she ever had.

"We always talk about doing the right thing," she said, "even if it's the hard thing. Well, this is the right thing. Bringing that poor man back from hell."

"What if something happens to you?"

"Don't you think I've been wondering about that every second? You think I want to go? This isn't a matter of want. I have to go."

Jack picked up the picture frame and stared at it, stroking the glass with his thumb.

"Why you?"

Her skin prickled with heat.

"What do you mean?"

"Why not a search-and-rescue team? Why does it have to be you?"

"They want a biologist on the trip," she said, the lie starting in earnest now. "They still want to know about the meteor. And they're not sure how he's going to react after twelve years. The psychologists think it will be better if I'm there when they find him."

He stroked his salt-and-pepper beard and studied her face. She held eye contact as long as she could, wondering how much easier it would be to just unburden herself of all of it.

*No, I don't know how I feel.*

*Oh yeah, there's an alien drone on the island, too.*

"Is it going to be easier on him when he finds out you're married with two kids?"

She considered this every day. Peter Abbott might still be alive, but his life as he knew it was over. His wife was gone. Even if Peter understood rationally that she had long believed him dead and had moved on with her life, it was going to be an emotional kick in the stomach. She wondered if he still loved her. Why wouldn't he? What if it turned into one of these *the thought of seeing my wife again helped me keep faith* deals? His re-entry was going to be tough, the heat of reality melting whatever shields he'd constructed to protect his sanity.

His house sold. The adorable Cape Cod they had bought together, where they had once talked about starting a family had already changed hands twice. After Peter's disappearance, a young couple bought it from Claire and lived in it for five years. They sold it to a middle-aged man fresh off a divorce, according to her old neighbor whom she stayed in touch with on Facebook.

Even Peter's job would be fundamentally different.

There had been so many breakthroughs and advances in astrobiology since he disappeared, he would be a decade behind in the field he had once dominated, even without accounting for the alien craft's presence. Second, the existence of the object had detonated the field itself. How would he come to grips with any of it?

"They're not going to tell him until he's back home," she said. "I won't be there for that."

She reached out for Jack's hand, enclosed it in her own. He let his hand sit a moment, then yanked it away, just hard enough to tell her what she needed to know. He tented his hands in front of his face, metronomically tapping his lips.

"He's not going to be happy," he said. "He's going to go batshit, no matter when or where they tell him. What then?"

"I don't know."

"Do you still love him?"

She opened her mouth to speak, but nothing came out. Her lips remained parted as she searched for the right thing to say, the thing that would keep the evening calm. And looking back on it later, it occurred to her that answering more quickly, that yes, part of her would always love him, would have been better than just sitting there mute, unsure what to say. Of course, part of her would always love him, that was to be expected of a woman widowed at the age of thirty-three in the most painful way possible. It would be clinical, distant, matter-of-fact. That would have been better than saying nothing because saying nothing was an answer in and of itself. Her silence, her equivocation was a loose thread in the marriage that perhaps neither knew was there. And now current events had started to pull on the thread, and things were beginning to unravel.

"No," she finally eked out. It sounded weak and pathetic.

"You're lying," he said, an edge in his voice. He took a long pull from his drink. "You are lying."

Each of those words was like a bullet to the chest. Maybe she was lying. If her primary motivation for going was to find the alien object, then why was she fucking this up so badly? It should have been easy to say the words in the right way, to assuage the fears of this lovely man sitting here with her, the man who had fathered her children, ease his mind so he wouldn't be wondering what his wife was up to on a tropical island with the other man she had married.

"It doesn't bother me that you love him," he said, his eyes cast downward to the rice on his plate. "It would be weird if you didn't. I can't imagine what it was like for you to lose him, and I won't pretend to know what it was like."

He paused, took a sip of his drink.

"But when you lie about it."

He looked up at her, his teeth biting into his lower lip.

"When you lie about it."

She took his hand again; this time, he didn't pull it away but instead left it lying there like a dead fish. It felt cold and clammy. The whole concept of love, on which she'd felt like she had a pretty good grasp a week ago, now seemed more slippery than ever. What did it mean to love someone anyway? Could you love more than one person in a lifetime, truly love more than once? Could you love two people at the same time, each fitting your soul in a different but altogether complete way? She loved both her kids equally. Why was this different? If your life were a series of interlocking stories, did that mean that Peter lived in an earlier chapter and that her love for him couldn't exist anymore? If she were single now, if she had never moved on or had never met Jack, would it be assumed that she and Peter would try to pick up where they left off?

She got a second tumbler from the cabinet and poured herself a bourbon, not bothering with the ice. She stood at the kitchen counter and drank it slowly, focusing on the burn in her throat as the liquor fireballed its way to her stomach. Her head was spinning from this discussion and she felt as lost as ever. If anything, things were worse than when they had started.

"So I've been thinking," Jack said.

"What about?"

"That maybe we need a little time to work all this out."

"I don't understand."

"You do."

"Just tell me," she said. "Don't you think we've had enough misunderstanding?"

"When you get back from your field trip, if you get back, I think we should take a little break."

"Meaning what?"

"I'll move out for a while," he said.

Her stomach dropped.

"Until you can figure out what it is you want."

She chewed the inside of her cheek as the import of his words hit home.

"I am coming back."

His head whipped around hard to the left and he bore into her with those eyes of his.

"Can you guarantee me that?" he snapped, his voice elevated. He wasn't a yeller, but he was yelling now. "Can you guarantee me that with one hundred percent certainty that you will come back from this trip?"

His eyes were red, his voice quivering. Again, her willpower wavered, and the truth was right there, right on the tip of her tongue. She could tell him that it wasn't only about Peter, that it was something bigger than that, much bigger than that. But even then, she didn't know how true it would sound. She was afraid that she would screw it up, that it would sound like a smokescreen, that Jack would know that even if she told him an interdimensional doorway was sitting on that island and an extraterrestrial army was ready to pour out of it, she was going for Peter.

He might not even believe her.

*Oh, an alien spaceship! Really? How dumb do you think I am, Claire?*

"Yeah," he sighed. "I didn't think so."

"And if I don't?" she said, her eyes welling with tears. "Make it back?"

"We'll figure it out," he said. "Kids lose parents all the time. What makes us so goddamned special? It'll just toughen them up. Make sure they know the world is unfair, get that out of the way early, make sure they learn that lesson before they turn seven."

She couldn't believe Jack, her Jack, was saying these things. It was like some terrible demon had possessed him and was trying to destroy her from the inside out. Make her doubt everything about herself, about who she was.

"Stop, please," she said, her voice thick with tears.

"And I'll tell you something else," he said, ignoring her pleas. "I will make sure those kids have your love forever, even if you don't deserve it. Because they do. They deserve to live their life knowing their mother had loved them above all else. I will make sure they never feel like you abandoned them."

"I am not abandoning them," she said, barely loud enough for Jack to hear. She wasn't even sure if she was saying it to him or to herself.

"I am not abandoning them."

He either didn't hear her or had chosen to ignore her.

For this, she was thankful because she didn't think she could hold up to another one of his verbal assaults. She was close to bailing now, bailing completely, even though deep down, she would be bailing for all the wrong reasons. Her desire to go was at the core of who she was, as a person, as a woman, as a widow, as a wife, as a mother. Not going would fly in the face of all that.

And if she didn't go, she would regret it. She would regret it for the rest of her life, and this regret would infect her, rot her from the inside out. It would spread from her to her work to her relationship with Jack (whatever remained of it at this point, it was like a goddamn bomb hidden under the comfy couch they cuddled on while watching movies and drinking wine had detonated) to her relationships with Hugo and Miranda, the ones she loved best, more than anything, more than Jack or Peter and definitely herself. She would die for them, she had known that from the moment the nurses had placed them on her chest, crying and wriggling in the first moments of their lives. She hadn't fully understood what that meant, that *you would die for your kids.*

People always assumed that meant you would step in front of a bullet for them, and, of course, she would do that in a heartbeat, without even thinking. But it went beyond that, she saw that now. And although she couldn't tell Jack the truth, and although Hugo and Miranda might never understand why she had left and what she had gone to do, that this was worth dying for in so many ways. It was worth dying for writ small. For Peter. His decision to go on that mission twelve years ago had made possible the lives they had now.

And it was worth dying for writ large.

The object.

Alien.

Her whole life's work validated.

And although it was easy to be frustrated that she'd spent the last dozen years in the dark, without the complete picture, the work had not been in vain. Every day had brought her closer to the truth, to being able to accept the truth. All the discoveries, all the knowledge, from everything the Mars rovers had sent back to the never-ending flow of information from the Jupiter missions, the discoveries of Earth-like planets that came in bunches now, like hitting on the slots in Vegas, but instead of coins and chips, they were getting exoplanets and gas giants. And this news would fit right in the center of the panoramic picture they were building. She had always expected to find evidence of extraterrestrial life and often considered her findings, her research, her study as part of a larger canvas. This line of thought also helped with the problem at hand. Focusing on her work helped distract her from her marriage as it cratered. Now, in real time.

Time.

It would take time to work through this.

To think otherwise had been foolish.

Whether she went or not, the fallout was always going to be severe. The idea there was an easy way through this was the fallacy Jack couldn't accept; maybe he didn't want to accept it. Claire too. Perhaps time apart was the best thing. Time didn't always heal all wounds, no one knew that better than Claire Hamilton, but it could heal many of them. They could use this time to remember the most important thing about marriage; you didn't commit your life to someone because you needed them; you did it because you wanted them.

It was why her relationship with Jack had worked. They had clicked right away after meeting at a mutual friend's fortieth birthday party. She didn't *need* to be with someone; she had become content by herself in the wake of Peter's disappearance, territory she battled hard for and that was why it worked. The pressure to meet someone and get married and start a family had faded; people gave you a wide berth on matchmaking when you were a widow. He had invited her out for a drink and she had found herself excitedly accepting, falling for him a little bit at a time, loving the way he told a story, the way he rooted for his beloved Ducks, the way he faked an Italian accent when he was making his excellent pizza dough, it got her going, laughing so hard she was afraid she would wet herself, it felt real and solid. She was with him because she wanted to be, not because she needed to be.

Marriage was like a bank account. You filled it with laughs and adventures and good times when the going was easy because there were going to be bad times and you would have to draw on that account to make it through them. And you needed to fill it early and often, especially in the salad days before real life started to creep in. The survival of a marriage, of any relationship, really, depended on getting through each day, each month, each year in the black, because if you got too deep into the red, the marriage would go belly up. And they'd managed to keep that account healthy over the years.

Jack had never been married before, but the end of a relationship with a college girlfriend had left him knowing what he wanted. Still, it was hard not to imagine this house empty and quiet a year from now. Claire sleeping alone, Jack living in some condo, the life of a single dad. The aroma of the Chinese food sitting untouched in the boxes made her sad; it was that scent that reminded her of her marriage to Jack, of all their happy carefree times together. That time was over now. They were making the biggest withdrawal on that account now; she could only hope there would be enough to cover the debt they now owed.

She walked over to him, still sitting in his chair, and wrapped her arms around his shoulders, pulling his head close against her chest. He did not pull away, but again, he did not engage in the embrace.

"Okay," she said.

"Okay, what?"

"You're right. We'll take a break while we figure this out."

He did not reply.

"I love you," she said, and that was the truth.

She kissed the top of his head. Then she grabbed her keys and went out to the car, leaving behind her warm house and that aromatic Chinese food behind, ducking out into the darkness, into the cold and the rain. She backed out of the driveway, edged her way through the gloom, sheets of rain shimmering in the light of the lampposts lining the main road out of the neighborhood.

She drove.

The research vessel *Kingsman* cut through the chop nearly a thousand miles east of Australia, bouncing from wave to wave like a kangaroo. She was a big ship, two hundred and thirty-six feet from bow to stern, three thousand tons, and currently home to fifty-five passengers and crew. Everyone from Claire's first briefing at Ames was on board, in addition to a number of soldiers.

The last two weeks had been the fastest and worst of her life, which wasn't how it was supposed to work. Usually, time zipped by when things were going well and crept along like molasses when they sucked. In this phase of her life, however, time had ceased to have meaning. The morning after the blowout with Jack, she picked up the kids from their grandmother's and took them out for pancakes, where she explained that Mommy was going on a business trip for a few weeks and that they would have to be big kids and help take care of Daddy while she was gone.

Miranda took it in stride, chewing on her pancakes while she let it be known how things were going to go down in Mommy's absence. She would pack her own lunch, and she would show Hugo how to pack his own, but she wasn't going to do it for him. Hugo remained quiet but tear-free, which told Claire that he was holding it together, but just barely. He poured syrup onto his plate until his pancakes and bacon were swimming in it. Normally, she would get after him about it but not today. He sat there, swirling his bacon in the puddle of syrup but not taking a bite.

"You OK, buddy?" she said, working hard to keep her composure. She couldn't cry in front of him because that would just tell him there was something to worry about, and that was the last thing she needed because there was a hell of a lot to worry about. He nodded without looking up, without making eye contact. Miranda kept talking, which served as a buffer between Claire and Hugo. Ball bearings. WD-40. Keeping things slick and moving.

"Why do you have to go?" he asked, dunking a chunk of pancake in syrup.

"It's the right thing to do," she said.

"So he was your boyfriend," Hugo asked.

"Actually, we were married."

"So is he our daddy too?"

"Hugo, don't be silly," Miranda cut in, sighing loudly.

"No, sweetie, he's not your daddy," Claire said. "Your daddy is your daddy, and I love all of you so very much."

After breakfast, she and Jack sat down and began the painstaking work of arranging for her trip. They did not revisit her decision to go; that was over and done with. No snide comments, no passive-aggressiveness. They worked in a demilitarized zone, sticking to the machinery of dealing with the prospect of Claire walking out their front door and never coming back. Over the next three days, they met with a Seattle attorney and updated their wills. She assured them that Peter's still being alive wouldn't affect anything because he had been declared legally dead, a legal technicality that had dissolved their marriage.

She called her father and told him she was going on a long research trip, but she didn't tell him about Peter because that was a discussion she wasn't ready to have yet. Then she met with her boss Jefferson and explained she needed to take a sabbatical, that NASA had come calling, and that was *easy-peasy-lemon-squeezy* because there was nothing he liked better than good publicity for the department and NASA coming for one of his top guys (he always called them his "guys," whether they were men or women) was the very best publicity there was. It meant that they were being noticed. He even volunteered to teach her introductory biology class for the last four weeks of the semester.

Somehow they crossed off every item on the to-do list without killing each other, without even arguing much about it. They let the work fill in the void between them. She spent every spare moment with the twins, packing in as much as she could in the last days before she left. While cuddling with Hugo on the sofa, while Miranda lectured her about this or that, she wavered, her willpower would begin to crack like ice bearing too much weight, and it would be so easy to call Murphy back and tell him she had changed her mind, that she could not leave her family behind, no matter what. She kept not doing it though, she kept not changing her mind until it was time to leave for Ames, where she would endure several days of briefings and training before they started the long trip to the island. They were both up early that morning, cranky but quiet. Neither had slept well. Jack made her the good coffee and she wondered when she would drink it again.

Her bag sat by the door. They stood on either side of the island counter, sipping their coffee. The kids were already at school, the bus gone, the final hugs and kisses and squeezes and promises to bring back presents already executed. Hugo had handled it better than she expected, probably because he didn't want to break down in front of his sister, who would torment him about it.

Jack drained the last bit of his coffee, and that was that. He rinsed out his cup and set it down in the sink with a heavy clank. There was nothing left for him to do but leave. She wanted to hug him but she wasn't sure how he would respond. She wondered if he would hug her, kiss her good-bye, but she wasn't getting a strong vibe on that front as he stood in front of the sink, his back to her.

"You will be careful," he said.

His voice was small but echoed through the empty kitchen.

"Of course," she said.

He set his hands wide on the edge of the counter, as though he were trying to hold himself up. Then he turned and stepped toward her, close enough that their faces were just a few inches apart. He smelled good, a swirl of mint toothpaste and soap and gourmet coffee. He was an inch shorter than her, so maintaining eye contact didn't require any neck gymnastics. She could just look at him. He was a handsome fellow, a bookish type of handsome, a guy who listened far more than he spoke. An old scar ran just under his left eye, a permanent reminder of a bar fight when he'd been in the Army; he'd been lucky not to lose the eye when a knife came screaming across the bridge of his nose.

Jack was shorter than Peter, who had towered over Claire. She had met many women who would not date men shorter than they were, but she never understood that logic. It didn't even make sense from an evolutionary perspective; there was no evidence that height was any barometer of superior genetic material. If anything, taller men were more prone to cardiac issues and certain cancers. No, that was a societal thing, embedded so deeply that it felt like it was the order of things. Thousands of years of sexual identity politics turning vanity into something atavistic and biological.

As she stood before him, her heart raced and she felt a lump in her throat, as nervous as she'd been the moment they had first kissed, all those years ago. Jack had been the first man she'd been with since Peter; in fact, he was the first man she had kissed since Peter. He kissed her on the forehead. She closed her eyes as he pulled back from her. Somehow, this was worse than his not kissing her at all.

"Please be careful."

She nodded.

He squeezed her shoulder and left.

She sat on the porch and smoked a cigarette while she waited for her ride, which arrived twenty minutes later. She got in the car without a second look back at the house; a second look would give weight and life to the fear that she would never see it again, that she had now seen her family for the last time. She wasn't going down that road. As the car made its way through the streets of Seattle on this unbearably bright morning, she made a few resolutions.

Number one. This mission was going to go by the book.

Number two. Four weeks hence, a car would drop her off here and she would walk back into that house and in charge of her own life.

Number three. Peter was the past. Fair or not, their time had come and gone. Fate or karma or kismet or the universe – hell, maybe it had been God - had intervened to push Peter out of her life, make room for Jack and, as a result, Miranda and Hugo. She was going for science and nothing else.

With those three directives guiding her, she was here, aboard this ship, preparing to drop anchor. They were just outside the island's exclusion zone, which had been quietly set up in the aftermath of the object's arrival. A secure perimeter ringed the island, protected by sea mines one mile in any direction from the shore.

In the morning, she and six Navy SEALs would load into a small patrol boat and paddle for the beach, the mines deactivated until they were inside the perimeter. The loss of the helicopters had convinced them that the anomaly affected electrical systems, which led to a decision to send Claire and her teammates with no electronics. They didn't know if this approach would work, but they did know that all the others had failed. They were going in with weapons, backpacks, knives, rations, water, matches, ponchos and not much else. If they ran into any opposition (and no one knew what that might entail), Claire would have to rely on the SEALs' skills in close quarters combat.

A storm was brewing to their south, churning up the sea like a smoothie in a blender. Claire was not prone to seasickness, but this tempest, combined with the stress pressing down on her, was putting her through the wringer as she lay on her bunk in her cabin. A framed photograph of the kids sat perched on her chest. She had snapped this photo at the pool when they were toddlers, almost half a decade ago now. They were eating popsicles, their hair matted and wet, their cheeks pink from a little too much sun.

It was close to dinner time, and despite her roiling stomach, she needed to eat, as her future promised nothing but protein bars, MREs and water pouches. Besides, it would get her mind off the photograph. She climbed to her feet and made her way to the mess hall. A kitchen worker plopped a spoonful of corn and a stiff slice of meatloaf onto her plate.

She took a seat across from Murphy, sitting alone at a small table. His food remained untouched, and he looked green. His fingers were tented at his lips, as though he were deep in thought.

"You okay?" she asked.

He nodded before taking a long deep breath.

"We're here," he said gloomily. "We're a mile away from the island."

Claire picked at her food, but she did not take a bite.

"How're you holding up?" he asked.

"It's a lot to digest, to be honest. Never thought it would break this way."

He took a sip of his lemonade.

"You're telling me," he replied. "Sometimes I'll be sitting in traffic or at dinner with my wife, and I'll look around at other people and I'll think about how they don't know. And I can't decide if I'd want to trade places with them. Because sometimes I don't like knowing."

Part of her didn't like knowing either, especially when they knew so little. And knowing more could be even scarier. Not all the possible outcomes of the object's arrival on Earth were good. Just its very existence had transformed everything in a way that she had not anticipated. Her entire adult life, she thought she had prepared herself for this eventuality; as she told that dad at the twins' soccer game, she had even considered it more than likely, a virtual certainty, that there was life beyond Earth. Now that the truth had been laid bare, however, she felt more disquiet than excitement. It was incredibly difficult to wrap her head around. Be careful what you wish for.

"Let's go over it again," he said.

He handed her a pen from his shirt pocket and a napkin.

"Draw the island."

Even though they had a dozen official maps of the island, satellite maps, topographical maps, relief maps, physical maps that they had studied *ad nauseam*, sometimes it was better to strip it down to the bare minimum. Deconstruct it so there was less noise. After a few minutes of sketching, she spun the napkin around toward Murphy. Her crude drawing depicted an irregularly shaped island, reminding her of a malignant mole on the skin. A number of coves dotted its perimeter. Sheer cliffs guarded the west and north sides of the island; sandy beaches dotted its southern and eastern edges.

"It's about twenty-six miles from here to here," she said, tapping on the island's longitudinal bulges. "And sixteen miles from here to here, east to west."

"Where's the object?" he asked.

She marked in the center of the island.

"X marks the spot."

He scratched his chin.

"Just keep in mind that satellite imagery has been unreliable," he said. "The crash sites. The object itself. We don't know what to believe. The object may be affecting our data collection."

He laughed.

"I'm a pretty educated man," he said, breaking his meatloaf into small pieces. "But this is beyond everything. We have our fancy briefings and research centers and strike teams and it all feels so fake. I really don't know what the hell we're doing. No one does. For all we know, everything we've learned about the sciences, about math and engineering, everything we've told ourselves we know, it could all be wrong."

"You sure know how to fill a girl with confidence."

"Don't tell me it hasn't crossed your mind."

"Touché."

Claire looked down at her plate. The food looked rather unappealing, flat and dead, like it had been cooked a year ago. Then she remembered that for Peter, this would be an unimaginable feast and guilt coursed through her veins. By this time tomorrow, this meal would seem like that to her as well, so she dug in. She ate it like someone who hadn't eaten a hot meal in twelve years would eat it, savoring the heaviness of the meat, the warmth of the thin potatoes. When her plate was clean, when she had used the hard roll to sop up the runoff, when her belly was full, she said a little prayer to a God she did not believe in that this would not be the last hot meal of her life.

Murphy lit a cigarette while she ate, but he had smoked very little of it. The heel of his hand was pressed against his forehead, the filter clamped between his two thick fingers. It had burned down quite a bit, a long cylinder of ash perched precariously at the tip.

"Any favorite theories?" she asked.

"What?" he replied, blinking hard, as though he had just woken up.

"What do you think it is?"

"I don't know."

"Come on," she said.

He shrugged.

"Maybe a drone. Maybe a Trojan horse."

"A Trojan horse?"

"We open it up, and an army pours out."

"Like in that comic book movie," Claire said, chuckling.

"I mean, can you say it's not?"

"No," she replied. "I guess not."

"It makes me nervous that it's on such a deserted island."

"Why?"

"Tells me it was intentionally sent here."

"How do you figure?"

"The center of that island is one of the most remote spots on Earth."

"That might be a good thing."

"How do *you* figure?"

"If they wanted to cause trouble, they could've just parked it on the White House lawn."

As they spoke, she started to feel a little better. The evidence before them suggested that whoever had sent the object had done so without any malicious intent. If that were the case, then the object was a gift to humanity. A glorious, wondrous gift. Sure, it had cost them dearly, Claire and the families of the others lost on the missions. But a gift that could teach them so much about the universe they knew so little about.

He looked up at her, his eyes wet with tears. The cord of ash from his cigarette had snapped off into a small salt-and-pepper colored hill on the table.

"It's just that-"

A loud boom interrupted him before he could finish his thought. For a split second, Claire thought nothing of it, assuming it was something routine, the way a house creaked at night while it settled. Very quickly, however, it became obvious that something was amiss. The ship groaned loudly and Claire felt her center of gravity shift underneath her. The chit-chat in the room stopped dead as two dozen people tried to process what was happening. She looked to Gene for a clue, but his face remained impassive.

Four crew members, two men and two women, were up on their feet before anyone else, streaming through the door into the passageway. Then: gunfire. Distant, on another part of the ship, but unmistakable. A klaxon alarm began to sound and the speakers crackled to life. Fear squeezed Claire tightly, making it difficult to breathe.

"Let's go," Murphy said.

"Where?"

"Our cabins," he replied. "We stay out of the way."

She started to ask about the gunfire, but the ship shifted a second time, flushing that query out of the queue. Somewhere in the back of her mind, the thought of the ship sinking scurried about like a rat. Murphy led her from the mess hall and into the narrow passageway. All around her, desperate shouts and the clang of boots on metal peppered the air. Murphy wasn't running, not exactly, but he wasn't walking either, and it took some effort to keep up with him. The lower levels of the ship were a maze and she could lose track of him.

At the end of one corridor, they ascended a narrow metal staircase and squeezed through the tiny opening in the floor. This brought them to the main living quarters, stern side, on the opposite side of the ship from the emergency. She recognized this section; her cabin was only a few steps away, immediately adjacent to Murphy's.

"We'll wait in here," he said, stopping in front of his cabin. "Until we get the all clear."

Claire paused behind him as he reached for the door, her heart racing, her skin slick with sweat. This didn't make any sense. Murphy wasn't thinking clearly. No good could come from waiting in their rooms, especially since they didn't know the gravity of the situation they were facing. For all they knew, the object was widening its sphere of influence. And either way, there was a good chance *Kingsman* was foundering.

"Maybe we should head to the lifeboats."

Then Murphy laughed, a shrill laugh that chilled Claire to her core. She had never heard anyone make that sound.

"We're not going to the lifeboats."

The hair on her neck stood up. Something was terribly wrong.

"What the hell is going on?"

When he turned back toward her, he was pointing a pistol at her face.

The *o* of the gun barrel stared at her like a mouth opened in surprise. Surprise that she shared because standing here at gunpoint, she could not fathom what was happening. Her eyes cut upward from the gun to Murphy's face, staring at her blankly.

"Inside," he said, waving the gun toward the door.

"What are you doing?"

"I said inside."

He took a step backward, keeping the gun out of her reach as she entered the small cabin and moved to the back. Before turning back around, she snuck a peek out of the porthole. The water line was all wrong, as the ship had begun to list heavily. Inside the cabin, there was barely enough room for both of them, which made the gun's presence all the more intimidating. It hovered in her face like a serpent.

"Have a seat."

She lowered herself down to the edge of the bed, never once taking her eye off the gun. Murphy closed the door with an unnerving click.

"Gene," she said softly. "What are you doing? Did you do this?"

"This has to end."

"What does?"

"These suicidal missions."

"Why?"

"It's finally become clear."

"What did?"

"I remember it like it was yesterday. I was so excited. It was the best day of my life. I mean, I was scared, of course, but mostly excited. Everything we had worked toward. It was happening. And there would be so much to learn, so many discoveries in the days and weeks and months to come. Then we lost Peter's team, and then we lost the other missions, and each time a little part of me died."

*Keep him talking, Claire thought. Just keep him talking. As long as he's talking, he's not shooting you.*

"But these things can be hard," she replied. "They can take time."

His face darkened.

"I know it can be hard," he snapped. "I know it can take time. But it's been twelve years. Twelve goddamn years and we haven't figured out shit. And then after the last one, I started to wonder. Maybe we're not supposed to."

"Not supposed to what?"

"Not supposed to make it to the island. It's cursed."

She struggled not to roll her eyes.

"I know that sounds crazy," he said. "But maybe this has been a test. Whoever sent it was testing us. And we've failed. What if we're not ready?"

"This is how science works, Gene," she replied. "We try something, we fail, we learn, we try again."

"We did all that. We did."

As they spoke, she began planning an exit strategy.

"Why didn't you say anything? That you were feeling this way?"

"I might as well have turned in my resignation."

She raised her eyebrows.

"No," he said, chuckling. "Someone else would have just kept going, this stupid quixotic quest, sending more people to their deaths."

"This isn't going to stop anything," Claire said. "You're right. They'll reboot and keep going. They'll never stop. They'll just restart the mission."

"No, Claire, they won't."

"What do you mean?"

He laughed again.

"Ames is gone."

She furrowed her brow in confusion.

"What?"

"We took care of it."

"What does that mean?"

"We took care of it," he repeated.

He sighed as Claire struggled to parse meaning from his words.

"We had no choice," he said. "You're right. If we didn't cut out the roots, they would just restart everything. We can't have that. We need to put this on the back burner for a long time. Years. Decades. We have to start from scratch. You know what some of the great writers do? They write a whole book and then throw out the whole draft. They don't revise it. They start from scratch, understanding that their internal filter will discard the garbage. That when they re-write it, it will be perfect. That's what we'll do. They'll restart without the burden of all the bad ideas that've weighed them down, that's led to the failure of all these missions."

Claire felt sick to her stomach.

"Did you kill them?"

"We had no choice," he said. "We didn't want to, but it all had to go. Personnel, files, research, data. Everything. No trace of the project could be left."

"You don't think they'll figure it out? They're smart. You might as well have put a bullseye on this place."

"We're smart too," he said chillingly. "You think we started planning this yesterday?"

"How many of you are there?"

"Enough."

She had to get out of here.

"So what's the gun for?"

He looked down at it, as though he'd forgotten it was there. He tapped the barrel with his knuckles. When he looked back at her, a wistful smile had spread across his face.

"We had to make some tough decisions."

"Why did you even bring me here?" she asked. "I never had to know about this. You could've just let me be."

He sighed loudly.

"I never wanted you to come," he said. "I figured you had suffered enough. But that decision was made above my pay grade. The powers that be decided that you deserved to know the truth."

He chuckled.

"Well, now you know."

He was going to kill her. In the tangled equation he was solving with this bizarre attack, she was a variable that had to be canceled out. His rationale wouldn't make any sense and so she didn't bother asking for an explanation.

"Is Peter even alive?"

The question broke free before she'd had a chance to

consider it. Perhaps this had all been a stunt to lure her out here, where they could get rid of her, write her off as yet another tragic casualty of the project.

He laughed.

"Yeah, I can see why you are asking that," he said. "But he's alive. That said, we can't continue to throw so many resources, human and otherwise, at saving one man while also trying to get to the object. It's too much. He's a distraction."

"He's smart too, you know. What will you do if he makes it off the island?"

"We've prepared for every contingency."

"You bastard," she said through gritted teeth.

He rolled his eyes at her.

"This isn't personal, Claire," he said. "It's like you said. Nothing is more important than the mission. Not me, not you, not Peter. We have to think much bigger than this."

The ship groaned and shifted again, and an idea dawned in Claire's mind.

"What did you do to the ship?"

"We placed a powerful explosive at the hull. Right now, the crew is trying to stabilize the damage, but it's too late. Too much water will get in, and *Kingsman* will go down."

Her breathing grew more ragged with each passing moment. Not here, she thought, she couldn't die here, her mission still in its crib. She had to find a way out; there would be no reasoning with Murphy. The man was broken mentally, and there was no time to try and put him back together. Death was nearby now, the closest she had ever come to it. All her life, she had wondered how she would react in such a situation, and now she was about to find out. She was quickly discovering the way was set, as though inscribed in stone before she had ever arrived at this juncture. Already, she had made decisions without realizing it. Escape. No pleading with Murphy. Just escape.

She just needed the right moment.

And she knew it was coming soon.

She closed her eyes and waited, on alert for a particular moment, a specific occurrence that could give her the tiniest step up on Murphy, a man who, it appeared, was waiting to sink to the depths of the vast Pacific Ocean.

Then it happened.

The almost imperceptible creak metastasized into a deafening groan, the loudest one yet, the ship listing and dipping hard to her right. Murphy stumbled for a moment, just enough to give her a chance. He was bigger than her, but the element of surprise was on her side. She lowered her shoulder and drove into him with her powerful swimmer's legs. The shifting of the ship threw his center of gravity off balance and their collision drove him toward the wall of the cabin; he stumbled across the rear corner of her bunk and toppled over. His feet flew up in the air as he somersaulted backward, heels over head. The gun came loose and clattered to the floor.

Down on her hands and knees, Claire scampered for the door, pausing to grab Murphy's gun. As she stood up, Murphy's hand clamped around her ankle. She grunted and kicked out hard. Her foot connected with the soft tissue of his nose, and he howled in pain.

"You crazy bitch!" he screamed through the blood filling his nostrils and throat.

She ignored him and hammered the door with her shoulder; which broke free from its track and hung askew like a broken wing. The force of her impact carried her into the passageway and hard into the wall opposite her cabin. The lifeboat. She had to make it to a lifeboat. She sprinted down the corridor, praying she was headed the right way. A ladder at the end of this passageway took her up to the main deck, which was strangely deserted. The air was humid and a strong wind was blowing from the west. The seas roiled behind her.

She risked a look to the front of the ship, now flooded, sinking by the bow. Shouts and orders caught up in the wind drifted back toward her. Then a large fireball bloomed from the engine room, the sonic boom reaching her ears a moment after she spotted the conflagration. The blast wave knocked her off her feet, down to her bottom; her stomach turned to water as she watched bodies and debris ejected into the air like confetti.

She clambered back to her feet and turned back to the stern, her eyes locked in on the lifeboats. This was her salvation, her only hope. She quickly studied the pulley system securing the boat to the hull, evaluating whether this was a one-woman job or whether she needed help.

A second explosion, this one from the middle of the vessel, deafened her and catapulted her off the deck. The warm blast wave lifted her high enough to give her a bird's-eye view of the *Kingsman* as it disintegrated into an asteroid belt of debris and body parts. Then gravity took over, and the uncanny sensation of rapidly dropping filled her belly and her throat.

She hit the water with a terrific splash.

## 16

Claire crashed into the ocean bottom first, kicking and thrashing as her momentum shoved her down a dozen feet into a watery grave. Her ears sealed up as the sea closed in around her. The urge to gasp from shock and the water's chill was strong, but she managed to catch her breath, a welcome byproduct of her thousands of hours in a pool. She waited until her body oriented itself and then kicked hard, surfacing amid three-foot waves, roiling enough to give them a whipped cream-like topping of sea foam. She breathed in hard, the sweet air delicious. The water was chilly, in the mid-sixties, but warm enough to survive in for a while. As her breathing stabilized, the enormity of the disaster struck her. The *Kingsman*, or whatever was left of her, was gone, already on her way to the bottom of the Pacific. Bits of flaming debris and detritus floated past her. A bloody stump of an arm, still in its sleeve. Then a corpse drifted past, but she couldn't tell if it went with the erstwhile arm.

Triage.

As she treaded water, she triaged her situation. She was

relatively unscathed, a little sore from her impact with the water's surface. Sharks were the second thing that came to mind, and the very thought threatened to take her breath away. The *Kingsman*'s final resting place would make for good feeding grounds, as the ocean's predators would soon zero in on the significant blood in the water. Quickly, she spun onto her back and extended her legs into the air, looking for any signs of bleeding. None. She rolled back into an upright position, checked her arms and her chest. Clear.

Fortunately, it was still daylight; sunset was still several hours away. She twirled in the water, looking for the island in the distance, perversely thankful that Murphy's group had waited to launch their attack. If they had pulled this stunt a day or two ago, she would have been floating in the middle of the Pacific, a hundred miles from land.

There!

Her heart soared as she spotted the island's hazy outlines, just visible enough to give her hope. The island was due east, but the current was pulling slightly south and could feel herself drifting. There was no time to waste. She swept a curtain of water clear and settled into the familiar freestyle stroke that had been part of her life since she was five years old.

Even after her competitive swimming days had ended, she continued to swim several days a week. In those dark days after Peter's disappearance, the water had been her refuge. The morning after she got the news, she found herself in her office, not even sure how she had ended up there, staring at the computer screen, staring at the blinking cursor on her computer screen. Blink blink blink.

*Blink. Blink. Blink.*

A knock on her door interrupted her. She got out of her chair, opened the door, and walked right past the bewildered co-worker standing in her doorway to the health club, a ten-minute walk from her office. She didn't even have a suit, but she needed to be in the water. After peeling down to her bra and underwear, she marched right out to the pool and dove in. She swam until her legs cramped. If anyone noticed her attire, they said nothing.

Every day for the next year, weekends included, she got up early and swam for an hour. She woke without an alarm, well before sunrise. She would lay there in the dark, still on the left side of the bed, never migrating toward Peter's side. His pillows were gone, tucked on the top shelf in the closet; the sheets were the same, the comforter was the same. Every morning, the routine had been the same; she would sweep her hand across Peter's side of the bed, the chill of the sheet jolting her to her feet. Even though she knew he wasn't there, something about the empty half of the bed drove her out of bed, to the pool, and into the water. She was almost always the first one there, the surface of the pool still a sheet of glass. Every day for a year.

Exercise helped swallow her grief, so she added running and cycling to her repertoire; she signed up for an Ironman triathlon and spent another year training for that, and when that was done, two years had passed and she felt like she could breathe again. The hole in her heart, in her soul, was still there, would always be there, but it was now just a part of her and not her defining characteristic.

The Ironman swim was two-and-a-half miles long, and this would be less than half that, so it really shouldn't be any problem at all. In fact, she should be able to pop up out of the water on that distant shore, climb onto a bike and bang out a hundred miles.

She swam.

She picked out a point on the island, a high rocky bluff

thick with trees, on the northwestern corner of the island, and maintained that heading as best as she could. She focused on her stroke, on keeping her form as clean as possible; that would maximize her speed through the sea-green chop while minimizing her expenditure of energy.

She swam.

Images of the kids tried edging their way into her mind, but she held them at bay. The list of things she would have to do if she were ever to see them again was about four hundred items long, and she was only on the very first thing. But she was back in the water, alive, her lithe body knifing through the waves, and that was something. A shimmer of warmth washed through her, a telltale sign that she was working hard in the chilly water. She took a quick break to check her progress; she was ten minutes into her swim now; if she was on pace, maybe a quarter of the way through.

As she rested, a flutter against her leg drew a gasp. Instinctively, her arms and legs flailed before she was able to settle herself down. Her head swung around like a disco ball; her eyes locked on a small grey triangle gliding through the water, away from her. To her left, another dorsal fin trailed behind the first one. Her body froze, her breath held tight. She could only hope the sharks were drawn toward the wreckage of the ship and that she would be of little interest to them.

She looked to the south, where another larger group of sharks was circling, roughly thirty yards away. She was pinned in for the moment. Great big shockwaves of fear rippled through her as she waited for them to do whatever it was they were going to do. They broke the circle and curled north toward her. Her breath came in ragged gasps, and she hated herself for making so much goddamn noise. Like a train, the sharks came in single file, swimming in that familiar serpentine glide. One by one they passed by her, and relief flooded through her.

Just a couple more and she would be in the clear.

Then one more.

Then the last one curled back again, directly toward her, its fin accelerating under the water. He was the smallest of the bunch; perhaps he was too young to understand that there was better eating up ahead. There was no doubt, though, that he had zeroed in on Claire, and he was approaching quickly. She had only a few seconds to act. Maybe a few seconds to live.

She dipped below the waves and kicked hard for the surface, breaching it just as the shark closed in, close enough that she could see its lips peel back from its teeth. She drew back a clenched fist and dropped it as hard as she could on the shark's pointy snout. Stunned, the predator changed its heading while closing its lips back around a stadium of teeth, turning just so and skimming past Claire's legs. The shark was close enough that she felt the water ripple around her as he gave her narrow berth. Then he turned back to the north to join his mates, having lost interest in this combative bag of meat.

Everything unfolded in slow motion as the shark swam away, leaving Claire alone and unscathed but for a red abrasion on her wrist where she had punched the shark's tough snout. As she floated in the water, she let loose a howl, barbaric and deep and desperate; it echoed loudly off the whitecaps, drowning out for a moment even the eternal susurration of the ocean's current. Her body trembled and she felt her bladder let go. She had survived.

Break over.

She took a deep breath and resumed her swim, refusing to look for sharks. Every moment spent looking for them was a moment of energy wasted. Hugo's sweet face forced its way into her mind, and this time she let it in. She was swimming for him and Miranda, after all. She had to make it through this because to not make it through this would mean to leave the twins without a mother. To abandon them. Just like Jack had said.

She swam.

Her legs burned and her shoulders ached, but she swam, a tiny insignificant dot in the vast ocean. Thirty minutes into her swim, the sun broke free of the clouds and she felt the warmth on her neck and shoulders. She paused again and took stock. The island was closer now, no doubt about it. Her beacon, the high bluff, was in sharper focus now, and Claire could make out individual trees.

Galvanized, she picked up the pace, her arms churning through the water like windmills. Just knowing she was making progress, that she wasn't spinning her wheels in the washing machine of the Pacific, jolted her with adrenaline. Everything fell away as she zeroed in on her target – Murphy, the shark, the kids, Jack, Peter, the object, everything. It was just her and the water now. Her whole life had been leading up to this moment, to this swim. She didn't know if it was destiny or fate or karma, but here she was, a fighting chance to get out of this particular mess because her dad had signed her up for swim lessons forty years ago. All the early mornings in the pool, her two years on the varsity swim team at Texas, her return to the pool to wash her soul of the grief from Peter's death, each brick stacked on the last to give her a chance to get to that far-off shore, maybe a third of a mile away now.

She was close enough to the island that she began thinking of the distance in meters, no different than a long training swim at the pool. Five hundred meters to go. Then four hundred, the island growing bigger by the second as she caught its profile in her metronomic head turn. It was time to start thinking about her final approach. The beaches were on the island's eastern side. Coming in from the west, Claire would have to deal with a cove surrounded by a sheer circular cliff and a rocky outcrop that would be difficult to negotiate.

At one hundred meters, the island in clear view now, Claire felt herself drifting north, although she was fairly certain she had not changed her heading. Alarm bells sounded in her head as she feared a cross current that could sweep her clear of the island, effectively dooming her. She pulled hard toward her original course, but she continued to drift, only more quickly now.

She paused for a moment to ascertain the current's true strength; the news was not good. Already she was a few degrees farther north than she wanted to be. She resumed swimming immediately, this time picking a far more southerly heading. This meant fighting against a strong current hellbent on flushing her out to sea. Panic shimmered in her belly and she feared that all this work would have been for nothing. That she would have made it all this way, that she would have survived her duel with a goddamn great white shark, and it would have been for nothing. She swam with all she had, her extremities feeling more and more like lead weights now, almost working against her. She wished now she had saved some of the energy she had expended during the swim; it wasn't like a medal awaited her at the end. She was now due southwest of a rocky tidal pool she'd spotted, which looked to be her only shot at a safe landing.

She'd be threading a needle. If she swam too far south, she might end up in the cove and she wasn't sure she would have the strength to swim back out, assuming the current didn't slam her worn body against the rock wall. Too far north, and she would miss the shoal entirely. Her mind was cloudy with fatigue, and every muscle in her body screamed for relief, for rest. But there was no rest to be had, the current strengthening as she drew closer to the island. The point of no return was rapidly approaching.

Her strength was just about gone, and she understood now how easy it would be to give up. You didn't have to keep fighting; you could just let the ocean take you. It would be over quickly. Just sink beneath the waves. She made herself a deal as she committed to her final trajectory. If she missed the target, that would be it. She would let it go. She had fought, she had fought like hell. Her kids could be proud of her, even if they would never understand what had become of their mother, even if they believed that she had died in the sinking of *Kingsman*.

The current picked her up and swept her northeast, and her swim was over. It would come down to whether she had picked the right angle of attack. A sense of peace washed over her, knowing her fight was over, that she had done all she could. The rock formation came up fast, more quickly than she had anticipated. The water level had dropped precipitously, and she could feel her toes brushing the bottom, but the current was brisk, too fast for her to gain any purchase.

A series of rocks, onyx, colorless, lay just ahead. She was coming in a bit shallow and might miss them entirely. She extended her arms as far she could, her fingertips brushing against the slick rocks, but she wasn't able to hold on. Her body came in hard, and she slammed into them, hard enough to take her breath away, but not so hard that she was able to grab hold.

Then the water deepened rapidly again and the current pulled her to the far side of the shoal, where the rocks climbed up into the mist surrounding the island. Soon the current would sweep her along the cliffside. Calling upon her fading reserves, she lunged one last time, digging her hand into a crevice carved into a large boulder; she was so surprised by the success of her gambit that she gasped. Her grip wavered as the force of the current yanked on her arm, almost until she could feel it coming loose from its socket.

She guided her free arm, her right one, toward the crevice, better anchoring herself against the rocks. Like a bug skittering on a wall, she slowly made her way to the base of the rock formation, one slippery stone at a time. The current pulled hard on her, as if the island didn't want her to make it, but she held fast. If she could make it another ten yards, she would be able to climb out of the water and get her feet, if not on land, then something closely resembling it. When the rocks flattened out, she swung a leg out of the water and planted a foot on a wide stone. This relieved some of the strain off her arms. With one final pull, she cantilevered herself out of the water and collapsed.

She lay flat on the rock, breathing hard, her lungs burning, her legs spent. The sun beat down hard on her neck, but a fine sea mist spraying the edge of the island kept her cool. It felt good to be out of the water, better than anything had felt in her life. Her exhaustion was complete. Every muscle, every ligament, every cell, every square centimeter of tissue had been called on to make this swim, and her reserves were at zero. Seawater brushed up against her lips, reminding her that she was profoundly thirsty and dehydrated. She would deal with that in a minute. There was more work to do. Now she had to get her sea legs back under her and get to higher ground.

With a grunt, she climbed to her feet and just stood a moment, enjoying being on *terra firma*. That alone rejuvenated her, filling her with a second wind. Okay, maybe more of a breeze than a second wind, but her strength was returning, albeit slowly. She glanced at her next obstacle, the stairlike series of rocks ascending to the island proper. She turned back toward the ocean, vast and empty, stretching endlessly in every direction. From her perch, the sea looked calm, the waves slow and lazy. It was a hell of a view. It was a lonely view.

A stitch of panic burrowed inside her, and for the first time, she wondered how the hell she was ever going to get home.

## 17

C laire pushed away thoughts of home, turning her back on the sea as the waves crashed against the rocks. Her legs were rubbery and her shoulders burned, but she needed to get to drier land. She took a few moments to study the rocks and saw that it would be challenging but not impossible to scale them. Her biggest enemy would be time. The sun had dropped low in the sky, leaving her only a couple of hours of daylight. She hoped she would have time to find some water.

After massaging her spent quads for a few minutes, she began climbing up the rocks. It was about fifty feet to the top, maybe a little more. She went slowly but methodically, keeping her center of gravity low, using the edges of the rocks as handholds. As she ascended the formation, she found it easier to almost slither along them, coming up to a crouch when it was time to elevate to the next level.

A light breeze came in off the sea, which, combined with the sun's powerful rays, helped dry her off. Even though her clothes were wet, the mere sensation of dry skin made her feel almost normal again. At the halfway point, she paused to rest, taking a seat on the rock's edge, her legs dangling over the side. Up this far, she was out of reach of the waves' backwash; it was almost uncomfortably hot up here. Then she remembered the chill of the deep ocean, and she was just fine where she was.

When she felt replenished, she started again, the temperature rising the farther she got from the cooling breezes of the ocean. Another twenty minutes, mostly uneventful but for a near slip in which she banged her hand hard, brought her to the highest rock; this one was long and narrow and tapered down to a narrow dirt path, flanked by tall trees. She was standing on the only sliver of land she could see that wasn't treed. To her south was the cove, the two ends of which looked like crab claws pinching together. She'd seen the satellite imagery, she'd studied the geographical dimensions, but now the island seemed much larger and much more beautiful.

Hell, if she were going to die, might as well do it in a place that looked like this.

There. She might die here. It was time to accept it. She was going to work her damndest to get home, but that was going to require a boat. A boat would require people, people who knew that she was here. And no one knew she was here because no one knew she was still alive. She would be presumed dead, like everyone else aboard *Kingsman*. Christ, she was going to have to build a raft like Tom Hanks in *Cast Away*. Become friends with a goddamn volleyball.

Her hand went to the hollow of her neck, where, inexplicably, the locket still rested. Somewhere on this island was the man whose photograph was secreted inside the locket. A photograph worn as a memorial to him. God, what would seeing him be like? It was still difficult to accept as reality. All these years she had lived as though he were dead, and once you lived with a belief long enough, it was hard to change course on it, no matter how much evidence was put in front of you. It physically pained her to accept that Peter was alive. Not because she wasn't happy that he was alive. Because his being dead had become part of who she was. A big part. But now that she was here, she was going to have to get used to the idea of a living, breathing Peter very quickly, starting right now and continuing as she made her way into the island's interior.

Her stomach rumbled and she became aware of a dryness crusting her lips, a bad combination of ocean salt, sun, and dehydration. She needed water. Without water, she couldn't do anything else. Everything began to feel very heavy all at once. Her legs and arms and eyes and head. She needed to sit. Just for a second. Then she would find water; if she had to suck the dew from the leaves hidden in all that wet tropical darkness beyond this path, she would find water. She sat, and it had never felt so good to sit in all her life. The island around her was so alive and vibrant, like it was breathing, like it was a beautiful living thing. Another breeze washed over her in the fading afternoon. She stretched out there on the path, on her back, rotating her spine, loosening her exhausted hamstrings and quadriceps.

Her eyes drooped, and she struggled to keep them open. It was too exposed to sleep here, too dangerous, and there was too much to do. But each blink of her eyelids grew successively longer until sleep overcame her and she slid down into darkness. She slept there on the path, her breathing even and deep; behind her, the sun eased toward the horizon, until it kissed the water and sprayed a kaleidoscope of pinks and reds and oranges across the sky. Twilight descended like a blanket, and Claire slept on, her body repairing the damage and strain of the previous twenty-four hours.

Around her, the island's nocturnal creatures came to life, hooting and squeaking and carousing. If she had been awake, Claire might have found this natural symphony unsettling. She slept, on and on, dreamless. Fourteen hours later, Claire started awake, bolting upright. Her head swiveled from side to side, eyes open and unblinking, taking in their surroundings as though she had woken up on an alien planet. Overall, she felt pretty good. She was pretty sore and stiff, and her shoulders were tight from the swim, but they would loosen up as the day went on. Still, she wouldn't have minded a couple of Advil and a bottle of Gatorade.

The tree line was about fifty feet ahead of her, a thick line of massive trees forming an almost impenetrable perimeter around the island's interior. An opening between a pair of giant sentinels caught her eye. As she slipped in between them, a perpetual twilight enveloped her, a dark world. Invisible life forms chattered.

A thought occurred to her.

She found herself hesitating.

She wasn't sure if it was because it was too silly to work or if she was afraid it actually would work. She cleared her throat and then cupped her hands around her mouth.

"Peter!"

It was worth a shot, after all.

The sounds of the jungle fell silent at this new sonic intrusion. Claire held her breath, waiting to see if she could find a needle in a haystack on her first try. Nothing. After a few moments of surprised silence, the jungle resumed its cacophony.

Water.

The branches hung low here, close enough that Claire could brush her hands on the green ceiling of this jungle. The leaves were damp, coating her hands with dew. Greedily, she lapped at her fingers before realizing there was a better way. A hard shake of the branches triggered a tiny little rain shower, spraying her mouth and face with water. She drank for a good five minutes as she beat back the demons of dehydration. Her lips moistened, and then her thick, cotton-laced tongue initiated a welcome retreat, the fading sensation that it was too big for her own mouth a stark relief.

She drank until her thirst was slaked. Good eating in these here hills. Only when she finished did it occur to her that she should have boiled the water first, but it was too late to worry about it now. Her thirst quenched, she considered her next move.

As best as she could tell, she had three options.

First, the alien object. The center of the island was a good ten or twelve miles to the east. With this terrain, it might take her a couple of days to make it that far. Part of her felt like it was more than she was ready for. It was weird, now that she was on the same little plot of land as the most significant discovery in human history, that she didn't want to race for it for all she was worth. The culmination of her career. All those years she had dreamed about actual contact, even knowing the odds were so slim, even thinking about the Drake equation, Fermi's Paradox, knowing the best chance was that future scientists would build on her work and draw them ever closer to an answer. But everything had been short-circuited by this discovery.

Option two was making for the beaches on the eastern side of the island, where she could start a signal fire. Presumably, someone would notice that the ship was gone, and they would have its final coordinates. But the beaches were more than twenty miles away, even farther than the object. The problem was that starting a fire here was likely a no-go; everything here bore a slick coating of mist, and it would be difficult to find enough dry kindling. The other problem was that the chances were good that no one was looking for a signal fire. The thought that Peter had probably had the same idea unnerved her. Of course Peter had built a signal fire.

Her final option was to hunt for the wreckage of the lost missions. However, even though the island was small, she was just one woman; it would be looking for needles in a haystack. It was, however, probably the smartest play; it was likely that at least some of the supplies had survived intact. First aid kits, MREs, perhaps even some weapons she could use to hunt. She hadn't seen any yet, but maybe there was game on this island.

Her thoughts drifted back to the object. It was here, perhaps no more than a couple days' hike from where she now stood. Whatever she decided, it was going to be a rough go. She was wearing calf-length cargo pants and a T-shirt. Luckily, a decent pair of running shoes adorned her feet. Trail shoes would have been better, but it wasn't like she'd had a chance to pack. The forest floor was heavily rutted with thick roots. Over the next hour, she picked her way carefully through the trees, stepping carefully around thick exposed roots and crossing small creeks. The jungle seemed to swallow her up like a prehistoric beast, but she was still close enough to the ocean that she could hear the waves crashing against the rocks. As she hiked, she kept a wary eye out for animals, particularly snakes. She hated snakes.

It was unlike any hike she had ever taken, something she and Peter had done frequently together. The island was breathtakingly beautiful, a swirl of dense forest and eye-popping flowering plants. At one point, the trees thickened enough that she was pushed a bit more to the east, back toward the cliffside ringing the cove. It was being entirely too generous to call it a path, but there was just a wide enough cut-through to negotiate. At one point, it narrowed so sharply that there was only enough room on the path for a single foot; her other one dangled precipitously over the cliff. She hazarded a glance only once, enough to send her heart into her throat; it was at least four hundred feet to the shimmering waters below.

One step at a time she went until she found another opening in the trees. As she turned to get away from the cliff's edge, something far to the east caught her eye. She turned her head but lost it in the sun. Her ears perked up at the sound of rushing water, somewhere to her northeast. After another half mile or so, the trees thinned out even more, opening up on a large glade dominated by bizarre-looking flowers. They looked like roses, but they were much larger, each one about the size of a bowling ball. She saw deep purples and fiery reds, blues that were bluer than the clearest October sky.

The volume of the rushing water increased in intensity as she navigated the flowers; on its far side, she crested a hill overlooking a small waterfall emptying into a reservoir to her east. That fed into a narrow river snaking its way into another copse of wide-leafed trees and twisting eastward into the heart of the island. The water was clear and cold and ran hard. She could see all the way to a smooth sandy bottom. She debated stripping down for a bath, but she couldn't bring herself to do it. That would call for a level of exposure, of vulnerability that she was not prepared for. Regardless, she made a note of this spot; a source of fresh water would be critical to her survival. Perhaps this was one of Peter's way stations. Certainly, in twelve years, he had mapped out the terrain, identified the island's hot spots. She studied the area, looking for any signs of habitation.

A chill ran through her as she considered Peter's life here. Twelve years. Half his adult life on this little chunk of dirt out in the middle of the ocean? It was difficult to fathom. Even harder to believe was the thought that he was the same man he'd been. This kind of isolation and hope-lessness would have taken its toll. It was one thing to discuss it with Jack, back in the safety of their kitchen. She had to accept the fact that Peter probably would be very different than she remembered.

Her stomach rumbled, reminding her that her last bite of food had come just as the explosion ripped through the hull of *Kingsman,* some twenty-four hours ago. She had taken care of her hydration needs, and now she needed to find some food. Her training before her research trip to the Arctic Circle five years ago had equipped her with a few survival skills in this department. Insects were usually edible, and while she wasn't exactly thrilled about the idea, she was in no position to be picky. Ants and grasshoppers and slugs and worms. Nothing with more than six legs. Nothing brightly colored. If she could make it to the beach on the east side of the island, hit the tidal pools for small crabs, eels, fish, and marine snails, she might have something.

She stood there with her hands on her hips, the water-fall crashing down behind her, vacillating between the options. As she leaned toward one option and then back toward the other, something to the east, beyond the curve of the river, caught her eye again. This time, she had a better view. An ugly gouge had been cut in the foliage upriver like some mythical beast had dragged its claw right through the forest. Then a glint of light, the sun reflecting off something. Perhaps a shimmer of light off a puddle of water, but she hoped it was something more. Something metal.

Wreckage.

## 18

Claire followed the shoreline around the lake, the north side of which opened up into a slow-moving river. Her nerves jangled as she drew closer toward the gouge in the forest and the shadowy gloom cast by the tangled web of trees and plants beyond. She would need to step carefully; without a waypoint, she could easily lose her bearings in these woods. Anxiety pricked her skin as the soothing sounds of the lake receded behind her. She had only spent a few minutes near it, but already it had felt like a home, a place to rest and recuperate.

Her clothes had mostly dried out, stiffening with a salty crust. They were going to ripen badly though, and she was going to smell like the dodgy end of an elephant with the runs. She made a mental note to get over her aversion to exhibitionism once she made it back to the waterfall. A good soak in that basin would help quite a bit. As she made her way through, she wondered if Peter had spent any time on this side of the island. If it was Peter's helicopter she had spotted, perhaps he had built a home base nearby. She wondered how much NASA knew about the island itself. Had it ever been charted, or did it owe its entire fame to its role as the landing spot for an alien craft? Had there been any previous activity on the island? All at once, thinking about these things made her conscious of her isolation, of her vulnerability. She had never been in a place like this, unspoiled by even the tiniest hint of human development.

It wasn't that her work hadn't carried her to some remote places. It was just that she had never been this alone. Even when she'd trekked to the Arctic Circle to study permafrost, she'd been part of a six-man team sleeping with a roof over her head in a prefabricated shelter. Here she was alone; no one was coming to help. This slowed her down, made her check everything twice, made her view everything as a potential threat.

A weapon. She needed a weapon of some kind. A stick, one that she could sharpen. It might not be as sexy as, say, an AR-15 rifle, but it would be more effective than cursing, skilled as she was in the profanities. She began scouting for a suitable branch. Something sturdy, at least two inches in diameter, but not so heavy that she couldn't wield it quickly. After twenty minutes, she settled on a solid prospect that she found lying in some brush. It was about six feet long, straight, knobby at both ends. It felt good in her hands.

It took longer, almost an hour, to find a suitable rock to sharpen her new stick with. Another hour went by, Claire sitting on a large tree root, working that sharp rock against the wood until she found the point hiding inside. When she was done, her hands hurt and her back ached, but she finally had a serviceable weapon.

As she resumed her hike, she felt better, more confident. It was the first time since this ordeal had started that she'd felt in control of something. Until now, she had been reacting to events, bumped along toward some unknowable fate without any say-so in the matter. The act of creating this simple tool, of taking charge, had made all the difference in the world.

The ground here was level and flat and made for easy travel; the downside was that she wasn't seeing any sign of the crash. The trees were much thicker here, the canopy denser, ensconcing her in gloom. Fear threatened to crash through her defenses, to turn her back into a scared little girl again, the one who had grown up virtually motherless in El Paso, a place that looked unkindly on scared little girls, a place where fathers were strong and gave their daughters no quarter. If those girls weren't up to the challenge, they were shuttled into a world of debutante balls and pageants and cheerleading. Then Texas A&M or Southern Methodist or Baylor, good schools for good Texas girls to meet their future husbands. It wasn't like that for all the girls, of course, it wasn't fair to paint with such a broad brush. However, Claire had known many girls like that, ones that wanted the life of the Texas belle, to love Jesus and Sigma Kappa all at the same time.

At her debutante ball, descending the stairs, the third of five girls at this particular introduction to society. She never quite understood what it meant to be a deb; did it mean she was now properly fuckable, properly assignable to some proper Texas boy, an oil-and-gas man from the right Texas family? Her grades had always been excellent, she'd had her pick of colleges to obtain that M-R-S degree, but she remembered deciding right then and there on that staircase, looking out over that sea of judgmental faces and gin-blossomed cheeks of old men who thought of little but getting their hands on that eighteen-year-old Texas beef, that she was getting the hell out of El Paso.

She had stopped being afraid that day.

She had never been afraid since.

Something about this sliver of the forest though. The hair on the back of her neck stood up at attention, sounding that interior klaxon alarm, telling her to get away, to get far away from this place, from this island. But she couldn't. To get the thing she wanted more than anything else, to get home, she had to be here and do this thing and not be afraid.

The trees here were huge and left to their own devices since time out of mind, they had gone wild, growing into and on top of one another. Their trunks were like the arms of a giant, thick and gnarled. Their green plumage appeared to defy all laws of physics and gravity, with heavy foliage extending in every direction, in some places suspended by nothing more than the skinniest of twigs. In those branches, she could hear the skitter of small woodland creatures, the heavy flap of birds of prey traversing the treetops.

An uneasy fog drifted across the forest floor, clinging to the ground and base of the trees. It was just the byproduct of the westerly breezes catching the warm water vapor evaporating from the cove just over the horizon. It still felt all wrong, like it might rise up and swallow her whole.

Her pace slowed as the fog thickened around her, dropping her visibility to arm's length. Every step was a journey in itself, each one wrought with fear and uncertainty. It was quiet now, deathly so. There was no breeze here, no rustling of the leaves surrounding her by the millions. Even when she primed her ears, she could hear nothing but the sound of her footfalls along the forest floor.

It was just an island. A big hunk of dirt. She repeated this mantra as she edged through the trees, but the fact that this was no ordinary island seeped into the edges of her consciousness. It was different because of what lay just a few miles to the east.

Despite the current state of affairs, it was hard not to feel a ripple of excitement. Her entire life, from the time she had fallen in love with space, that day she watched a solar eclipse in eighth grade, the zone of totality cutting straight through El Paso, space had hypnotized her. She had stood out there in that bizarre twilight, similar to the one in this forest, as the moon had slid in front of the sun, turning the star into a negative of itself, a black hole of nothingness.

Just an island.

What was it?

What was it doing here?

Where had it come from?

Who had sent it?

Why?

These questions could very much occupy the sciences for decades. And it would be partly because of her. She had made it here when so many others had failed. She and Peter. They'd been the ones to make it. She wondered if Peter had been able to learn anything about it. The Peter she'd known would have risked all to study the object, to learn what he could from it. Hell, after twelve years, he probably had mounds of data from his observations. She wondered if he'd been able to open it, to look on the inside. He would have tried, no doubt.

She paused to rest, gather her bearings, confirm that she wasn't walking in circles. Ahead, further east, something caught her eye. The forest had brightened, this section awash in a bit more sunlight. From her current position, she could not tell if it was a natural break in the trees or something else. She set off again, ever more slowly, ever more cautious.

A hundred yards farther up, Claire came across her first chunk of wreckage, a fire-charred rotor section. It sat alone atop a thicket of brush. The rotor was large, about the size of a recliner, intact, although most of its blades were badly bent. Claire knelt beside it, caressed it with her fingers. Her breath froze in her chest. Here it was. A brutal reminder of the lives that had been lost here. As she studied it, a thought shimmered but disappeared just as quickly, a lover disappearing around a dark corner.

She looked for more debris, but seeing none, she resumed her trek, on full alert now. A few minutes later, she came across a bigger debris field, this one comprised of tangled and twisted metal. Parts of the rotor blade, an engine block, a broken skid. To her right, a giant gash in the trees where the helicopter had knifed through during its final violent descent. She followed its likely flight path through the woods; it had probably crashed through the tree line before coming to rest somewhere out of sight.

A longer trail of debris ran deeper into the woods. At the edge of the trees, she scampered up the berm, back into daylight and into an open glade where the river cut east. Just out of full view, at the top of a hill, was a large piece of the fuselage, including the passenger cabin. Her heart was in her throat as she crested the hill and came face to face with the wreckage.

The sun was high in the sky now, its rays beating down hard on her. She missed the gloomy chill of the forest; standing here exposed, near the crash, the jungle had felt like a protective cocoon. Now she was in front of the tragedy. She drew closer to the wreckage, one step at a time. Her bare shoulders cooked in the sunshine, but she barely noticed as she neared her first body. It looked to be a man, but in this stage of decomposition, it was hard to tell for sure.

She kept moving, now in the shadow of the fuselage, walking its perimeter. Another two bodies, also badly decomposed. As she completed the circuit around the chopper, her confusion grew; the nagging thought that had skittered through her mind in the woods was back. She approached the cabin door and poked her head inside. More carnage. Six more corpses, including the two pilots, still strapped in their seats. Footlockers and packs had been strewn about the cabin. She moved gingerly through the wreckage, mindful of the broken glass and twisted shears of sharpened metal. She checked the name patches on the bodies, the names unfamiliar to her. Kent, Davis, Simmons, Keaton, Ramirez, Ryland, Hankinson, Harris, Miller, Smith, and Brown.

No Peter.

She was confused. As badly decomposed as these bodies were, the key fact was that they were *still* decomposing. These people had died recently. Murphy had told her there had been no missions to the island in what, two years? This helicopter had crashed much more recently than that. A week ago. Two at the most.

Murphy had lied to her.

They hadn't stopped trying to get here. Why would he lie about it?

To what end?

There had been much she didn't know about Murphy, about any of this. She felt like one of those vacationers scammed by a tour company. You checked into not a resort hotel with clear views of the sparkling water, but a rat-infested motel a mile off the beach.

As the shock of finding this tomb faded, she went to

work, focusing on the supplies. She hoisted a full rucksack onto her back and made her way back to the door. Several assault rifles were scattered through the cabin, and she grabbed the closest one, dusting off her father's gun lessons from decades past. She paused in the opening, sweating heavily in the heat. As she prepared to step back outside, a flicker of movement to the north caught her eye. Her heart skipped a beat.

*Peter.*

No.

It *could* be Peter. It could be a low-flying bird. It could be some wild animal looking for its dinner. Just because she hadn't seen one yet didn't mean there weren't any. For all she knew to the contrary, it could be a man from Mars. She took cover inside the cabin once more, peeking around the corner of the doorway. This time, she got a better look. A cloud passed over the sun, removing the glare and making it easier for her 20/20 vision to pick up the source. When she saw, her breath caught in her throat.

It wasn't a man from Mars.

It wasn't Peter, either.

But it *was* a man.

It was Agent Berry.

## 19

No doubt about it.

The man approaching the helicopter from the east was the DIA agent who'd come to her house, the one who had secured her release from jail, the one who'd let her decide for herself whether to come here. He was here too, dressed in green battle fatigues and black boots. He was approaching the chopper from the east, moving slowly, his head on a swivel as he scanned his surroundings.

What the hell was he doing here?

Had he been on the *Kingsman*?

Did he know about the bombing?

Was he in on it?

If so, then she couldn't let him know she was here. At his current pace, he'd be at the chopper in thirty seconds, a minute at the most. Gingerly, she stepped back to the opening on the other side of the helicopter and slipped outside. She scanned the terrain for an escape route. The river was about fifteen yards away, down a shallow hill, the land dipping away from the chopper. She grimaced. Rivers freaked her out much more than oceans. Oceans were predictable. Waves, schools of fish, dolphin, sharks. A river was like the Mona Lisa; you never quite knew what was hiding under its smile.

She debated abandoning her newly acquired pack, but she dismissed the idea just as quickly. The pack was going with her. If it turned out to be too heavy, she could dump it during the river crossing. Getting as low as she could, she scurried down the hill, checking over her shoulder every few seconds. The hill was steeper than she had first calculated, and the helicopter quickly receded from view. Briefly, she considered holding her position just under the crest of this hill and spying on Berry; perhaps she could discern what he was doing here.

If the chopper was not his final destination, if he was river-bound, then he might catch her. That was something she could not risk without knowing what he was here for. But what if he wasn't headed her way? The only reason for her to ford this river was to escape from him. She was willing to bet whatever was in her pack that Agent Berry was nothing if not a practical son of a bitch. There would be purpose in everything he did. An end game. He was the kind of guy who packed exactly what he needed and nothing more or less, whose shirts were starched just right, whose necktie knot was always perfect.

She decided to do some reconnaissance. Carefully, she eased out of the straps and crept back up the hill, just shy of the crest. At the top of the hill, the land flattened sharply, giving Claire a bit of a spot to spy on Berry. She edged up until her eyes were level with flat ground, her hair just a shade above the plane. Berry was about thirty yards away, his back to her; he was crouched, examining the first body she had spotted. He rubbed the fabric of the man's uniform between his fingers. Then he searched the man's pockets, one at a time. Several items went into his pack. Then he made a slow circuit around the helicopter, stopping every few yards to check the ground. She didn't know what he was looking for, but if she had to guess, this was his first visit to this crash site as well. There was no way to know if he knew what she suspected about this crash – that it was, at most, a few weeks old.

He spent another fifteen minutes scavenging. Claire was relieved she had stayed, relieved she'd managed to abscond with the pack. He had shown no interest in venturing beyond the crash site. After completing his circuit of the crash site, he sat in the shadow of the wreckage and repacked his rucksack, carefully finding a proper home for each item. Then he got up, brushed off his hands, a man who had finished his work. In mid-swipe, he paused. Quickly, Claire ducked her head down below the crest and held her breath.

Everything fell silent.

Claire pressed her body flat against the incline, trying to make herself invisible. Her heart pounded relentlessly against the ground beneath her; it was a wonder it hadn't caused an earthquake. He had seen her. Maybe he had sensed her. Hell, maybe he had seen her even before she'd cleared out of the helicopter. Regardless, it was a Schro-dinger's cat situation now. Inside the shoebox that was her life, this moment, he had both seen her and not seen her, and the only way for her to find out what had happened would be to open the box.

He might be just over the crest, waiting for her, taunting her, torturing her with the most terrifying thing of all – the unknown. Not knowing something was the worst. When a noise jolted you awake at night and you didn't know if it had been in your dream or if it was an intruder who'd jimmied the lock and was on his way up the stairs right now to murder your children in their sleep and make you watch. When you had a mole removed and they sent it off to the lab just to be sure, and you couldn't think about anything else, and it drove you crazy because no one in the chain of custody of that little sliver of cells cared whether you had cancer or not and you really were alone.

She was frozen against that hillside, encased in terror. She was on her side, curled up in the fetal position, which she hoped would give her some extra cover. The gun was snug against her, her finger curled gently over the trigger guard. Her stomach churned with hunger and nausea. Beads of sweat traced rivers down her flank, down her back, down her cheeks. Time lost all meaning as she lay there; it was impossible to tell how much time had elapsed.

Count to one hundred.

Two hundred.

Two hundred would be enough.

She counted slowly.

As she approached two hundred, her breathing grew shallow and ragged. Then it was done. She rolled back into a prone position and edged her way to the top of the hill. Schrodinger's cat. He was there and he wasn't. The only way to collapse to one reality or the other would be to look. She poked her head up enough to break the invisible plane, just long enough to steal a peek, before dropping low again. Nothing appeared in her field of vision. Maybe she had looked too quickly. She would have to risk another glance. She poked her head up a second time, like in one of those whack-a-mole games from her youth, holding her gaze this time.

There.

Berry was leaving the crash site, heading east toward the woods. Following him would be risky, but she had to know what his end game was. She climbed up over the hilltop and made her way slowly back toward the helicopter, the muzzle of her newly acquired rifle up and ready. The safety was already disengaged. There were so many variables at play here that her head was starting to swim. Berry's presence on the island had cast a shadow over everything.

As she considered this new development, it occurred to her that perhaps things weren't that complicated at all. Either Berry was in on Murphy's conspiracy or he wasn't. One of those two things was true. Maybe Berry was here on the same mission she was. It was possible that he wasn't involved in the sabotage aboard the ship, that someone higher up Berry's food chain had built him in as a redundancy to account for this very contingency.

If he were part of the conspiracy, on the other hand, then his mission here was something very different. Obviously, he wasn't here for her. Perhaps he was here to kill Peter. Murphy's warning to her, that they had planned for every contingency, loomed large in her mind. That made a perverse sort of sense. If Murphy and his confederates believed the project had to be shut down, then Peter was a loose end they needed to snip off. Berry might even have orders to try and destroy the object. That prospect chilled Claire to her core. There was no way to know if such a thing were even possible, or what the ramifications would be if it were.

What was her mission, now that Murphy's gambit had been exposed?

It was a simple question, and it had a simple answer.

To save Peter and get off this wretched island. The alien object had to be secondary to that goal. Getting home would mean stealing Berry's transport, assuming he had come ashore in one; otherwise, they would have to construct their own means of egress. As for Berry himself, he was the ghost in the machine; she could do nothing but consider him a lethal threat to her survival. So every action she took going forward had to be with that end goal in mind, at the expense of all else, including the object. It was a painful thing to come to grips with. She would have to set her pride to the side as well. Peter and the knowledge he had accumulated in his twelve years here had to come first.

Strangely, she felt a bit better about things. Having a plan filled her with confidence, with purpose, and it helped dissolve the sense of her own forsakenness that had enveloped her since the moment Murphy had turned the gun on her. She was the mother-fucking cavalry now.

And she had the upper hand. Berry didn't know she was here, which left him vulnerable. The gun felt good in her hand. It reminded her of the days her father had taught her to shoot; if there was one thing Texas fathers taught their kids, especially in the border towns, it was how to fire a gun. He wanted her to be able to defend herself, to never need a man to do that for her. Her father had a strange take on gender equality; it had to do with his revulsion to weakness. No daughter of the Judge would ever need to lean on anyone for her own protection.

She'd gotten rid of her gun after the twins were born, believing that the risk far outweighed the benefit of having them in the house. A gun was no good if it wasn't loaded and at the ready, and you could not have that in a house with small children.

*No, you had to store the gun in one safe and the ammunition in another safe, and excuse me Mr. Axe Murderer, do you mind giving me a second to get my shit together so I can blow a hole the size of a pie in your chest?*

But that was okay because it was a mindset too. To accept that protecting yourself might one day involve violence, real and terrible violence. When you shot a gun on the range enough times, it became part of you, this understanding that you would be as *pure* when it was a real target and not a paper one. And that was the problem. Privately her father had supported strict gun control laws because he believed people were too lazy, too careless to maintain proficiency with their weapons.

As Berry he re-entered the forest, she emerged from the cover of the chopper and followed as far back as she could without losing him; after all, she had no idea what she was doing. For all she knew, he was baiting a trap, drawing her in like a spider lured a fly. If nothing else, he would be more skilled at tracking Peter on the island. Perhaps he could lead Claire right to him.

A rumble of thunder rippled across the island, and it began to rain. For this, Claire was grateful. She was no tracker, and the sounds of the storm would help mask whatever noise she made in her amateur attempt to stay on Berry's trail. Over the next hour, the weather deteriorated slowly, the canopy above awash in the susurration of the rain. Heavy trains of rain sloshed down on her, sluicing down her back, along her arms, splashing up into her shoes.

Her pace slowed, and she feared losing Berry's thread entirely. Her eyes swept the ground, looking for any sign of him. *There!* Half a footprint in a spot of ground between two thick roots, the tread of heavy boots. Fresh tracks, although they were already dissolving into the mud. They gave her waypoints to follow.

Ahead, a flicker of movement stopped her cold. She

ducked behind a large tree, lowering herself onto her haunches. Staying close to the tree's massive trunk, she risked a peek. Berry was close, no more than twenty yards away, tucked behind a tree himself. Something out of Claire's line of sight had caught Berry's fancy. Without taking his eye off his quarry, he removed the component pieces of a rifle from his pack and quietly assembled it. Claire clapped a hand over her mouth as Berry's gambit became clear.

The storm worsened, the thunder relentless, the rain deafening. A stiff wind had picked up, sending the foliage into a ripple. Frequent lightning fractured the sky in a gaudy harsh white, creating a photo negative of the way the world really was. Claire's clothes were heavy and clingy with rain.

Her heart had reached overdrive. Had Berry spotted Peter? Was the man she lost a dozen years ago right there, just out of view? The idea that Peter was close by added a second difficult dynamic to the situation; she had to set aside her emotions and focus on the problem at hand. A single mistake on her part could jeopardize both of their lives. As it was, death was on its way for Peter, that much was clear.

Berry resumed his hunt, cutting southwest. After he dipped back into the woods, Claire scampered across the clearing and took haven in the spot he had just vacated. Here the land sloped downward toward another glade, where the river emptied into another lake. The trees had thinned out significantly, and without the buffer of the canopy, the rain was coming down in sheets, like a curtain shielding her view.

A trio of tall rocks, arranged in a U-shape, covered by a thick tangle of brush and branches lay ahead; it was behind these that Berry hid. Her eyes flitted over the area, her heart in her throat. She spotted a small bundle of wood, maybe ten yards off the lake's edge.

It looked like a shelter.

*Dear God.*

She turned her attention back toward Berry, lying in wait now, ready to pounce. It reminded her of one of those nature shows, the camera crew filming a large cat quietly hunting a blissfully ignorant gazelle. It was nature, and, it was their duty to observe, but part of her always wished that one of the cameramen would call out a warning for the doomed animal. Berry lifted a pair of binoculars to his face. He locked in on the shelter, but from his vantage point, she wasn't sure if he could see inside. She couldn't. She couldn't risk trying to shoot him; she hadn't fired a gun in a long time, and the odds were excellent she would miss.

They waited.

The storm continued, drenching Claire, soaking her, washing her clean of the grime and the sweat and the salt caking her body. She remained hidden behind that tree, wondering if her entire life had been prologue to this moment in time. She looked down at her hands, pink and clean and fresh. She licked her lips, savoring the taste of the water, clean and pure.

Was Peter in there right now? Such a thing seemed impossible. He was dead. He was gone. It was a bright spring afternoon, the day they had come to tell her, and she'd been in meetings all day, so many that the substance of them had swirled together into a miasma of nothingness. She was sitting on the front porch with a book, planning to order some dinner later. Peter had been gone ten days and was scheduled to be gone another fourteen. Then they had come in their black Suburban, dressed in their dark suits, their faces hidden behind mirrored sunglasses.

Life had moved on, slowly and painfully at first, when every day, every hour, every minute, every second felt like an eternity. Every sliver of time, no matter how thinly carved out, no matter how closely shaved, served as its own plane of existence with no easy way to cross over to the next and the next and the next. Then time had accelerated, slowly picking up momentum, a tiny puff of snow moving down a mountainside, growing in size and speed until a year had gone by in the blink of an eye.

As she stood here under these open skies, she couldn't help but wonder if it had all been a lie, if she was still stuck in that moment that Murphy had told her that the chopper had gone down, that Peter and the others were dead. That she had stayed where she was and the world had continued without her. The shell of Claire Hamilton had moved on through those moments, through those countless fractals of time, each containing a lifetime, but Claire Hamilton herself, the woman, the young scientist, was still there in that moment, broken into a million pieces. She didn't know.

As they waited, she and Berry frozen in this strange diorama, the storm began to fade; the clouds broke apart and sunlight spread across the landscape from west to east, like some invisible being was coloring in the vista with a golden marker. Then a shimmer of movement. A figure emerged from the shelter as the rains died away. Even after twelve years, she knew. The way he moved, the way he blocked the sun from his face with the back of his forearm.

*Peter.*

## 20

There he stood, this man to whom she'd committed her life, his hands on his hips, not doing much of anything. The storm had cracked the shell of humidity cloaking the island and now he simply seemed to be enjoying the breeze that had risen in the storm's wake.

*Tick, tock, tick, tock.*

Her eyes flitted back to Berry, who remained locked in his crouch, waiting for his moment. It was all about to change for Peter, one way or another. The end of this chapter was upon them, and the poor guy didn't even know it was coming. Countless sunrises and sunsets now behind him. If things went really bad, if she wasn't able to rewrite a history that Berry undoubtedly believed was already written, Peter's whole life behind him.

She wondered if Peter still dreamed about a rescue. Of course, in those first days and weeks, such a dream had been big and vibrant. Someone would come. Hell, he was on the most important mission in human history. There would be contingency plans in place, a search team on the ready line, chomping at the bit to save their fallen brothers and sisters.

Had he seen the failures of the rescue missions, of the chop-pers losing altitude, of the sonic booms of them crashing into the ground, of the clouds of smoke rising above the treetops, that achingly lush backdrop of his life falling apart?

Eventually, the dream would have started to die. What had been impossible, unimaginable, that no one was coming for him, had slowly morphed into the possible, into the real. Perhaps he had marked the days with hatches on a thick piece of wood, and one day had become a month, and a month had become a year, and he would have needed a new stick because all that time had passed and no one had come for him.

She pictured him sitting on that beach, his legs criss-crossed, looking out over that endless ocean, nothing but blue wherever he looked, waiting for a rescue that would never come. He would scoop up a handful of sand, as he had done when they had gone to the beach together, and then let it pour out slowly. That detail came rushing back to her right then, this habit of his when they were at the beach. He dug into the sand like a backhoe and came out with a palmful; then he would tip his hand and the tiny grains swirled out like an hourglass emptying itself out. He might be reading, they might be chatting while having a drink, but without fail, that hand would be at work, scooping up the sand and letting it go again. It was soothing to watch him do it, that's probably why he had done it.

A cough broke her out of her trance, brought her back to reality. Peter was still standing there, still unaware of the situation developing around him. Claire raised her weapon; her hands were shaking so badly she could not settle the sight on Berry's back. And if she fired, there was no guar-antee she wouldn't hit Peter as well. Then, to make things worse, the opportunity vanished; Berry had moved out of her line of fire, shielded by the boulder.

Peter disappeared back into his makeshift shelter for a moment. Its primitiveness struck Claire. Had he been living here this entire time? Peter was one of the smartest men she had ever met; certainly, he would have constructed a more permanent shelter by now. Perhaps this was a satellite shelter, one that he used for his journeys to this part of the island. That would make more sense.

He emerged a few minutes later with a pack strapped to his back and began making his way up the hill toward their tree line. Berry was in a perfect spot, prone; he drew up his rifle. There was no doubt he would hit his target. It was now or never.

"Peter!"

She fired a burst into the air, in the opposite direction. Berry's head swung around, desperately looking for the source of the gunfire.

Peter froze.

She fired again into the air, driving Berry from his hiding spot. He bolted for the woods and disappeared into the tree line. She howled at the top of her lungs, breaking free of her hiding spot and racing down the hill. The ground dropped quickly, pockmarked with little stones and roots and jungle brush, making her descent treacherous; her balance held as she drew in on Peter.

"Claire?" Peter said breathlessly, her name laced with a healthy dose of skepticism, as if he should be careful simply saying her name aloud.

"Yeah."

"Claire."

A gunshot broke the silence between them, a round

pinging off the boulder near Claire. A piece of rock chipped off and struck her in the arm.

Time to run like hell.

"We have to go."

She followed Peter's lead, using long parabolic strides down the hillside toward the water. Additional rounds peppered the air as they ran. The ground leveled out as they approached the riverbank. Peter did not pause for even a second; in he went with a terrific splash. Claire followed moments later, the icy water taking her breath away as she knifed beneath the rippling surface. She kicked hard for the surface, noticing with amazement how far they already were from their point of entry.

The current ran hard here, sucking them downriver with the force of a vacuum while Claire worked to keep her head above water. She turned her head from side to side, scanning the water behind her for any sign of their would-be killer, but it was difficult to triangulate on any one point for more than a second or two.

The rapids were deafening, the manic rush of countless gallons of water probing, searching, hunting for an outlet, hunting for release. Peter's head bobbed above the surface ahead of her. He seemed to be trying to slow his pace, letting her catch up to him, but the current was too strong. They would have to run the current's course and hope they didn't drown.

It was quite a tour through the island's interior. The terrain was ever-changing, its topography lush and varied. Massive tropical trees. A small mountain. Over there a series of caves. Eventually, the waters began to calm, the slowing river dumping into yet another large lake, the biggest one she'd seen yet. As the river funneled her into the calmer waters of the basin, she turned back to check for Berry, but she saw no sign of him. Behind her, Peter had begun to swim for shore. She followed him, her heart in her throat as she steeled herself for a reunion she never imagined possible.

Closer to shore, her feet scraped the bottom. She stood up in hip-deep water and looked up at Peter, who awaited her on the bank of the lake. A breeze blew across her body, sending chills through her, making her skin ripple with gooseflesh. It was the most surreal moment of her life. The prayers of those first minutes and days and months following his disappearance pinging out in the ether, in the dead space of the universe, everywhere and nowhere, finally answered.

He was tanned, but otherwise, he looked much like she remembered. His hair, which had grayed at the temples when he was in his late twenties, looked about the same, perhaps a bit shaggier. A thin layer of stubble darkened his face. He wore cutoff camouflage shorts, the cuffs badly frayed, and a dark-blue t-shirt. If he was surprised to see her, he was hiding it well behind those haunting blue eyes of his.

"You okay?" Peter asked.

Her body recoiled at the sound of his voice. Time had inoculated her from it, made her immune to its power over her. Now it seemed like an interloper, here to disrupt the stasis that she had worked so hard to build. For years, she had kept the last voicemail message he had left her, just before he boarded the ship to make the trek to the island. Eventually, she had deleted it, deciding it was too strong a link to the past to keep alive. It was fine to remember the past, sure, that was fine, but too many links to it kept you rooted there, unable to move forward, unable to continue living. Part of her did not like this, not one bit, rebelling against this invasion from the past. Her primal self was struggling to reconcile these two things, this life she had now and the fact of Peter being alive. She didn't know if it ever would.

"Yeah."

He looked past her, back out toward the lake, which filled her with a sense of relief, gave her a chance to recover as she exited the water. Seeing his face was too much right now, too overwhelming. Her heart was racing, pressing up against her throat.

"I don't see him," Peter said, extending his hand to hers. "But we need to get out of here."

They fled.

———

## 21

They ran for an hour, zig-zagging, doubling back, starting trails in divergent directions, anything to throw Berry off their scent. They took a break at to the top of a rolling hill, giving them a nice view of this section of the island. The ride down the river and their subsequent flight had scrambled Claire's brain, so this helped her regain her bearings. They were on the eastern half of the island, the beaches miles away.

Claire's lungs burned and her legs were jelly. She was bent over, her hands on her knees, sucking in big gobs of air. A run like that was hard enough under normal circumstances; doing it when their lives depended on it added another dimension of misery to it. When her breathing began to stabilize, she reared up and took a good look at Peter, who was himself struggling to catch his breath.

Peter fucking Abbott.

There he was. In the flesh. Close enough to touch. Their final morning together unspooled in her mind, from the moment she had given up on sleep until he had gotten out of the car. Those memories had been altered by the passage of time, of course, shaped by her grief, by her anger, by her denial, the way a nor'easter could reshape a beach, even if didn't look all that different after the tempest had blown through. She searched those memories for the last time they had touched. The brush of a hand. A quick squeeze of the hip before they got out of bed. A pat on the bottom as he walked behind her to his side of the sink.

"You okay?" he asked.

She nodded, his voice staggering her again. My God. Did it sound like she remembered?

"You?"

"Yeah," he said, his face scrunched up in a grimace. "What are you doing here?"

It was insane, just talking to him. This conversation should not be happening, but yet it was all the same. How many times had she dreamed about one last day, one last conversation, one last kiss? More than she could count. Now that the wish had been granted, however, there was no palpable sense of relief; there was only confusion and shock.

"I don't know," she said. "They told me you were still alive, wanted me to come on this mission to find you."

"What about our friend? Who is he?"

"His name is Berry. He's with the DIA. He's here to kill you."

"What? Why?"

"Murphy, he's crazy. They blew up the ship. I had to swim here."

Peter held up his palms in surrender.

"Wait, this doesn't make any sense."

"I know," she replied, "but we have to get off this rock. If Berry came on a boat, we need to find it."

"Claire, slow down. Start from the beginning."

"They came to my house," she began, "told me you had survived, told me the truth about the meteor. When we dropped anchor outside the exclusion zone, there was an explosion. Then Murphy tells me they wanted to destroy any evidence of the object. They killed everyone back at Ames."

"Jesus," he said. "Why?"

"I don't know," she said. "Murphy was talking crazy."

"Okay," Peter said, taking a deep breath. "Let's just deal with the problem at hand. Are you telling me no one knows we're here?"

"Basically," she said.

Peter began tapping his hands together, as he often did when facing an intractable problem. Just seeing it again made Claire's head spin. A dozen years gone and still the old idiosyncrasies were running like a computer program.

"And you say this guy Berry came on a boat?"

"Possibly," she said.

He considered this, rubbed his hands against his face, which was dark with the early seeds of a beard. Something about this struck her as odd, but she couldn't quite put her finger on it. Perhaps it was seeing him with facial hair; he never liked it, always complained about how much it itched if he went more than a couple of days without shaving. He particularly enjoyed the cool burn of Old Spice, a scent that always reminded Claire of him, even all these years later. Just this semester, one of her students wore it regularly, a bright kid named Justin, and if the draft in the room caught it just right, it would tickle her nose and shatter her focus briefly, just long enough that she worried her class would wonder if their professor was going to pieces.

"I still don't understand. Why would they do this?"

"Murphy said something about us not being ready for the implications of first contact."

Peter guffawed at this.

"That's nonsense," Peter said. "He was jacked about this. He was like a schoolboy."

"After you crashed," she said. "I guess he changed his tune."

"I don't know what to say about that."

They fell silent. A breeze had picked up, rustling the leaves and the grasses. In the heat of the day, it was refreshing. Claire kept a wary eye out for Berry, but there was no sign of him.

"So what now?" Peter asked.

"Have you seen it?" she asked, her heart pounding as she waited for his answer. She was likely talking to the first person to ever make contact with an extraterrestrial intelligence. Her Peter had been the one.

His eyes cut to the ground, surprising her.

"No," he said. "I never found it."

For reasons Claire could not articulate, a small needle somewhere deep inside her, a scrape against her soul, she found herself not believing him.

EXHAUSTED, they made camp several hours before sunset. Neither wanted to risk a fire, so they hunkered down in a thick grove of trees a bit higher uphill near the island's southern bulge. Claire's legs were sore from the hours spent traipsing across the island. Peter sank to the ground and leaned back against a thick tree trunk with a big sigh. It was still fresh, this shock of seeing him; she did a double take every time she caught a glimpse of him out of the corner of her eye.

"God, it's good to see you," he said.

Her eyes welled up as she considered how good it was to be seen by him, and yes, how good it was to see him too. It was fucking great to see him, to lay eyes on him and not a picture of him inside her locket and not a memory that had faded over time. The real thing was much better.

*Like fuck those low-fat potato chips, give me all the fat and the salt, bitches.*

"I can't believe it," she said. "I mean, I know I'm sitting here with you, but it seems impossible."

"Yeah, the crash was intense."

"How did you survive?"

"Not sure," he said. "The engines quit just as we made the island. Hard crash. The pilot kept us airborne almost long enough to clear the trees. Then we must have caught one of them and that was that."

"Anyone else make it?"

"No," he replied, his stare distant and vacant. "The crash knocked me out. It was dark when I woke up. I was scratched up, bleeding, had a terrible headache. I scavenged what I could, started waiting. Guess we'll get to wait together now."

The defeat in his voice was evident, a sense of foreboding she shared. God knew how long before NASA could piece together what Murphy and his co-conspirators had done. She could only imagine the scene playing out on social media, on the cable news networks, as pundits fell all over themselves casting blame on the attacks on Islamic jihadists, on white supremacists, on anti-government survivalists, never once suspecting that it was the scientists themselves that had turned on each other. Certainly, the whereabouts of two lowly scientists wouldn't be high on the priority list.

"What did they tell you about it?" she asked, her earlier suspicion about his honesty still niggling at her. "The object?"

"Not much to tell," he replied. "At least that's what they said. That a non-naturally occurring object had landed here and that it was most definitely not local."

"They give you any idea where it was from? How it got here?"

He shook his head.

"You know, it's amazing how little we know about anything," he said. "We barely know the things we do know, and there is a whole universe of things we know we don't know. And that doesn't even count the things we don't know there are to know."

"Yeah," she said softly.

"I mean, I guess I can understand why Murphy panicked. You dream about something like this your whole life, but then when it happens, it's so much bigger and scarier than you thought it would be."

Claire smiled in the afternoon sunshine. She knew something about that, about a dream coming true, but it's not at all like you had hoped or it's just too fucking late. Perhaps there was a reason the past was to be left in the past, why it was better for certain dreams not to come true.

"Sorry you're in this mess now," he said.

"It is what it is."

He had moved closer to her, which made her nervous. Did he still consider her his wife? Did he have any idea how long he had been here? At some point, he had certainly lost the thread of the calendar. It was unlikely he knew what day, what month, even what year it was. Had it occurred to him that she might have been living her life as though he were dead, that the world had moved on without him?

These were all questions she was afraid to ask him.

Then he was even closer to her, crouched in front of her, close enough that she could feel his breath on her face, and somehow close enough she could smell that Old Spice, even though he hadn't used it in more than a decade.

"I wasn't sure if I would ever see you again," he said softly. He reached out and caressed her cheek with the back of his hand. "When we were going down, that's all I could think of, that I was never going to see this face again. I was so pissed. I was so pissed that I wasn't even afraid. I was pissed that it was all being taken away from me, and there was nothing I could do about it."

"I'm sorry," she said.

She was sorry. It was all so very unfair.

He was going to kiss her, oh my God, she thought, Peter was going to kiss her, and she wasn't ready to tell him about Jack and the kids and her little house in Seattle, and to stop him would mean she would have to tell him the truth about all of these things. In his mind, her lips, her body were still zoned recreational for him. This part of their relationship had always been easy and fun, she as into him as he was into her.

Then his lips were on hers, and it felt wonderful, that brush of electricity racing through her body, awakening long-dead circuits, and that confused her because things had been good between her and Jack in this department as well, but now she was seeing each operated on a different plane of her soul, of her heart. Just thinking about Jack made her tense up, flush with guilt, as though he were sitting on that thick root over there, watching his wife cheat on him with her dead first husband.

Peter must have sensed the tension because he broke off the kiss, although his face remained mere inches away from hers. His hands dropped from her face to her shoulders, to her arms, down to her legs.

"What's wrong?"

She shook her head.

"I don't know."

He placed his hands on her legs, gently, stroking the tops of her thighs. It felt the same, like no time had gone by at all. He had not forgotten how to touch her, that was for sure.

"Aren't you happy to see me?"

She cupped his cheek with her hand, stroking it. Yeah, he would want a blade and some aftershave when they got back right quick.

"Of course," she said. "I thought you were dead."

He rubbed her legs, a thing he had done after she'd had a hard day. They would sit on the couch, her back against the armrest, her legs draped over his lap, and he would rub them while she sipped wine. Peter did not drink; he hated the taste of alcohol. Every now and again, he would try something she'd ordered and would immediately regret it.

"I missed these legs," he said, gently tracing his fingers from her upper thigh and down her right leg. Then he stopped, something catching his attention. He raised her leg by the ankle and gently turned it toward the sun.

"What's this?" he asked, rubbing his thumb against the small tattoo she had there, ink of the moon, three stars, and the Earth. She'd gotten it on a lark, not long before she'd met Peter, just when she was beginning to feel like she'd made her way out of the darkness. The question depressed her, sending a wave of melancholy crashing through her. Soon it would be time to start peeling back the layers of time, showing him a little bit at a time that she was no longer the woman who had yelled at him about the trash can so many years ago.

"Got it a few years ago," she replied.

"I don't remember you getting a tattoo."

His comment stopped her cold. She began to wonder about his mental state. Science had proven that extreme isolation had profoundly negative effects on a person's state of mind, and Peter had been subject to it for longer than virtually anyone on Earth. His sanity might be in a far more advanced state of decay than she thought.

"No, honey, you wouldn't remember it."

"I think I'd remember you having a tattoo," he said, a bit of heft in his voice.

Her confusion grew. She could feel her mind splashing about in a deep dark pit, the sides slick and lacking purchase, unable to latch on. It was as if Peter was protecting himself from the reality of his isolation. Refusing to accept that he had missed out on a tattoo would shield him from the fact that he had missed out on so much more. It was a bunker, an outer defense to the truth. A truth that he would want to avoid confronting as long as possible.

"I got it a few years ago," she said again.

"A few years ago?" he said.

A hunch began to form in her mind. Suddenly, little bits of discrete data she'd collected that, standing alone, had not made sense, coalesced into a picture that she did not know was there. The young age of the crash site she had explored. The stubble on Peter's face. The makeshift shelter he had built by the lake. His relatively casual response to seeing her after twelve years. The way he had talked about the helicopter crash like it had just happened.

His seeming confusion about her tattoo was about to be the final nail in the coffin.

"Pete," she said, choosing her words carefully. "How long do you think you've been here?"

"What do you mean?"

"How long? How long do you think you've been on this island?"

He leaned away from her, his face tightening.

"I started keeping track on the first morning after the crash," he said. "I found a black marker in the wreckage, made a mark every morning at my campsite."

"How long have you been here?" she asked, feeling like she was in freefall, like she was in an elevator whose cables had been cut and was plummeting to a nasty end.

"What's wrong?"

"How long do you think you've been here?"

Each word was a struggle, and her question came slowly. It came slowly because she had a strong hunch that she wasn't going to like his answer.

"Fifteen days."

## 22

Fifteen days.
Fifteen. Days.
Fifteen.
Days.

"That can't be. It cannot fucking be."

"Jesus, Claire," Peter said, "you're white as a sheet."

"No, no, no," she kept saying.

She scrambled to her feet, dizzy, the world spinning. Everything became too much at once, the island, Peter trying to talk to her, the sounds of the bugs and birds hidden away in the grasses and the trees. Her legs gave out and she fell to her hands and knees. She took a deep breath and let it out slowly.

"Claire."

She ignored him. She didn't want to look at him and have to tell him the truth. She could stay here in this downward dog position forever and never have to tell him that he was a ghost. That's what he was. A ghost in the flesh. Dead to the world. The world had no need for people it had left behind. It wouldn't know what to do with them.

"Claire, goddammit, what's wrong?"

She rolled over onto her seat, crossed her legs, drew them tightly against her body.

"How long has it been?"

She laughed, a short, loud, hysterical bark. Was that the first stage of a psychotic break? Maybe she would go insane and it would no longer matter whether she made it off this island or not. Crazy back at home would be no different than crazy here.

"Claire," he said, grabbing her by the shoulders and lifting her to her feet. "How long have I been here?"

She looked up at the sky. They had arrived. The moment was here, the moment she would open a doorway and unleash a stream of horrors on this man she had once loved or hell, maybe still loved, and the jury was out on that right now. She was about to destroy him in a way that did not seem possible, that seemed so utterly cruel that it would defy comprehension.

"Twelve years."

He shoved her away like she was on fire and staggered backward, taking two giant steps away from her. His legs buckled, dropping him to his knees. When that seemed to be too much, he leaned back onto his seat.

"Peter," she said, stepping gingerly toward him.

He held up a hand, waving her off.

"No," he said. "Get away from me."

"Peter."

"What are you doing here?"

"Peter."

"They send you to check on me?"

"What? No."

"Then why are you here?"

"I told you."

"You're lying."

"No, I swear to you I'm not."

"How is this possible?"

"I don't know," she said. "But it's the truth."

"Twelve years?"

"Yes."

"Twelve years," he said. "Twelve years. Twelve years. Twelve years."

He said it over and over, repeating it so many times it sounded like the whisper of a wind carving its way across the hilltop. Claire herself was having a hard time processing what Peter had told her, even though in her heart she knew it was true. Facts were facts. The helicopter she had found. It had crashed two years ago, just as Murphy had said. It should have been rusting and brown, there should have been vines and grasses growing up around it; in this heat and humidity, the poor crash victims should have been nothing but bones and dust. Murphy had told her the truth about that. You didn't lie about something unless you had a good reason; there was no reason to lie about the timing of the crashes.

Claire Hamilton had faced many challenges in her life. The death of her mother. Bradford Hamilton's overbearing nature. The unrelenting sexism in the hard sciences. Peter's disappearance. Jack's lymphoma. Quite frankly, in many ways, her life had seen its share of shit downpours. This was something else, though, so far beyond what her puny human mind was capable of comprehending. For Peter, a mere fifteen days had passed. Two weeks since he'd last seen his wife. It was nothing. A long business trip. He had just seen her. She would look the same because that's what he would expect to see. He would not see the wear and tear of the intervening years she had endured because those years hadn't happened for him.

She had been spun back through the years, back to a moment when she was still young, when her life was still unwritten, when she wasn't a young widow struggling to put back together all that had been torn asunder. This was the Peter she had dropped off at the airport, not one driven mad by isolation. Had she not imagined a couple of weeks away from Jack and the kids? Alone with a stack of books and a case of wine? Hell, he was still hoping for a rescue.

"Peter?"

He was standing awkwardly, as though he'd been kicked in a sensitive spot, his hands on his head. He was facing her, but he wasn't so much looking at her; he wasn't really looking at anything at all. She drew closer to him, one step at a time, anxious not to spook him. At this point, she had no idea what his mental state would be. Another step. And another. And another, until she was within arm's length. Slowly, she reached out and touched him on his hip. He flinched, seemingly unaware that she was there.

He blinked twice and gave his head a good hard shake. Then he locked eyes with Claire.

"It's gonna be okay," she said, although the jury was still out on that, and to be honest, she really didn't know if it would be.

"You're lying," he said coldly.

"What?"

"It's not true," he said. "It can't be."

"Why would I lie about this?"

"I don't know," he said. "But it doesn't make a damn bit of sense. You're just here to check on me."

That claim again.

"Why would I be here to check on you?"

"Because you think you're a better scientist than me," he said. "You think you're smarter than me. You think they should have picked you to come. Now you're here to take all the credit."

He was rambling now, tears silently streaming down his cheeks.

"Peter," she said. "Honey, I am not lying. I came here to get you."

"Like that guy? Berry? Were you in on it together? Were you fucking him?"

She took a deep breath and let it out slowly, letting his barbs pierce her. There was no playbook for what he was going through at this moment. She had to ride with him like a junkie coming down from a high.

"Why on earth would I make something like that up?"

"I don't know," he said. "I haven't thought that far ahead. But what you're saying is impossible. Impossible. You're talking about, shit, I don't even know what you're talking about."

"I know it sounds insane."

"So why aren't you freaking out?"

"What?"

"How long have you been on this island?"

Claire's stomach flipped. Of course. How could she be so stupid? She'd been so focused on Peter, she'd forgotten to consider how the time anomaly had affected her.

"Since yesterday."

She'd been here roughly one day. Her brain quickly ran the numbers.

"Ten months," he said, beating her to the punch. "Give or take a few days."

He'd always been good at math.

"Oh my God."

"If what you're saying is true," Peter was saying, "then ten months have gone by."

He was right. Ten months. Immediately, her thoughts ran to Hugo and Miranda. Nearly a year of their lives, gone like a puff of smoke. Jack, left a widower just like he'd predicted, left alone with an unlimited supply of *I-told-you-so's* and no one to spend them on.

*Goddammit, you were right, and the price of that was losing your wife.*

*I'm sorry, Jack.*

*I'm sorry, Miranda.*

*I'm sorry, Hugo.*

Hugo.

*Good night, love you, sweet dreams, see you in the morning.*

It was a thing he said to her every night before he went to sleep, just when she'd crossed the threshold from his bedroom into the hallway. It had developed slowly over the years, until she realized it was a thing they said every night, with the same cadence and rhythm, a coda to the day. Even Miranda had gotten in on the action, unbeknownst to her brother, because she didn't dig that kind of outward display of emotion. She whispered it into Claire's ear, not wanting Hugo to know that it was part of her bedtime routine as well.

Now bedtime was an empty thing for the twins like it once had been for her; once upon a time, she had been a little girl in Texas whose mother wasn't always there at bedtime. Usually, Ashley Hamilton was asleep on the couch at the end of another day of pickling herself with the gin she had managed to sneak into the house over the Judge's strong objections.

In their living room, there had been a brown recliner she had favored, her mother, in their little house that many people believed was beneath the stature of a federal judge. But treatment for alcohol abuse was expensive, especially when it didn't work and you kept having to get that treatment. The living room bore horrifically ugly wallpaper, with its weird pattern of blooming flowers that Claire detested; even now, if Claire saw flowers that looked like it, she could smell the booze on her mother's breath when she leaned in to kiss her on the cheek before putting herself to bed without a story or goodnight kiss of her own.

She clapped her hand over her mouth.

"Hugo," she whispered, hopefully below the range of Peter's hearing.

"Oh, Jesus," Peter said, breaking her out of her daydream.

"What?"

"You're not lying," he said. "I can see it on your face."

"No," she said. "I am not lying."

He stood there, his mouth opened as though he were going to say something.

"I'm sorry, Peter."

"Has it really been twelve years?"

"Yeah. Really."

"The way you pulled back when I kissed you," he said. "I should have known something wasn't right."

Guilt coursed through her veins. That sense that she had done something terrible, that she had been living a lie at Peter's expense, that she had built her wonderful life on the back of Peter's suffering. It was nonsense, of course, but she couldn't help but feel the universe was laughing at her now, mocking her, judging her. Peter had not taken the step of inquiring whether his wife was still his wife because until five minutes ago, he had likely believed that a loaf of bread he'd eaten from still sat in their breadbox.

And there was still so much bad news to cover with him.

"We have to get off this island," she said. "Right now."

A clock was running now, faster than she could comprehend, but running nevertheless. If she were lucky, she would only miss a year of the kids' lives. She could only hope the temporal anomaly was contained to the contours of the island, a very unhappy byproduct of the alien object, and so she needed to get as far away from it as possible. She had so many questions about how such a thing was possible, but now was not the time for that.

Okay," he said, nodding his head, a hint of panic in his voice. That was unlike Peter Abbott.

"We need to get to the beaches," Claire said.

A million different things were running through her mind, and it was a struggle to stay calm. The beaches were several miles away and, assuming nothing went awry, it would take a couple of hours to get there. Already she was doing the math in her head. Three weeks off the island. Maybe four. If they didn't get off this island soon, she would become a ghost herself. A memory. A picture in a frame. They'd probably already held her funeral.

"Let's go," she said.

"Wait," he said.

"What?"

"You're in an awful hurry to get out of here."

"What?"

"We're back together," he said. "So what if a little time slips by?"

"Goddammit, we need to go right now!"

He flinched at her outburst, which was not normal for her. The woman he'd left behind was quiet, a thinker. He was having a hard time accepting the gap in time, that this mountain for her was nothing but a speed bump for him.

On that mountain that he could not see was the life that she had built for herself.

They started down the east side of the hill, Claire leading the way without even looking back to see if Peter was following. She didn't care much if he came. Panic was crawling up from her belly, scraping her insides until she felt it in her ribs, in her chest, all the way in her throat. Her mind was locked on those two sweet faces back home; each step across this God-forsaken island was like a flamethrower to their childhoods.

"Claire!"

*Momma's coming.*

Her kids were the only thing that mattered. Not the alien object, not Peter being stolen away from her, no matter how unfair it had been. Getting home to her kids, to Jack. There was a painful truth to face as she stood here; had she come for Peter or had she come for herself? She was glad that Peter could not read her mind because it was very possible she had come for herself. She had told Jack that she had come for Peter.

What if it had just been a meteor?

*Would you still have come?*

Her cheeks flushed with shame. She didn't know. Maybe she wasn't the altruistic saint she had tried to sell to Jack after all. Maybe she had put her own ambition above Peter, above Jack, and worst of all, above those two kids. Pride. That's what had brought her to this point. Instead of accepting the contours that parenthood placed on one's life, or rolling with the randomness of life's dice, she had made the mistake of believing she could operate outside those contours without consequence. Saying no to this mission would not have compromised her ability to be a scientist. No, she had come here because she wanted to be the one.

At the bottom of the hill, Peter's hand closed around her elbow and stopped her dead.

She wrenched away from him.

"Goddammit, I said we need to go."

He pulled her close to him, their faces inches apart. The face she had dreamed about for so long after he disappeared, here now, in her worst nightmare. *Be careful what you wish for*, what a dumb goddamn saying that was.

"What are you not telling me?"

"You were dead," she said. "You were dead. I had to move on. I had to move on."

She cried. The sobs came in earnest now, the first time she had cried since Murphy and Berry had come to her house to tell her Peter was alive.

"You were dead. Do you get what I'm saying?"

His face softened. The joy that had filled it upon seeing Claire drained away, leaving nothing behind, a deflated balloon.

"You have a family," he said softly.

"Yes," she said firmly.

The waterworks stopped as she looked him squarely in the eye.

"Two kids," she said. "And I have got to get home to them before it's too late."

## 23

The words hung in the air, so heavy that it felt like they were dragging him down, burying him right here and Peter would die of shock and misery on his sixteenth day on this island. When she had told him it had been twelve years, that was bad, of course, it was terrible, but there was part of him, the clinical scientist inside him that helped steady the vessel, keep him calm. After all, it was a remarkable event and what scientist didn't want to be part of something remarkable? They would write books about him. His name forever entwined with this most fantastic of discoveries, this fountain of youth, this place where he could live forever. He would be a household name, he would return to civilization a goddamned hero.

It didn't occur to him, however, that this development meant far more than the world chewing up and spitting out a dozen calendars; it never occurred to him that Claire had left him behind. The love of your life waited for you. That was what the love of your life did. Maybe it would have come to him eventually, this ridiculous notion that she had waited for him. Here in the harsh light of reality, he saw it had been silly to think such a thing. Time waited for nothing, for no man. The future kept coming, time kept gobbling the life behind you, hurrying you along like an impatient tour guide.

*Lots to see folks, lots to see, can't linger for too long, you'll get left behind. Everyone in the group needs to stay together.*

He hadn't been ignorant of the risks in coming here.

But first contact!

How lucky had he been to be in the right place at the right time in history? How fortunate to be the one fate had shined her spotlight on? How many scientists, living or dead, would have traded places with him instantly for that spot aboard the *Kingsman*? Any scientist would have. His son of a bitch father would have. Claire would have, he knew that. She would have gone in a hot minute, no doubt about it. But while science itself was fair and always played by the rules (well, it had until he set foot on this godforsaken island), the business of science was far less equitable. Contributions from women like Claire were frequently hitched to a male colleague's wagon.

Part of it was the rise of the internet as a breeding ground for the complaints of whiny men, like a bucket of fetid water for mosquitoes. Social media brought them together, creating strength in numbers, an unprecedented ability to sabotage the advancement of women's careers by attacking their work relentlessly (if you looked long enough you would find something worth attacking), by leaving them off panels, by not inviting them to social gatherings, digging up their backgrounds, even going so far as to sabotage their data. He'd known scientists who had done that, even friends of his from graduate school; he had never participated himself, but he hadn't stopped them either.

You had to go along to get along.

That all changed when he met Claire.

She was the smartest person he had ever met.

Compared to Claire's, his intelligence was Cro-Magnon level.

That hadn't been easy to accept at first. Perhaps he had never accepted it. But he learned to live with it.

"Peter," she said, breaking him out of his daydream. "Babe, I know you've got questions, but we have got to go. I am not going to wait for you."

*Babe.*

She called him babe.

That's what she called him. That was her name for him.

He looked over her shoulder, out toward the island. Dusk was falling. Darkness would be upon them soon. Darkness. Darkness had fallen on him too. He was lost. Everything had been ripped away from him.

"I'm going now."

He was going to lose her again. If he didn't get his shit together, he would lose her again. He had just discovered he'd lost her once, and now he was about to lose her again, this time for keeps. A memory of their wedding flickered in his mind. They had gotten married in the Dominican Republic. Neither was religious and so they asked a friend to perform the ceremony. They'd written their own vows, words that had come so easy. That he would stand with her to the very end.

He had to stand with her right now.

He wouldn't ask her about her family. Every answer was liable to break him. Did he need to know about her two kids or fixer-upper house or her husband the surgeon or best-selling author or whatever he was. Her husband would be something impressive, of that he had no doubt, because she would accept nothing else (*except him, ha-ha*). She was drawn to greatness. He was never quite sure why she had picked him; perhaps one of those times that the universe hadn't been looking. Besides, it wasn't like the universe hadn't gotten its revenge. Exhibit A, *take a fucking look around here.*

There was no going back. All you had to do was see the look on her face. But to not help her would be turning his back on her in her hour of greatest need. He had to stand with her.

"Claire," he said.

"What?"

"I know a shortcut to the beach."

THEY STOPPED to rest at a small but fast-moving creek about three miles east of the hilltop. It ran through the center of a low valley, grassy and damp and studded with huge black rocks. The creek, a tributary of the river they had forded while fleeing Berry, wound around them.

"Five minutes," Claire said. "Make sure you hydrate."

His face flushed with annoyance. He sure as hell didn't need her telling him to drink enough water. He knelt by the edge of the creek and scooped it into his mouth; the water was cold, so icy that it hurt his teeth when he swallowed it. The moonlight reflected off Claire's face. In the splash of silvery gossamer, he really saw her face for the first time since they'd reunited, and in it, he could see the lost years etched into her skin. A scatter of crow's feet framing the rims of her eyes. A hint of hardness in the jawline that had once been soft.

He glanced back up at the moon, which had lost its luster for Peter. He didn't know what he was looking at. Was this the moon from right now or two years ago? The ramifications of Claire's bombshell were replicating faster than he could process them. Did the temporal anomaly affect just him and Claire or every living thing on the island? What if it only affected one of them? What about plants? Animals? How did the sun rise and set here? Was he imagining it? Was the object making him see things that were not there? Or blinding him to things that were there?

All at once, he was exhausted.

His legs were tired; she had allowed them five minutes to rest and rehydrate at this small but fast-moving creek that they had found. The water was cold, so icy that it hurt his teeth when he swallowed two palmfuls of it. They had been on the move for two solid hours. Little had been said, which was fine with him. Better to keep this professional.

"Time to go," she said.

## 24

Claire set the pace as they continued onward, the ticking clock in her head looming large. Time with her kids. Time with Jack. She was already in far too deep, and every second here was costing her bedtimes and weekend getaways and cuddles on the couch. At best, she would lose a year of their lives. A year! And if too much more time got away from them, if they encountered any more trouble, that would be it. Another few hours, and her kids would be on the other side of the mountain, having made peace with their mother's disappearance, having moved on. Perhaps a new stepmother had entered their lives. It wouldn't be new and raw anymore; her sweet Hugo would be tougher, made tough and leathery by his mother's selfishness.

She was jogging now, keeping the sun over her left shoulder, her singular focus on the island's eastern beaches. There was a lot of ground to cover, but if Berry's vessel was here, she felt confident they would find it. They had to. To believe otherwise was to admit defeat. At least Peter had come around; he trailed just behind her, within earshot, the steady footfalls of a man on the move.

"I just thought of something," he said, somewhat breathlessly.

"What?

"This island is the most important piece of real estate on the planet."

"What do you mean?"

"It's basically a fountain of youth," he said. "Imagine the ramifications of that. Whoever controls it would control time. And they don't even know about that, do they?"

"They didn't mention it to me. Besides, how could they?"He was right. The island was now a weapon of staggering power. The U.S. government could park assets here, both human and otherwise, the way you froze a roast to use later. It could become a playground for the wealthy and well-connected, those who would pay anything for a taste of immortality. It would take time to sort things out, such as addressing the failure of electronics on the island, but she was sure they could figure that out. It was pretty clear that the temporal anomaly was the cause of the choppers going down. That's why nothing worked. The notion that time on Earth was now moving at two different speeds was difficult to comprehend. Time had always been the constant of her life, of everyone's life. In many ways, it was the ultimate enemy. Racing along, chewing up their lives, an insatiable monster. Moving quickly when you least wanted it to, crawling by when you needed it to zip by. It seemed like just yesterday they had brought the twins home from the hospital, and here they were, already one-third of the way to adulthood (if not more, given her current situation). Time was her work's greatest enemy, in fact, the one thing that had once convinced her that contact with another civilization would never happen. They'd be just too far away.

Thinking about it was maddening, so she told herself that it didn't matter. She wasn't going to be on this rock much longer. The closer they drew to the beach, the more confident she became that they would find Berry's vessel. If he had come here to silence Peter, then they had made sure he had gotten here safely. It was the only thing that made sense.

Because the alternative was too horrible to contemplate.

What if there were no boat? What if Berry was on a suicide mission and had destroyed the vessel that had brought him here? There was no other way off the island, at least not one that got her back to her kids before they died of old age. A sliver of doubt edged its way into her like a knife. The clock was moving too quickly here. No matter how fast she moved, it would cost her too much time; even if every single thing went by the book and she was right that Berry had left a seaworthy craft behind, it wouldn't be enough.

Clouds darkened the sky and the wind freshened. The skies opened up, the rain washing down her neck, under her shirt, down her arms, coursing down her stomach.

"I'm sorry," she said as the rain poured down. She hated herself for saying it, but it came out almost of its own accord. She didn't have to anything to be sorry about, but she'd said it so many times over the course of her adult life that it was almost a reflex for any situation that had been rendered askew. It was a thing women said, she noticed, never men. Men knocked things off their axes, they were the ones who rendered things askew, but they never apologized for it.

"Sorry for what?"

Everything. For this goddamn thing landing on this island, for believing he was dead, for moving on, for getting married, for having kids, for leaving him locked in her past, forever trapped in this locket hanging from her neck. She sighed deeply and let it out.

"For all of it."

"What's he like?" he asked softly.

Her stomach flipped at the question. How did you tell the love of your life about your new husband?

"Do you really want to know?"

"Not really," he said. "But it's better than not knowing."

She considered her response. There was an urge to exaggerate, let Peter believe that only a perfect man could have replaced him. But that would make her like one of those idiots she saw on Facebook, the ones who sang the praises of their perfect spouses even though the truth was that deep down, if they left the bowl of oatmeal in the sink without rinsing it out one more goddamn time, they would murder their beloved in their sleep.

She didn't want to undersell him either. That wouldn't be fair to Jack, a man in emotional hell because he'd had the misfortune of falling for the scientist with the tragic past. If she didn't sell him strongly enough, she might leave Peter with the impression that their shared past was like that comfy pair of old pajamas you couldn't wait to climb back into at the end of a long day.

"He's a good man."

"What's his name?"

"Jack."

"Jack," he said "Good strong name.

"Jack.

"Jack," he said a third time.

A tickle of discomfort brushed against her, like an unexpectedly chilly breeze in September, when the memories of summer were still strong and you could smell the sunscreen and the salt air.

"Two kids?"

She stopped on the narrow path they were blazing through the jungle at the mention of Hugo and Miranda. Her heart swelled with panic at the thought that she might not see them again. A strange thought bloomed in her head like a lit match before extinguishing just as quickly. Her skin prickled with anger.

Anger.

Anger at Peter.

For coming here.

It didn't make sense. Of course he had come. She would have. Yet she was angry all the same, angry that his decision to come here had brought her here and away from her kids; for some reason it didn't quell her rage that her kids would not even exist *but for* his decision to come here. That was a mother's love for you. Irrational and pure.

"Yeah," she said dismissively. "Let's keep moving."

She didn't want to discuss the kids. Feelings of hopelessness and anger ignited inside her like renegade fireworks.

"What are their names?"

"I said we need to keep moving," she said again, conscious of a little fire in her voice.

Peter huffed. Something she was all too familiar with - the Peter Abbott huff. When a discussion didn't go his way, his little signature huff was the capper, the door closing on the argument. It normally drove her crazy, even when she wanted to keep talking, but she was A-OK with it right now. She wasn't ready to let Peter inside her life just yet. She wasn't sure she would ever be.

The terrain began sloping upward as they came across a

ridge of hills guarding the southwestern corner of the island. She paused to assess the changing dynamic, cursing yet another obstacle in her way. An uphill climb would certainly cost her more time. Every goddamn step was killing her, literally. As she took a deep breath, readying an attack on this hill, she felt herself trembling. Her hands shook. Hell, maybe she would have a stroke right here, a big juicy aneurysm that would drop her right here. That might even be better than having to suffer through this nightmare, one whose ending was perhaps already preordained.

She was never getting off this island.

*You'll die here*, a little voice whispered. *All this is just busy work. Make you feel good about your current situation, make you feel like you actually have a chance to prevail. Even though you don't.*

As a little girl, Claire had been terribly afraid of clowns. In the fourth grade, she'd gone to a classmate's birthday party. They hadn't been that close, but Alisha's mom had made her invite all the girls in the class because that was the right thing to do. Alisha had actually said that to Claire, that she was inviting her because her mom said it was the right thing to do. The party's main attraction was a clown named Jingles; he wore baggy yellow pants and giant red shoes and a puffy white shirt. His face was painted white, of course, his eyes windowed by bright blue diamonds. A red nose completed the picture.

Claire never knew for certain, but she felt like Jingles had watched her the entire afternoon, filling her with that strange creepy-crawly feeling of someone staring at you and then looking away an instant before you caught them. Maybe he had been, it wasn't like the Lodens had run Jingles the Clown through an extensive background check.

It felt like Jingles was here now, staring at her, making

her feel uncomfortable, reminding her of the darkness in the world. There wasn't always a happy ending. Sometimes young joggers did get snatched from the side of the road, left in a ditch with terrible things done to them; sometimes fathers who had become distracted, who hadn't slept well the night before, forgot their toddlers in hot cars.

The same sour milk feeling Jingles had left in her stomach was back.

Four decades left in the bank, and Claire was going to have to cash them all out now. Perhaps someday someone would crack the code, unlock the mysteries of the island, and they would find her corpse. They would collect her remains and send her home, and they would give her a hero's funeral for being one of the first.

*We're here today because of the sacrifices of people like Claire Hamilton and Peter Abbott. A new era in human history. A dawn of a new age, blah, blah, blah.*

They would say something like that, and perhaps they would hand her great-grandkids a medal and an American flag folded just so, and seven soldiers would turn and fire their weapons thrice each.

She had to keep going, despite the inevitability of it all. Even if it proved futile, she would keep going until she could go no more.

The hill crested, tapering off into a grassy flatland. Here the scent of the sea was strong again, the salt air tickling her nostrils. The ocean was always welcome because it melted away the real world, reminded you that there were things bigger and older and deeper than you, than your problems. This was the pull the ocean had on her, even here at the edge of the world. Simply coming up on it filled her with hope. As they made their way through the grasses, the ground underneath their feet transitioned from dirt to a kind of rocky clay before its final transformation into sand.

The ground sloped gently downward, giving Claire a wide vista of the beach. Here the island's southern and eastern shores came to a point, demarcated by a small cove protected by a long narrow natural bridge sweeping from one side to the other. Below, the water gently lapped at the cove's rock walls. It was more tranquil than the western side where she had come ashore. As Claire considered her options, the decision was suddenly made for her. Something underneath that salt tang found its way to her nose. Her brain sorted through its catalog of smells and settled on its identity instantly. Weird how the way the mind worked, delivering you the news even when you wanted to reject it as fake. You lied to yourself when you didn't want to accept the truth, not because you didn't know what the truth was.

This was a truth she did not want to accept.

It was smoke.

She cupped her hands around her eyes, turning south toward the shoreline stretching away from her. Nothing. Then she turned back east, her eyes scanning the shore as it crawled north to the horizon. There. Two or three miles away. A wisp of black smoke, the noxious thin cloud drifting offshore like an apparition.

"Shit."

She broke into a run, the hot sand shifting under her feet as she angled down toward the cooler packed sand at the water's edge. She ran like she had never run before, not waiting for Peter. There was no way to gauge how far she had gone or how much farther she had to go. There were no landmarks to fixate on, nothing to give her any sense of place. Even when her lungs burned and her quads and calves trembled with fatigue, she seemed no closer to her destination.

There was nothing to do but run. She took a short break after a mile or so, bending over, tugging at the edges of her shorts, gasping and clawing for fresh air. Instead of pacing herself, she continued full out, each sprint shorter than the previous one and requiring longer and longer rest breaks. At one point, her legs gave out and she flopped to the ground, rolling in the shallow waves as her muscles screamed for oxygenated blood. The smoke was thicker now and much closer. The outlines of a structure burned about fifty feet from the water, up high in the sand, back toward a large dune guarding the beach.

She resorted to crawling.

Behind her:

"Claire, wait!"

She ignored him. He kept calling after her, even as she continued staggering down the beach. The fire came into stark view now, burning like hell, consuming a structure that was still recognizable but only just so.

She drew close enough to feel the heat of the blaze, radiating toward her. It crackled and split, arms of flame licking the air for its precious fuel. Lower down, the core burned like an open furnace, taking with it Claire's last good hope to ever see her family again.

Buried in the cloak of the conflagration was the outline of a small boat.

## 25

As her absolution burned, Claire found herself thinking about the day the twins had been born. Her doctors had scheduled a C-section for early June, but on May 22, at about thirty-four weeks, she had gone into labor while she and Jack were streaming a stand-up comedy special. She laughed so hard at a bit about cable companies and how the comedian was comfortable hating his current cable provider and simply did not have the time or energy to devote to learning how to hate a new provider that she peed herself a little. She marveled at a comedian's skill to mine the mundane and find the humor in it, to wring joy from a joyless situation.

The contractions began slowly, but by the time the comic was thanking everyone for coming out, they were six minutes apart (she had kept track via the digital clock of the DVR) and sweeping from her back to her front. She phoned the on-call physician, who told them through a tired yawn she'd meet them at the hospital. A mad dash through their to-do list followed as the reality began crashing in on them;

when they next returned home, they would be parents. They made it to the hospital a little before midnight; a waiting nurse wheeled Claire to her room in Labor & Delivery.

As Jack finished checking her in, she couldn't help but think about Peter; she didn't mean for it to happen, but he had snuck in while she took in her new environs. The harder she tried to eject him from her mind, the stronger her memories of him grew, and how unfair it was that she was here doing the things they had talked about doing while he lay dead on a deserted island. She had been pregnant when Peter disappeared, just past the first trimester. Peter hadn't known. Jack never knew. But a miscarriage two weeks after Peter vanished put an end to all that.

When Jack found her with tears running down her cheeks, she lied to him about why she had been crying, she had lied right to her husband's face, and she didn't know why she had done that.

She had a roommate, a young girl who couldn't have been more than seventeen and was ready to pop. The girl was scared and alone but for her disinterested boyfriend, a pale, twitchy guy with the letters SYKO (*psycho*, Claire deduced one night several weeks later while feeding Miranda) tattooed on his stringy but tough-looking bicep. On the rare occasion he wasn't outside taking a smoke break, he sat in the chair next to the girl's bed, engrossed in his phone and never once looking up to see how the mother of his child was doing. Jack had raised holy hell about the roommate, since the hospital had promised them a private room, but there had been a full moon and a heavy line of thunderstorms earlier, and *that was the kind of thing that just triggered labor, hon, I know that's not real science, but damned if it doesn't happen every time,* the nurse had said.

Finally, they administered the local anesthetic after explaining the risks, such as a one-in-a-thousand chance that Claire might experience partial paralysis in her upper legs, but she didn't care because by then the pain was so bad that she would have been okay with a one-in-three chance of all life on earth being extinguished. Her lie to Jack had haunted her through the surgery, even through the first moments she had held her babies close, feeling their warm wriggly bodies against her skin, throughout her four-day stay in the hospital. The babies stayed in the NICU until the doctors were comfortable with their lung development, and that had been a hard week for Claire. She cried constantly, wondering if the universe was punishing her for moving on with her life, that she was not supposed to do this, and fate would take her babies from her for her insolence, just like it had stolen her pregnancy a dozen years ago.

The twins improved steadily, however, and their week in the neonatal intensive care unit had gone off without any complications. Then they were home, which was filled instantly with exhaustion and bodily fluids and short tempers and laundry undone and lots of takeout boxes, but every once in a while, the four of them would be together and the babies would be awake and happy and fed and dry, and it would seem to Claire in these moments that her heart would burst with joy. It was during these moments that Peter seemed very far away – never gone entirely, but when she felt the least guilty about how it had turned out. It was these moments she stitched together to create the tapestry of her life; how easy it was to dismiss the sleepless nights and the stomach bugs and the saggy belly when Hugo batted at her nose while she fed him a bottle or when Miranda laughed her belly laugh while Daddy tickled her chin.

Now it was gone.

The fire burned and crackled and popped, breathing its dragon breath on her face. It did more than consume this vessel; it burned away her entire future. Jack and the kids would be on their own now, just as he had feared. He had been right all along, and she was mad at him, mad at herself for her selfishness, and then she got mad for being mad at herself because she was a scientist, and this is what scientists were supposed to do. They were supposed to go to dangerous places to study things that would help humanity better understand its place in the universe.

A flicker of movement caught her eye.

Her pulse quickened when she saw Agent Berry stumbling around the far edge of the fire. He looked unsteady on his feet and did not seem particularly focused on her.

"Berry?"

His head snapped to attention. Until that moment, she wasn't sure he'd noticed she was there. She shivered as a breeze slipped around her like the touch of a lover in the dark.

"Oh," he said matter of factly. "I thought you drowned."

A smile curled across his face like a big red slash, but it wasn't a happy smile, exactly, or one that could be described as sane. She didn't reply. Downwind, she detected a hint of booze radiating from him.

Something behind her caught Berry's eye. She spotted Peter drawing up behind them.

"Maybe you did," he muttered, mostly to himself. "Maybe she's dead and this ain't real."

"Are you drunk?"

He started weeping. He buried his face in his hands and sobbed. The boat continued to burn.

"Did you do this?" Claire asked.

The question froze his tears; he looked up from his hands with a furrowed brow and a grimace on his face, as though her question had insulted his very intelligence.

"No one can know about this," he said, glancing at the flames, dancing and popping. "No one can know what goes on here."

"Why?"

"We are not ready for this," he replied, his eyes bright and wet. He was slurring his words now.

"Why do you get to be the judge of that?"

"Because I am trained for this kind of thing, and I cannot handle it."

"You saw the object."

His eyes flashed downward before re-engaging Claire's gaze.

"I saw it."

From the corner of her eye, she could see Peter nodding in agreement, his hands on his hips.

"You," Berry said, pointing at Peter. "You know what I'm saying."

"Peter?" Claire said, turning toward her former husband. "You said you hadn't seen it."

"I didn't," Peter replied softly.

"No, he saw it," Berry said. "I can see it on his face. I went to a class for that, you know. Tells, tics, that kind of thing. He saw it."

"Peter, why did you lie?"

"I didn't lie!" he snapped. "I said I didn't see it."

"Well this is fucking great," Claire said, snapping at both of them, putting aside her growing suspicion that Peter was indeed lying. Fucking men. Always viewed as possessing the superior temperament, and maybe that was the case when nothing important was happening, but when the shit hit the fan, they froze, they locked up because they didn't know how to deal with the cascade of emotions that came with a stressful situation. She wasn't afraid to admit that women were more emotional, more in touch with their feelings; they cried more, they melted down more, but they did that and they still got shit done.

Men, though, men were good, men had a plan, at least until they got punched in the face, as the saying went. Then they just went to pieces. Exhibit A. Right here. This current situation, if you will. She had to calm these idiots down, these teenage boys acting like it had been three hours since their last meal, acting like they had just seen their first boob. Women's lives, on the other hand, were nothing but a daily punch in the face. At home. At work. In school. At the PTA. Women learned pretty early how to deal with being punched in the face. A woman's plan was to take the punch and then get shit done anyway.

"What do you know about this place?" she asked.

"What do you mean?"

"You keep saying that we're not ready, that we have to keep this place secret, but I'm not getting it."

He shook his head slowly.

"This thing, it topples everything over," he said. "This balance of power that keeps the world calm-"

"Calm?"

"Admittedly, a relative term," he said. "The thing that keeps the world calm is the idea that we are in charge of our own destiny, that at the end of the day, there is no reason for anyone to go off cockeyed. But we've come to understand that if word of this got out, all bets would be off. Our government will not allow that to happen. That's why no one can be allowed to leave this island alive."

"Do you know about the temporal anomaly?" Claire asked.

There was a risk in asking him, a chance of setting him off. On the other hand, it might calm him down, knowing that what they did here no longer mattered back in the real world. Either way, she wanted to keep him talking.

"What are you talking about?"

"Time works differently here," Peter said.

"Meaning what?"

"I've only been here for two weeks."

Berry laughed a strange little laugh.

"See?" he said. "Proof that I'm right. This is way beyond what we're capable of dealing with. They should nuke this place."

"They're going to figure it out eventually," Claire said. "Eventually. They have to start somewhere. You don't get to decide how humanity deals with this discovery. We do not get to decide."

"The hell I don't," Berry snapped back. "People are dumb and panicky, prone to violence, especially when faced with something they don't understand, with something that doesn't fit into their carefully constructed paradigm. For all we know, it's a doomsday device."

His mood had darkened considerably.

"The one thing we know," he continued, "this thing has sat here peacefully for twelve years. We've proven we don't know what to do with it. Even if the sender's motives were benign, it's clear we are not ready for whatever gifts it might bestow upon us."

"That is not our call to make," Claire said.

"The hell it's not," Berry snapped. "The hell it is not."

There would be no changing his mind, if it even mattered anymore. She looked out over the water, toward the horizon, painfully aware that just beyond her reach, time was rushing along like a roaring river; where she stood, however, still waters. The die was cast. There was no way off the island, not anytime soon. They could build a raft, but that would take weeks, if not months; if they were lucky enough to be rescued, decades would have slipped away.

A flicker of movement caught her eye; before she could react, Berry was on her, grabbing her, pushing her toward the fire. Pain rocketed through her shoulder as he pinned her arms behind her back. She was too stunned to even scream, watching with horror as he drove them toward the flames. Finally, her fight instinct kicked in, and she began thrashing against him, but he was too strong and had too much leverage on her.

Within seconds, it felt like she was at the front door of hell; the flames leaped out and singed her arms. Then, just as suddenly, Berry's grip on her loosened, and she stumbled to her right, toward the water, desperate to remain clear of the flames. She turned and saw Peter and Berry wrestling in the sand amid a blur of punches and kicks. They were close to the fire; one wrong move by either of them would propel them right into its hellish belly.

Claire looked for some way to help Peter, suddenly aware of her status as a damsel in distress and having none of it. A piece of driftwood by the water caught her eye. As she scrambled after it, Peter and Berry began circling each other; she charged at Berry, who had his back to her, and swung the piece of wood with all her might. It connected solidly with the back of his head, staggering him. Peter rushed him with both hands out, giving him a mighty shove. Berry stumbled at an angle, toward the fire, tripping on a piece of boat debris and falling into the flames, engulfing him.

He managed to crawl out of the fire, his body ablaze. It was horrifying to watch, this man-shaped thing creeping toward the water's edge. She looked on, frozen, knowing there was nothing they could do. Berry made it to the water line before collapsing. Gentle waves lapped at him, dousing him, extinguishing the flames, leaving the husk of his ruined body smoldering and smoking. He did not appear to be conscious.

Claire collapsed to the sand, far away from the fire. Peter sat next to her, and they sat quietly, not saying a word, as the boat fire burned itself out, as the water gently rocked Berry's body back and forth. The sun dipped below the highlands, unrolling shadows across the beach like blankets. As dusk fell, the tide came in. A little bit at a time, darkening the sand a bit higher with each successive wave. Eventually, the water reached Claire's toes. It was cool and refreshing, a moment of peace after a hellish twenty-four hours.

On its whispery way back out, the tide gently gathered Berry's body and carried it away from the shore. Berry exited the stage not all at once but in fits and starts. A few yards out, and then a few back in. She watched, transfixed, as his body slid up a small wave and then down its backside. She kept thinking it would slide back toward shore, that the waves weren't big enough to take the body out to sea, but within a few minutes, his remains were receding from view. She watched as long as she could, even cupping her hands around her face to better track Berry's progress. Eventually, he was but a dot on the horizon, and then a few minutes later, he was gone.

At some point, Claire realized that her fingers were entwined with Peter's. She didn't remember him taking her hand or her taking his, but nevertheless, they held hands as the darkness fell around them, as time beyond the island raced by, as the life she had worked so hard to build since the last time she had held this man's hand left her behind, in the past, in a place that perhaps she had never left and where she was now trapped, possibly forever.

## 26

They slept on the beach.

Peter woke with the sun, just as it edged up over the horizon and flooded the island with light. Several more months had elapsed while they slept, a reality that was difficult to wrap his head around. If he was watching the sun rise now, what was anyone beyond the island's grip seeing at this moment? How could time be one thing here and another thing out there? Was there time within time? Could you control it somehow, the way you could rewind or fast-forward a television show? What effect would all this have on humanity, on the planet, on their solar system?

Time.

The destroyer of all things.

Humanity's unifying constant.

Good or evil, black or white, Muslim or Jew or Christian, Satanist or atheist. Time bound them all together here on Earth. Einstein's theory of relativity posited that massive objects distorted space-time, which they felt as gravity. Space and time were woven together in a continuum, like a tapestry of the universe, and an object in motion experienced time at a slower rate than one at rest. So did that mean that the island was in motion in a way he did not understand? Perhaps the object was so heavy that it was bending space around it. But if it were that massive, wouldn't they have felt the effects of it off the island? Wouldn't it have altered the shape of the planet? Or had it accelerated the world beyond like some a temporal turbo booster? After all, if they all experienced the passage of time at the same rate, then they wouldn't notice that it was moving faster than it should have been. Both possibilities were ludicrous and yet possible at the same time.

"Earth to Peter."

He did a double take as he realized Claire had been speaking to him. She was on her side, her head propped up on her hand, not unlike the way she would lie in the bed they had once shared.

"You okay?" she asked.

"Fine," he said. "Just thinking."

"About what?"

"About what we're going to do next."

A quiet moment followed, one in which he took in her face. The passage of time was apparent now, at her eyes, at the corners of her mouth. Yet she looked as lovely as ever. Lovelier than she seemed even two weeks ago. She would be forty-four now, maybe forty-five. He could not believe that of all the men in the world, she had chosen him. Of course, the price for that was falling into a goddamn wormhole or whatever this place was and losing her to some lawyer, probably. He bet her new husband was a lawyer. Maybe the guy she'd hired to handle his estate. Yeah. He could just see some slimy lawyer sliding into her broken heart while he processed the machinery of Peter's untimely death.

"We'll need a long-term shelter," he said. "A steady supply of food and water. Is that what you were thinking about?"

She pursed her lips and hummed her apparent disagreement.

"You don't agree?"

"No, not really."

"Well, what do you think we should do?"

"Are you serious?" she snapped, sitting up. "The object. We need to find it. Like yesterday. It's not too late for me to get back for part of my kids' childhood."

Her anger and delusion caught him off guard. She was still thinking about getting off the island. Did she think that finding the object was going to buy back all the time she had lost with her kids? Time was an arrow, flying in one direction only. It had left her behind, just like it had left him.

"Claire," he said, "honey, we need to be realistic. We need to take care of ourselves."

"What do you mean?"

"I mean, what difference does it make? It's a day's walk to the other side of the island. By then, another year will have gone by."

"What difference does it make?" she repeated in disbelief. "It's because of that goddamn thing we're in this mess. Maybe there's some way to undo it. I don't know. It's worth a shot."

She wasn't being reasonable. That was a woman for you, but *holy shit* would he never say that out loud. The thing was, he wasn't trying to be an asshole. He wasn't trying to be mean. He was being realistic. They were hungry and dehydrated and exposed to the elements. These were immediate and real concerns. If they didn't address those concerns, and that right soon, it wouldn't matter if the object turned out to be a fucking DeLorean equipped with a flux capacitor. They would be dead. And if the object really could make a difference, then would it matter if they got there this afternoon or two days from now?

He got up and stretched. His mouth was dry and he was hungry, and he made a note to backtrack toward one of the various springs they'd seen along the way. One of their top priorities would be locating the various crash sites and scavenging for supplies. After all, none would be more than two weeks old.

"Are you coming or not?"

Peter sighed loudly. There was no harm in humoring her. She could scratch this itch, and then they could move on with their lives.

"I don't want you alone out there," he said. "Maybe you're right. We should go to the site."

SHE WAS quiet as they trekked northward through the highlands back toward the center of the island. Peter noticed there was less urgency about her, less pep in her step, and he wondered if his words had taken a toll on her hopes of getting home.

"I'm not saying there's no chance," he offered when they paused for a five-minute break. They were back in the forest and had stopped at a quick-moving spring that held the clearest and coldest water he had ever tasted. After their thirst was slaked, they sat side by side on a large low-slung boulder.

She didn't reply.

"I mean, you think I'm thrilled about losing twelve years of my life? About losing you?"

She looked at him with a wistful smile. Then she reached out and squeezed him gently on his flank, just above his hip. They had held hands on the beach the afternoon before, but this felt different. That had been two people in the aftermath of a crisis, survivors of a terrible disaster. Not because it was Claire and Peter. It electrified him, sent him back home, erased all the horror of the last twenty-four hours, made Peter feel like himself again. In that touch, there had been no failed mission, no new husband and new family; in it, they were both still young, living in that little house, and their whole lives were in front of them.

"I'm sorry, Peter," she said. "I know this is hard."

He struggled with what to say next. It was tough making conversation with someone you loved when that person wasn't part of your life anymore. Probably why they said you should never be friends with an ex. If you wanted to be friends, then why were you exes? For God's sake, they had once had sex in the bathroom of a Chili's in El Paso while at dinner with her dad, and now they were supposed to be friends, shake hands and say *hey, how are the kids, good, good, everything's going really well*? The memory brought a smile to his face. She had surprised him in the bathroom, locking the door behind her; she had told the judge that she had to make a quick phone call to get away from the table. When you became intimate with someone, all the masks came off, for better or worse, and there was no hiding who you were.

"It's not your fault," he said.

"It's not really anyone's fault, I guess," she said.

"Except for NASA. Those assholes."

Claire laughed.

"Still got your sense of humor after all this time."

"Claire."

"Right. Dammit. I keep forgetting."

There it was. The gulf between them. Not distance but time. They were separated by time, Peter frozen in place, Claire rushed along to middle age, to the peak of her career, to suburban life, to runny noses and supper clubs and PTA and soccer games, and all the things they had talked about barely three weeks ago, suddenly rendered irrelevant.

Didn't matter whose fault it was.

It was what it was.

It was never not going to be twelve years for Claire, any more than it was never not going to be a few weeks for him. It was only going to get worse; she'd only given him a taste of everything he had missed. All the things that had happened to shape her into who she was, these tiny changes carving her soul. Like a parent who didn't notice their child's day-to-day transformation and then a distant relative sees them and marvels at how big they've gotten. Claire wasn't the same person anymore.

They resumed the journey, Peter leading the way through a narrow, winding valley that ascended to an open glade, where the wreckage of his helicopter came into view. The sight of it still made his heart race, the tangle of twisted metal now a tomb for eleven brave men and women. It was here he had made his home, in the shadow of the crash, for the last two weeks, waiting for rescue, waiting to live, waiting to die. He had not done much in the way of a long-term shelter as that was tantamount to accepting defeat, to accepting that no rescue was coming.

"Oh my God," Claire said, coming to a halt.

Her hands were on her head, pushing the hair away from her face. He found himself staring at her, at the line of her face, at the angle of her jaw, at everything that he loved so much. That was the current state of affairs; he loved her.

Would she understand that? Would she be able to comprehend that he still loved her just as much as he had when she dropped him at the airport? The issue had not come up, perhaps because it had not occurred to her. But it would.

"Peter," she said. "How on earth did you survive this?"

He didn't know. With each passing day, it felt more and more unlikely that he had. Maybe he was dead. Maybe he had died and gone to hell and his hell would be an eternity on this island, stuck with the woman he loved who did not love him back and that's how it would be for all time. Why not? Shit, it made as much sense as surviving an unsurvivable crash and finding out he was stuck in a time warp.

The crash had been horrible. He had never liked to fly, it always put him on edge, but the scientist in him had usually handled things, kept him calm. The final moments of the flight before it all went bad kept replaying over and over; Rodriguez was telling him a story about a previous mission, about this meal they'd had in a local village when he'd dined on sheep testicles. Then the chopper had fallen silent as its electrical system and engines had failed and it began its rapid descent. Rodriguez had stopped mid-story, right about the time Peter started wondering if they were putting him on, every conversation suddenly going silent but for a steady stream of profanities as the pilots struggled to regain control of the aircraft.

*Goddamnit, goddamnit, goddammit*, over and over again, it played in his head, over and over again, his stomach dropping into his shoes and he kept waiting for the pilot to regain control; that's what you thought about during a crash, that it wasn't going to happen. Was that what people who died in plane crashes thought, up until their very last moments of life? Nothing frightened Peter Abbott more than the prospect of dying in a plane crash; it unnerved him so badly that he took a Valium whenever he flew. The chopper kept dropping, catching the edge of a tree and somersaulting twice, scattering bodies and gear and equipment through the cabin before slamming into the ground.

The crash knocked Peter unconscious.

He woke up several hours later, pinned under a rucksack on the ceiling of the chopper. He touched his head; his hand came away tacky with drying blood. It was still daylight, but this part of the island was in shadow, the sun behind the trees on its western side. His head was pounding and he was covered in blood (his own, it turned out, from two dozen cuts and scratches, none severe, miraculously enough). It hurt to move, so he lay there quietly.

Silence greeted his calls out to the other passengers. With a mighty shove, he knocked the rucksack to the side and inched upward to a seated position, his back against the curved metal skin of the helicopter. Bodies were strewn about the cabin, blood splattered every which way. He crawled from victim to victim, checking for any signs of life, finding none. They were all dead.

That's when it hit him. He was all alone, the thin veneer between adventure and disaster ruptured, panic pouring in like ocean water into a doomed ship. You told yourself you knew the risks, that this was dangerous work, and you were okay with it because the payoff would be worth it. Especially once they had told him what awaited them on the island.

He crept out of the wreckage on his hands and knees; when he touched *terra firma*, he began to cry, awash in a strange and terrible joy that he was still alive. A hot chaser of guilt vaporized that joy, followed by a profound confusion as to why he alone had survived. He had barely known them, but he could right then and there recite each of their first, middle and last names, his grief a key unlocking a cabinet in his mind.

Around him, giant trees spiking high into the sky rustled in the breeze, the air thick with salt air and humidity. The island was alive with hidden activity, birds chirping, small animals traipsing about, twigs and leaves crunching underfoot. These ordinary processes of nature calmed him down. Life. Real life all around him as he sat on his haunches, watching it play out as it had for eons. They would come for him. This was a contingency they had planned for. He needed to remain calm, keep his wits about him until they came for him. Right now, back on the ship, they were scurrying about, trying to figure out what had happened, monitoring the data from his biomonitor, grieving the lost but jacked for the opportunity to bring one home, preparing a rescue. He just needed to stay close to the wreckage.

"Peter, are you okay?"

*Claire.*

Her voice snapped him back to reality, the pair of them standing before the wreckage. See, it was better that Claire hadn't come. She could've been killed. No, this way was better. Both of them still alive, a reunion in their immediate future.

He told himself this because the truth was something else entirely.

He hadn't wanted her to come, he was a terrible person for thinking this, but he hadn't wanted her to come. He hadn't wanted to share this discovery with her; he needed to catch a break, pull even with his more successful, more well-known wife. There were more white men in the hard sciences than you could shake a stick at; nothing about him stood out. Claire, on the other hand, could become the face of science. A former athlete, beautiful, brilliant, a fierce warrior who'd slashed her way through the jungle of their patriarchal, sexist, chauvinistic profession. Her face was made for the covers of scientific journals and how long before television came calling, before she made the leap to popular science while he continued to toil away for this foundation or that one, constantly begging benefactors for money, doing the filthy dance of fundraising. This mission was going to change all that. His name, his face would become synonymous with science. He would get the big book deal, the TV appearances, hell, maybe even a movie!

In the ultimate irony, she had made it here after all.

Wouldn't it be just perfect for it to end this way?

That she would become the hero?

Hell, standing there, looking at this horrific crash site, perhaps she wished he had died here. He saw now that his being alive was the complication. Dead was easy for her; she'd lived more than a decade believing he was dead. She could do Peter being dead in her sleep.

"I'm fine," he said.

But he didn't feel fine.

## 27

Claire kept one eye on Peter and one on the debris as they gathered supplies for their push toward the island's center. He was quiet, which was normal, but there was a brooding underneath the surface that she didn't like. Like his mind was running a fever.

Of course, what else could she expect? That he wasn't running around naked talking to a coconut was probably a miracle in and of itself. It was a lot to take in. The crash alone had probably triggered post-traumatic stress, a fact that was easy to overlook in the shadow of her unexpected appearance and the devastating news she had brought with her. How was he processing all three of these variables?

She'd known Peter to be a strong man, rattled by little. He never got too up or too down, a personality trait that people often equated with cold aloofness. But that was wrong, it focused on the wrong thing. He cared a great deal. He was passionate about many things. He did not, however, get revved up about things he could not control. Traffic, bad weather, illness, shitty politicians, corrupt bankers, other people's drama. He did not use social media and had had a print newspaper delivered to the house every morning. She kept the subscription after he left; she couldn't bear to cancel it. He had too many other things to worry about. Ambitious, of course he was, what scientist wasn't? He wanted to make a big discovery, they all did; for some reason, people were always surprised that scientists were ambitious, that they weren't automatons solely dedicated to furthering human knowledge.

While Peter continued picking through the wreckage, Claire divided the supplies into two rucksacks. As she worked, she stole glances at him. It was becoming more and more obvious that very little time had passed for him; his body was still as lean and lithe as it had been at the airport. This wasn't a man who had been struggling to stay alive for years.

Fifteen days.

Once again, the revelation left her temporarily frozen. It wasn't something you could get used to; your brain kept telling you it was wrong, kept trying to substitute what it believed should be there, that he was Robinson Crusoe, stuck on this island for more than a decade. She gave her head a good hard shake and returned to the task at hand, dividing the MREs between the two packs, following Peter's work to make sure they left nothing behind. Matches. A first-aid kit. Canteens. Knives. An analog compass. This item she studied a little more carefully, wondering if the object would have any impact on it.

She pointed it at the window of the chopper, which faced southeast, keeping her eye on the compass' pointer. The disc, notched with eight different compass points, began to spin in its solution like a centrifuge, faster and faster until Claire could not make out the directional markings. She continued to watch it, mystified by the newest quirk the island had seen fit to reveal to them. It began to make her dizzy so she snapped the case closed and placed it in her pack.

"Claire?"

She looked up to see Peter glancing over his shoulder.

"You ready?"

She nodded.

After one last pass through the cabin, they set off again, making their way up a shallow hill. He took the point, Claire bringing up the rear. As they made their way, her eyes kept flitting to the backs of his legs, burnished with sun during his time on the island, remembering suddenly how sexy she had once found them.

*Oh come ON, what the hell is the matter with you?*

She looked away quickly, hot with guilt, hot with something at least, convinced that he could feel her eyes on her, that he would figure out that somewhere deep down, in that place of self-awareness that you did not want to acknowledge, a tiny fire for him continued to burn. She had no desire to learn what awaited her if the barrier to that place was breached.

Her eyes locked on their surroundings, this hillside, its flora, full and rich. To her left was a thick ridge of ferns lining the incline. They paused at one of the island's higher points, its topography rolling downward toward a heavy forest, green and rippling, much like the one she had navigated upon her arrival. A cross breeze freshened the air, filled it with the sounds of nothing and everything. A flicker of movement to her left. An iguana skittered across the face of a large boulder before disappearing behind it.

Her chest tightened with panic as she surveyed the landscape, painfully aware that this might well be the last home she would ever know. A flash of memory, the day she and

Peter had first seen the house they would buy together, move into two months before they got married. It was a first for both of them, their lives to that point consisting of short-term rentals. The itinerant path of graduate students. She had never lived with anyone before, and she had been apprehensive of this step, perhaps even more so than of getting married. Standing next to Peter, however, in the small foyer of that little Cape Cod, which the owners were selling in advance of a move to Florida, it immediately had felt like home. It was right at the top of their budget and it needed a little work to boot, but she couldn't shake the feeling that this was the right place.

There was a checklist, of course, no self-respecting scientist, let alone two, went into a decision like this without a checklist. A decent kitchen, because Peter liked to cook. Ideally, a Florida room, but a screened-in porch would do, a place she could sit in the evening and have a drink; even though it was a cliché, sometimes there was nothing better than sitting with a glass of wine to would take the edge off just a little bit as the late afternoon bled away the remaining light and softened into the low purple sky of evening. A backyard for the garden and the dog they planned on adopting, and of course for a little runt or two down the road. Way down the road, ha-ha, they would joke, but it couldn't be too far down the road because she didn't want to start gambling against Father Time. The house started winning early and the odds only grew longer as the years slipped by.

But that was for a different day.

They made an offer that evening and she was even more nervous than she had been defending her dissertation, worried the sellers wouldn't accept it, worried that someone else would swoop in with a better offer or a briefcase full of cash. But the sellers had taken their offer, ten grand below asking price; they'd wanted to unload it quickly because they didn't want the place where they had raised three kids and welcomed their grandchildren to turn into a cold financial negotiation.

The closing followed sixty days later and just like that they were homeowners, standing at the threshold, surveying the little slice of the world that was all theirs, much like it felt this island was all theirs, that it was going to be home whether they liked it or not. Kind of a fixer-upper, a real estate agent might say, but with good bones. You could make this place a home.

They were never getting off this island.

Not in time for it to matter, at least.

Maybe it *was* time to start thinking about a long-term plan.

She was a scientist, she dealt in facts, she could see the writing on the wall. But she wasn't ready to give up just yet. Not until they played out the string, the last thread of hope, followed it to its very end.

They descended the hill toward the forest, falling into a bit of a rhythm now as they walked. A ripple of optimism curled through her. Just doing something. Just doing something got the juices flowing. Attacking the problem. Predator not prey.

"How was my funeral?" he asked.

She chuckled.

"It was nice."

"Did a lot of people come?"

"Yes."

"Even Vable?"

Eric Vable was another astrobiologist at UW, where, unbeknownst to Peter, Claire now worked, and a longtime foil of Peter's. They hated each other, each thinking the other was no more than a well-trained primate.

"Yeah, he was there," Claire replied. "He even shed a few tears."

"Get the hell out of here."

"Seriously. He was in bad shape. He said you made him a better man."

"Nice. Who gave the eulogy?"

"I did."

"Wow," he said softly. "How about my dad?"

"He was there," Claire replied, suddenly filled with horror at the idea that Peter had not been sure whether his own father had attended his funeral. This drew down his excitement over Vable. It had been one thing to discuss the impact of his death on professional colleagues; mentioning his dad, however, brought home the damage his disappearance had done.

"How is the old man anyway?"

Claire squeezed her eyes shut and let out a long sigh. All his life, Peter had been trying to impress Fred Abbott, a high school science teacher back in Ohio. He had never understood what Claire saw all too clearly. Peter's father wasn't distant because he wasn't impressed with his son; he was distant because he was impressed. He hated knowing that his son was his professional superior, that Fred Abbott wasn't half the scientist his son was.

"Oh," he said softly. "When?"

"Four years ago. Stroke."

"Damn."

"I'm sorry, Peter," she said.

Peter ran a hand through his hair and let out a long sigh. Just another reminder of how much he had missed in these last twelve years. There was going to be no good news, no matter how you sliced it. He stepped off the train for a moment and had been left behind. It was so brutally unfair.

"I'm really sorry," she said.

It seemed to catch up to him all at once. He placed a hand over his mouth, his chin dropped to his chest, and he began to cry. Her Peter, the stoic scientist, stood there, crying loudly. His sobs were amplified by the desolation of the island, the absence of ambient noise, the low-level buzz that humanity's existence created. He sat down on the ground, his legs crisscrossed, and disappeared into a cloud of unrelenting grief. It took Claire aback; she had never once seen him cry in their time together. It just wasn't something he was wired to do.

How much would they have to pay? How big a sacrifice did they have to make for the privilege of being first? They would find the object and pat each other on the back and that would be it. For all they knew, it was just some interstellar drone that had gone off course. A stunning discovery, to be sure, but was that going to get Peter back the dozen years he had lost? Would it get Claire back to her babies?

She sat down next to him on the hillside, close enough for their shoulders to touch. She didn't know what to say, so she slipped her arms around his waist and held him while he cried. It felt good holding him again, she didn't like how good it felt, like a key in a lock. There was something magical about finding someone whose body fit with yours, not at a physical level necessarily, although that was nice too, but at some other level. A level where you had not two halves making a whole, but two wholes melding together to make a better whole.

He buried his face in her hair, his body trembling. The ferocity of his breakdown frightened her a little, but before she could think to say, okay, Peter, take a deep breath, she began to think about Hugo, would he be seven or eight now, she didn't know, and who snuggled with him on the couch and who sat with him at bedtime until he fell asleep, goddamnit, and Peter infected her with his grief. It spilled into her like a virus, breaking her down, and then she was crying too.

They sat there crying for a while and she didn't even notice when he kissed her on her forehead, it didn't seem weird at all, and then she was kissing his face and his lips, and that didn't seem weird or wrong either because she knew now that she was dead, lost aboard the mysterious sinking of the *Kingsman* eighteen months ago. That's what they would have told Jack, who would be moving on, playing the role of both daddy and mommy; he hadn't deserved this, not one bit of it and she hoped he could find happiness again. If they ever got off this island, she would ask to be a part of the kids' lives, as much or as little as they wanted. She would not ask or expect him to be waiting for her; she would not do that to him or the kids.

Peter's hand slipped behind her head, returning the kiss as an ancient desire broke free. A desperate heat bloomed inside her, one she did not want to admit had been simmering these last twelve years, locked away in one of those dark corners that you pretended didn't exist at all. Black ops, classified intelligence, Eyes Only. Then her shirt was off and his hands and mouth were on her skin, warm and tight with sunburn, on her neck, on her breasts. It happened quickly and in slow motion, a series of flashes, Claire wrenching his pants down, Peter peeling her shorts off. His hardness was against her, and then he was inside her.

As he rocked above her, everything slipped away, the object, the *Kingsman*, Berry, Murphy, Jack, the kids, until it was just the two of them on this island, entwined together the way people had tangled together since time immemorial. She didn't even know if it felt good, if it was supposed to feel good, or if this was just the embrace of two survivors of a disaster, a cataclysm of time, the calendar upon which they both stood, the one constant of their lives, of all their lives, of their universe, totally and utterly obliterated. His pace quickened as her orgasm burst forth without warning, and then he finished a few seconds later, and the two of them lay side by side, in the falling darkness, and with the darkness falling all around them, looking up at the stars twinkling in the vast emptiness above them until they slept.

## 28

P eter woke before sunrise, cold and needing to pee. Claire was still sleeping soundly. He got up, stretched, and toddled off behind a tree near the site. The sex loomed large in his mind; sex was what made it different between two people. There was no place to hide, there were no more secrets. He wondered if she would regret it. He didn't, of course. Maybe he should have, a little bit? After all, she was another man's wife. Kind of, but who the hell could say, given this temporal mind fuck they were dealing with. Yeah, she might have been married to someone else, but for God's sake, in his reality, in his place along the river of time, they'd had sex less than three weeks ago, two nights before he came here. And in the two weeks he had been here, she had been fucking this other guy, loving this other guy, marrying this other guy and....

*Stop.*

*Just stop.*

This husband of hers, this Jack, this life she had, was a ghost, an apparition, a thing that wasn't real, a bad dream. Or maybe they were the ghosts now, the negative, the void in their lives. Either way, it didn't matter anymore. She was here, he was here, and those kids of hers, that husband of hers, were thousands of miles and years away. That's just the way it was now. He made his way back to their campsite and lay back down next to a still-sleeping Claire, on her side, her back to him. Her breathing was slow and even, her flank rising and falling like a metronome. He watched her for a bit, happy that she was getting some rest. Maybe this was a good sign. Maybe she was coming around. When you slept hard, your mind was at ease. You had made your peace. The nights you spent tossing and turning, those were the ones to worry about. That was how she was, an all-or-nothing kind of sleeper. If something was troubling her, she would toss and turn for a bit and then she would get out of bed and read journal articles in her study.

Her future was here, with him. It would be hard on her, and he would need to be patient. It would take a little time. He hadn't wanted to push her; she needed to come to these realizations and epiphanies on her own. They were still a day's walk from the object, another ten months off the island. Then what? They would spend days studying it? More time would rocket by.

He had already been down that road. Claire was right; he had lied to her. He had spent five days with the object and hadn't learned a goddamn thing about it. He had lied to her because she would know he was a fraud. He so badly wanted to be the one to crack the code, solve its mysteries. Of course, the deaths of his crewmates had hit him hard. They were good people, brave men and women, supporting characters in his story. But the grief faded. He hadn't known them, after all. They were strangers. There was an undeniable joy there as well. Joy that his place in history would be secured. Peter Abbott alone would find the alien craft.

As he zeroed in on the site, two days after the crash, he was that excited little kid on Christmas morning, the same areas in his brain lighting up, the pleasure centers tickled by the chemistry set, by that first bicycle, the first real one with twenty-one speeds and the oversized knobby tires. His entire body was sore, he was limping, and he suspected one of his ribs was broken. But when he had come into the clearing and seen it, put his eyes on this thing that no human eyes ever had, all the pain and the memory of the crash had bled away. He stood there before it, then knelt before it, crying, its presence humbling him. He hoped there were no sentient beings aboard because he would look ridiculous to them, primitive, on his knees, weeping. His heart was racing and a lightness filled him, the certainty that he had made the right call all those years ago to pursue science, to show his father that his was the superior intellect.

Eventually, he made his way around its perimeter, mentally cataloging his observations. The object reflected no sunlight, kicked off no glare. No sound emanated from it. It simply just was. The ground beyond the object's footprint appeared undisturbed. At some point, he decided to touch it. He stepped toward it, within arm's length of it, a hand up, his body trembling. Humanity physically intersecting with another civilization for the first time. For eons, these separate civilizations, operating on tracks that were not parallel but nearly so, drawing closer together at a maddeningly slow rate, as though they would never meet. But meet they would, billions of years after the stars and planets had emerged from the ooze of the galactic soup, when fate had pointed her finger at Peter's ancestors, at his family tree, following the trunk down to the correct branch and then out toward that baby boy who would grow up and do all the things to bring him here, to this moment.

He touched it. His palm lay flat against the object, feeling the resistance of an immovable object, but somehow it felt like he was touching nothing at all. It was neither cold nor hot. The temperature seemed to match that of his palm. He stood there for another few minutes, until his arm began to ache, waiting, waiting, waiting. He spent hours at the site and discovered nothing. His human eye could discern no way to dismantle it, to open it, to do anything but look at it. Look at it he had, until he was near the point of madness. Overwhelmed by its beauty. He'd never felt so powerless, so incompetent, so utterly impotent. It was as if his years of study had been for nothing.

A voice in his head, far away, the words unintelligible, like someone shouting from down the street. The longer he stood there, the longer he puzzled over it, the louder the voice became, the clearer it became. It was the gravelly harsh voice of his father, the one that baked fear into the hearts of the eleventh-grade science students at Beechcroft High School back in Columbus. He had never been in his father's class, but he hadn't needed to be.

*You stuck, baby boy?*

He had hated it when his father called him that. Perhaps it had once been a term of endearment when he was small and his daddy was his hero, but that had changed over time, as Peter had gotten older and the permanence of his father's station in life had hardened like concrete. He grew more bitter, the nightly gin-and-tonic growing progressively ginnier and less tonicky, and that term of endearment took on a darker tone, one of condescension and contempt and envy.

And hate.

His father hated him.

*You stuck, baby boy?*

Over and over he heard it, caught on a loop in his mind.

That would be just what his dad would want. For Peter to fail, to be stuck, especially here, at the most critical moment of his life. Choking in the clutch, he would say, like baseball players who never seemed to get it done in the playoffs. Here the voice was loud and clear, like it was being broadcast from hidden speakers. Only when he put some real estate in between himself and the object did the voice quiet down. When Claire had magically appeared here, he knew he didn't need to understand it.

It wouldn't be easy, of course not, but they would be together. The object would be background music.

Early retirement!

Just like they had once joked about, living out their golden years on a tropical island sipping fruity drinks with garishly colored little umbrellas. So it would start a few decades ahead of schedule and without the fruity drinks. Perfect, actually, since they were still young and vibrant enough to enjoy it. He would entertain her, he would go with her to the object if that's what she wanted to do. Let her scratch that itch. He didn't care much about it anymore. Their alien benefactors wanted the object to be unknowable, unreachable, a Sphinx? Fine. The hell with them. With Claire here now, he didn't need them. He didn't care about them. He would pick Claire over the object every day of the week and twice on Sunday.

Family first!

Funny how your priorities changed. Maybe when he'd seen her face again his love for her was crystallized, imprinted upon him like a brand. They *(who? They, the mysterious They)* always said that times of distress revealed your innermost truths, peeled back the curtain in front the things that were most important to you. As the chopper had plunged to the ground, his teeth clenched together so hard that his jaw remained sore for days afterward, all he could think about was Claire and their life together. The way she laughed at his jokes, the way she curled up against him in bed on cold mornings in their perpetually drafty bedroom.

Yeah. It had been Claire all along that he had thought about as the chopper went down.

He wanted to shake her awake and tell her these things; he was so excited to tell her these things. He had never been a particularly emotional man; it was something that people ribbed him about from time to time. It didn't bother him so much, he didn't love it exactly, it was just who he was. It was like teasing someone for their eye color.

Dawn broke, eating up the darkness around them. He had only slept for a few hours, but he felt refreshed, cleaned out. He was a man on a new journey, a great adventure. The world they had left behind continued to recede in the rearview mirror of his life, and he felt no sadness, no nostalgia for it. Everything he wanted was right here.

He debated waking Claire up for another roll in the hay, but he thought better of it. It was like dealing with a frightened puppy. Too much aggression would scare her off. She would need time to process this rekindling of their romance. It was a big step she had taken. Coming across too strongly would backfire. No one told Claire Hamilton what or how to think, and to do so was to court disaster. It was a self-defense mechanism, one she had honed during her years in such a patriarchal profession.

Claire was stirring as the day brightened around them. She sat up, yawning, blinking the sleep out of her eyes. His heart, filled with love, felt it like it might burst from his chest. It was going to be a great day. The first day of the rest of their lives.

Everything felt right.

The universe worked in mysterious ways.

It was as if all this had been fated to happen. He survived the helicopter crash when he should not have; she survived the sinking of the *Kingsman* when she should not have. Even fracturing the stream of time into separate tributaries had not been able to keep them apart. He did not know where they were, he did not even know *when* they were. All he knew was that they were together.

"Good morning," he said.

*W*HAT HAD SHE DONE?

She offered up a smile in reply to his salutation, but it felt forced, phony.

*What in the hell had she done?*

Her final confrontation with Jack mocked her. Two days with Peter and she had been unable to keep her hands off him. What did that say about her, her life, her marriage? She understood at a rational level that she was dead to Jack now, but that was for him. In her time, in her reality, she had managed to keep true to her vows, to her promise to Jack, for the length of a weekend, if that.

Just bravo, missy. Bravo.

Her kids would be so proud of her.

As she sat there, her body slick with morning dew, she felt empty. Circumstances had scooped out her old life and dumped it into a landfill like a backhoe. Left behind was her clear-cut soul, left in this terrible limbo. The sex, rather than bringing her closer to Peter, now felt like a mistake. Not because it hadn't felt good, not because it hadn't taken the edge off the growing sense of isolation here. It had. That was something they had always been good at. It felt like a cop-out. Like they couldn't think of anything better to do. Like she was hiding from reality. The problem at hand would come roaring back.

It was never going to go away.

She missed her babies.

It didn't matter whether they were six years old or sixty years old, they would always be her babies, and she would do anything to see them again. She had slept hard, a deep dreamless sleep because she was sure of what she had to do. It was tempting to take the easy way out, of course, to fall back into the warm embrace of the past, where Peter was.

But that was the past.

Peter was her past.

"Good morning," she said.

"How did you sleep?" he asked, handing her one of the ready-to-eat meals.

There.

She could hear it in his voice. It was the tone of a man who was latched on to a reality that no longer existed. She would have to be gentle and careful. Where he wanted to go, she could not join him.

"Good," she replied.

They ate in silence. The food was salty but otherwise bland. She had to look at the label to even know what it purported to be.

Salisbury steak.

She took another bite and tried to match its taste to anything resembling Salisbury steak that she had on file, not even the bad Salisbury steak she'd eaten in elementary school.

No Match Found

*Salisbury steak my ass.*

"Like old times," he said.

Her stomach flipped.

"Mm-hmm," she said. She was thankful she had a mouthful of food, which provided good cover for her noncommittal response.

It never changed, the fact that sex changed everything. Whatever paradigm was in place, sex blew it all to hell. Sex was a high-stakes poker game; all your vulnerabilities, all the worries pushed to the center of the table, daring your opponent to call your bet. That's why it was so dangerous, and that's why last night had been a mistake. She couldn't say that now, not when he was so fragile. She stole a glance at him as he ate, taking note of the twinkle in his eye, the first time he had looked at ease since they got here. This was her fault.

"Yeah."

Would he want to do it again?

Of course he would.

She would have to buy herself a little time.

"I know it was weird for you," he said.

"Maybe a little."

"I'm sorry," he said. "It hasn't been that long for me."

"I know."

"But I know, I understand that it hasn't been three weeks for you."

"Thank you."

Did he understand? How could he comprehend such a long passage of time when he himself hadn't experienced it? While he was counting a handful of sunsets and sunrises, hoping for a rescue, she had been mourning and putting together the broken pieces of a life shattered and growing and loving again and loving Hugo and Miranda beyond any plane she believed were possible.

It couldn't happen again.

The gap between them was too wide. She had been places he had not, places to which they could no longer travel together despite all their plans otherwise. It was in that moment she understood that getting off this island was her quest, her sole reason for being. It didn't matter how long it took, it didn't matter if she made it back to visit her great-grandkids or their great grandkids. If she could figure out how to fly the spacecraft, she would do it; if she had to build a raft and sail out of here, she would, and if her raft foundered and she drowned or the sharks made a pizza roll out of her, then that's how she would die. Not here, not growing old here with Peter, not making a go of it here on this tropical paradise.

They finished their breakfast.

"You ready to go?" he asked as they cleaned up the remains of their meal.

"You bet," she said.

As she hoisted her pack onto her shoulders, he leaned in for a kiss. She saw it coming, the way women could see these things a mile away, the way his head was tilted just so, his lips parted, his nostrils flaring. A dozen years away from him and her early-warning system was still operational, those little radar dishes of instinct rotating around her soul.

She turned her head just so, catching his kiss on her cheek as he palmed her other cheek with his hand. It was meant to create intimacy at a moment he needed to compensate for the turned cheek, that door slamming closed. Her jaw was tight, her teeth clenched together, and he withdrew wordlessly.

"Let's get moving," she said.

They moved out.

## 29

P eter puzzled as they hiked. The vibe wasn't right.
They'd been on the move for hours, Claire
setting a murderous pace. Peter was desperate for a
quick rest, but he kept his mouth shut. He did not want her
to think that he was interfering, that he was standing in her
way. He would ride the wave with her until it crashed on the
inevitable shore of reality. Stalling or giving her the impression that his heart wasn't in on the whole giving-her-a-hand
thing could sever their tenuous connection.

The vibe. He was getting a bad vibe.

Did she sense his deceit? Phony sincerity would be just
as bad as throwing a tantrum. Reading people was one of
her strong suits, something that came naturally to her. It
had helped her a great deal in her career, knowing without
knowing who was on her side and who was just trying to get
into her pants. A valuable skill in a male-dominated profession like theirs. No, if she was going to accept her fate here,
she needed to come to that conclusion on her own.

It was hot today, perhaps the warmest day he'd experienced yet. A juicy air mass had settled over the island,

enveloping the landscape in a thick cottony embrace. They were traversing a wide plain, grassy and rocky. His shirt, already gamey, was soaked through with sweat and was ripening with a broken tang of decay. They had passed a series of caves near his crash site on the way and he bet they were just as damp and cool as anything; instead, they were out here hoofing it through this blast furnace.

This was dumb, that's what it was. He couldn't be so subservient to Claire's wishes that they just threw caution to the wind and died of thirst. No, they still had to be smart. She wasn't being smart right now. She had gotten it in her head that the object would provide her with salvation, and that was affecting her judgment.

"Let's talk about the object," she said.

"OK."

"How come you haven't been out to see it?"

"I didn't want to break the protocol," he replied. "They were very adamant about no one going to the crash site alone. They had a very specific plan in mind for the first encounter. Video, photography – of course, that was before we realized the electronics wouldn't work – everything documented. Plus, I had a lot to do. I didn't want to venture too far from the crash site."

She paused to think, chewing on her lower lip as she did when she was deep in thought.

"I gotta say, I'm pretty surprised," she said.

"What do you mean?"

"You know, the discovery of a lifetime, and you didn't go to see it."

"Yeah?"

"Just curious is all."

He did not like her tone at all.

"How long before you got here did it crash?" she asked, changing gears.

"About two weeks."

"Or two minutes," she replied.

He honestly did not know if the craft had been here for twelve years or three weeks. He did not know if *he* had been here for twelve years or four weeks. Fancy doctorate you've got there, Pete. Claire would think of things he hadn't. Her brain worked in a way that he didn't understand.

"What if the temporal anomaly isn't consistent?" she asked.

"Meaning what?"

"What if there's a kind of Doppler effect in play?" she asked. "Clearly, at some distance from the object, time has continued to run at its normal pace. So the effect gets weaker the farther from the object you get. And then it completely dissipates."

"Then the entire concept of time, or at least our understanding of it, is screwed."

She fell silent for a bit, scraping at her lower lip with a thumbnail.

"What do you think time is?" she finally asked.

"It's how we measure and quantify."

"Measure and quantify what?"

"The relation of the occurrence of one incident to the occurrence of another," he replied. "Quantum mechanics 101."

"Right," she said. "And although we know that time can get funky under certain conditions, one thing we accepted was that, on Earth, in our galaxy, in our solar system, virtually anywhere but near a black hole, it flowed in one direction and at the same rate, more or less. This place bends that somehow. Imagine a piece of paper with two dots on it.

The paper is space-time. What's the most direct route between the two points? A straight line, right?"

"Right, I guess."

"But what if you fold the paper? The paper is curved, bringing the dots closer together. What if this place does that?"

He didn't reply, considering her example. He flushed with heat, annoyed with himself for not considering it, a little angry that she had considered it before he had.

"That works both ways, too. Fold the paper the other way and the dots are farther apart."

"And if you're right?" he asked.

She laughed.

"No clue."

She went on.

"And why is it here in the first place?" Claire asked. "This huge, stunning, amazing discovery and we don't know what to do with it. We don't how to interpret it. We can't get anyone here to look at it, study it. We can't get it off the island. You and I are possibly trapped here. It's almost irrelevant."

For this Peter had no answer. But that was fine. That was good news. It belied a certain understanding of the way things were. That was good. A way station on her journey to acceptance.

"But maybe it can get us off this island," she said. "Maybe you can think of something I haven't."

"Maybe," he replied.

There. There it was again. That vibe. They were discussing the utter impossibility of her mission, its guaranteed failure, and yet he could detect a hint of defiance in her voice. The sense that she welcomed this challenge, that if there was a way through it, she would find it where he had not. This brought up his hackles a bit again, a ripple of annoyance washing through him. It was because she believed she was smarter than him. As though she were patting him on the head like he was a small child, telling him to step aside because the grownups were here now.

"Time," she said. "Time, time, time."

She was talking to herself now, not to him.

"Lost time," she continued. "Losing time every second."

Muttering now, he only understood what she was saying because he was familiar with her quirks, her little idiosyncrasies, the things that made Claire Claire.

"We need to keep moving," she said.

He turned to follow her when a flicker of light caught his attention, stopping him cold. It was green and shimmery and wildly out of place here in the dark, well after sunset. The light varied in intensity, deepening into a dark green before cycling back to a thin translucence. Almost as if it were pulsing, beating. It was circular, about four feet high and about as wide.

"Claire."

"I see it."

He stepped gingerly toward the orb of light. It hovered there like a giant beach ball, cycling through its color spectrum. The light was warm and inviting; even at its peak, there was no cause to shield his eyes. The scientist within him floated a reminder that he might well be frying his corneas, but that seemed incidental right now.

He stopped next to Claire, close enough to put his hands on it. He had been too afraid the last time, a flare of fear that he regretted now. He wasn't going to let this opportunity get away from him.

"It's beautiful," he said.

"That's what they want you to think," she said with a

hint of that Hedwig wit. "Right before you get sucked into another dimension. Classic alien invader stuff!"

Peter was barely listening, his attention zeroed in on the orb now. His heart racing, he reached out slowly with an open hand.

"Christ, don't touch it," she said, her voice heavy and severe.

"I have to."

She grabbed his hand just inches away from the light.

"Don't."

He looked over at her.

"It's okay," he said. "It's why we're here, right?"

She released his hand, which hovered close to the orb's breathing, pulsing shell. Peter's heart was racing, his body electric with excitement. He was about to make first contact. Not how he'd pictured it, but hey, you danced with the one who brung you, as the saying went. Fingertips extended, his feet shoulder width apart, his weight on his back foot in case he needed to pull away quickly. The green light swirled and rippled around his hand, then up his forearm, like he was rolling on a shimmery evening glove. He glanced at Claire, who watched him intently.

"Well?" she said.

"Nothing."

Which was true. Nothing was happening. For the moment, it was merely an unusual light show. A minute passed, then two. Claire shifted her weight from one foot to the other, crossed her arms in an X across her chest, signs that her patience was running out. His arm started to ache, and he started to feel a little silly.

Screw it.

He started to pull his arm out, but the translucent glove held it fast. At first, he thought nothing of it, but when a second yank proved unsuccessful, a ripple of panic crawled up his back.

"Shit," he muttered.

"What's wrong?"

"My arm is stuck."

"What?"

He tugged harder, but his arm would not budge.

"Shit, I can't get it loose."

"Goddammit, Peter."

The more he tried, the tighter the light gripped his arm, snug enough that he could feel his fingers tingling. Worse, it looked like the light had swirled farther up his arm, reaching his elbow, sweeping across his collarbone, enveloping him in.

"Pull me out, pull me out!"

She stepped behind him and locked her hands around his abdomen, bring every bit of her one hundred and twenty pounds to bear, but it didn't work. The green light, now bright and intense like a Vegas marquee, now cloaked his body from the neck down. Terror dripped from every one of his pores as the light crept up his neck, into his mouth, up his nostrils, into his eyes; he was screaming now, begging for help, the orb swallowing him into a vortex of green light.

Everything fell silent around him.

The island looked far away, as though he were looking through the wrong end of a pair of binoculars. Claire was there, calling out to him. He couldn't hear her, but her hands were cupped around her mouth, which had widened into an O shape.

"Claire!"

No indication she could hear him either; in fact, she began to fade from view, as did the island around her. The orb's color began to drain away as well, and darkness seeped in from the edges. Soon he was encased in it, unable to see his hand in front of his face. The only thing he could hear was the sound of his own ragged breathing as he trembled in abject horror. He was in a small room, sitting down. He was looking out a window, out over some green space. A courtyard ringed by bushes, boxwoods by the looks of them. They were ragged, overgrown, blanketed by spiderwebs, these gossamer veils glinting in the morning sunlight. A pair of hands wrinkled and gnarled by arthritis lay in his lap like abandoned old tools. He wore a pair of thin blue pajama pants and a yellowed white t-shirt.

*Oh my God*, thought Peter. Was this him? The portrait of Peter Abbott as an old man? The scene blinked out for a moment before coming back into view. He looked back up, glancing around, giving Peter his first view at his surroundings. It was a small room, spartanly furnished. From the corner of his eye, he caught a glimpse of the large spoked wheel attached to the side of his chair. Jesus, he was in a wheelchair.

Behind him, a heavy door screeched open. Footsteps and commotion.

"Good morning, Mr. Abbott," said a male voice, quite matter of factly. "Time to change you."

*Change me?*

"This here Mr. Abbott," said the man. "This our most famous resident."

That's when the smell hit him. He hadn't noticed it before, possibly because he didn't want to notice it. The ripe smell of human excrement; the fact that he was smelling it at all befuddled him, given that he wasn't even here, wherever the hell here was. Then he was moving backward, a male nurse wheeling him back toward the bed. He and another nurse lifted him to the bed, laying him on his back atop a changing pad. Although his aged doppelganger stared blankly at the ceiling, Peter struggled to watch the nurses work, hitching his pajama bottoms down. He could feel the cool air of the room on his legs.

"This old fucker shits himself every morning like clockwork," one said.

"Yeah?" replied the colleague.

"Yeah, always check him after breakfast," said the first. "Management go crazy if you don't."

"OK."

"Hard to believe he some kind of famous scientist."

"Really?"

"Yeah, he found the thing on that island."

"No shit?"

"Yeah."

"Where his family at?"

"Naw, man," he said. "No one ever come visit."

The nurses continued, lifting his legs like he was a goddamn infant so they could wipe his ass. Peter tried not to watch, but no matter which way he turned, his field of view was filled with the image of these two young men changing his diaper.

"Three-wipe morning, Mr. Abbott," said the nurse.

The newer nurse turned his head, holding his fist to his lips as he gagged. Peter couldn't blame him. Deep inside, he felt something break, something shatter, and he didn't even know what the hell he was watching. Was it his future? A possible future? A nightmare? A hallucination? The nurses finished their work, securing the diaper snugly against his wrinkled abdomen.

They moved him back into his wheelchair and rolled him back to the window. As he sat there, a cardinal landed on top of a bush to his left. He watched it intently, his view interrupted only when old Peter's head drooped downward momentarily, as though he were nodding off. A crushing sense of isolation filled him like wet concrete as he sat there watching that goddamned bird. It was difficult to breathe, to focus on anything but his surroundings.

Slowly, color filled in from the edges, like a Polaroid picture blooming to life. Claire. Trees. Rocks. He moved his arms freely. Whatever Chinese finger trap had held him fast had disappeared. The light was gone too.

"What happened?"

The replay of their fight loomed in his head.

"Nothing."

"How long was I gone?"

"What do you mean gone?"

"Didn't I disappear?"

"No," she replied. "I pulled you as hard as I could, and then all of a sudden, you came loose."

He blinked and looked around. The nursing home, the airport, these places seemed far away. Living sculptures carved from smoke, holding together just long enough for him to see before dissipating. Had he dreamed it? A hallucination triggered by his interaction with the anomaly? The nursing home. Had that been real, a picture of a Christmas yet to pass but that very well could?

It felt real. It felt as real as anything he'd ever felt in his life.

"What happened in there?"

He blinked again.

"What did you see?"

"Nothing."

~

SHE WAS quiet for the next two hours of their hike, lost on her train of thought as it steamed through their dilemma. You could almost hear it clacking down the tracks, a phantom locomotive. On their next water break, they drank in silence. She barely acknowledged his presence.

"How are you feeling?" he asked as she refilled her water can.

She flashed him a thumbs-up but didn't throw a glance his way.

"We can stop a little longer if you'd like. We don't want to overdo it."

"I'm fine," she said, hitching the rucksack onto her back.

She was on the move, leaving Peter behind again. He scrambled to follow; it reminded him of those days growing up in Columbus, chasing the school bus because no matter what he could not make it out the door in time; it drew the ire of his mother, a patient woman whose patience did not extend to those last five minutes before the bus was scheduled to arrive. It didn't matter what time he woke up; the time, whether it was an hour before the bus arrived or five minutes, would fill with the day's duties and no more than that. If you had three tasks to do and eight hours to do them, it would take you eight hours; if you had an hour, it would take an hour.

As he pursued her through a grassy glen bursting with wildflowers, he considered and discarded a dozen topics of discussion, something to get them back on the same page. He was playing both a short and long game here. It was difficult not to get irritated with her when she got like this, when she just ignored him. He didn't understand why people did that. Even when feeding her delusions of flying the object off this island and landing at LAX, she should still respect his opinion, try to work together with him.

As they walked, he stepped on a rock, and his ankle buckled underneath him; he recovered his balance before he did too much damage, but a bolt of pain shot through his foot as he called out. He tested the foot. A bit tender, but it wasn't too bad.

"What's the matter?" she said, turning back toward him.

He grimaced as he lowered himself to the ground.

"Twisted my ankle."

He looked up at her, hoping to find a little sympathy on her face; instead, he saw blank annoyance.

"Can you walk?"

"Give me a minute," he said. "Let me see if it's swelling up. Can you help me with the shoelaces?"

She glanced back toward the trail ahead before kneeling next to him. She helped him work the shoe off, bringing him close enough that he could smell her. Even after two hot days on the island, her scent was intoxicating. Beneath the grime and the sweat was the vanilla sweetness of her perfume or soap or whatever it was she last used, the shampoo fruitiness of her sandy-blonde hair. He placed his hand on her shoulder, ostensibly for balance, but wanting to be close to her, to remind her what it felt like for him to touch her. Then the shoe and sock were off. His ankle was a smidge puffy, but it was not serious. Already, he had to admit, the pain was fading, down to a twinge.

"Thanks," he said, sliding two fingers under her chin and turning her face toward him.

They held the gaze for a long and moment. His insides twisted and ached as he drank in her face, her eyes, her lips that remained pressed together, an implicit warning that now was not the time. There was conflict there, too, he could feel it; her breathing was shallow and a bit ragged. Near him, her defenses wavered, each in the other's orbit again. Outside it was her other life, the one she had left to come here. Inside it was the two of them. If the fire were not still smoldering, at least a little bit, why had she made the trip to the island at all?

Did she not understand how much he loved her?

Did she not understand the isolation both would face back home?

She needed to get it, she needed to understand the fix they were in. The object was a dead end. He had once thought like she had, that despite the object's non-terrestrial origin, he could extrapolate the steps needed to raise the conn and bring in the cavalry. He was a bright guy, paid to think at another level; hell, that was why he was here in the first place.

He had not been back to the site since. Would the voice still be there, waiting for him?

His anxiety deepened as they drew closer to the object. He was trembling, and it felt like his body was rattling to pieces. Metal filings drawing closer to a giant magnet, starting to shimmy, rattling. He didn't want to see it again. His pace slowed, imperceptibly at first, but then slow enough that it drew Claire's attention.

"Something wrong?" she asked, her words clipped and cold.

He took a deep breath and let it out slowly. It came out raggedly at a time he was hoping to display a sense of calm. He needed to buy a little more time.

"The object," he said.

"What about it?"

"It's wrong, all wrong."

She crossed her arms, clicked her lips together, considering her reply. They were still on the same side, for now, but he was pushing his luck. Her patience was not infinite.

"What does that even mean?"

Her tone was firm but gentle. There was an opening here, greased by the goodwill they had accumulated in their time together. He looked for the words, the argument that would stop this train before they got too far down the track. He was afraid. He was afraid of what would happen if the same thing happened to Claire, if she failed as he had. If the object kept its secrets hidden like a demure lover, that might push Claire completely over the edge, to a point of madness from which she might not return.

He was even more afraid that she wouldn't fail.

What if she pulled it off, succeeded where he had not?

Jesus, what was the matter with him? He was afraid she would save them?

He was afraid of that. Yes, indeed. Because then the thing he had feared above all else would come to pass. That she would be the one. The idea that he would claim credit for her discoveries was laughable because he would be immediately outed as a fraud when he wasn't able to explain them. She would be famous and wealthy and they would name schools after her, just like he had predicted.

*You stuck, baby boy?*

His father would have had a good laugh at that one. A lady scientist. He didn't think much of women, of their ability to deal with the technical realities of the sciences. He often described them as too emotional for such a rational discipline. His father had never met Claire, which was for the better. He had begged off the wedding at the last second, claiming some mystery illness would preclude his appearance.

"I don't know," he finally said, exasperated.

She huffed and rolled her eyes. Her lips were pressed

together in annoyance, the regret that she had granted him this quarter evident on her face.

"I don't have time for this, Peter," she barked. "I do not have time for this."

She spun on her heel and continued along the trail.

W orry had evolved into annoyance. Yeah, things were bad. They were really bad and liable to get worse. Peter was now pushing fifteen years on the island; it was getting away from him in a very permanent way. She got it. She was sympathetic. If too much more time passed by, they would be in the same boat. Would it matter if he lost fifty years and she lost thirty?

This was for both of them. Hopefully, he would figure that out, but she couldn't do it for him. So she persisted through this narrow valley, the rocky passage so tight at one point she had to turn sideways and shuffle along, the stone wall scraping her abdomen before widening a bit. He stayed close behind, quiet, lost in his own thoughts, probably pissed at her. That was fine. She could deal with that. When you were in your forties, there was little more precious than some goddamned peace and quiet. Didn't matter if it was back home with two precocious six-year-olds or here on this deserted island with a moody ex-husband. Maybe that was the problem they were having. It wasn't just time separating them; it was life. She had earned these last dozen years.

They had been paid for and then some. She'd done post-graduate work in life, things that no one should have to go through. She had the right to dispense with his thirtysomething bullshit, even though it was because of him that she had earned that right.

The terrain climbed sharply, eating away at the red blood cells in her legs until her muscles burned. The crest of the hill opened up on a circular grassy glen. In the brilliant sunshine, gilding everything with golden light, she saw it.

There.

Her pulse quickened as the object came into view for the first time.

It was disorienting to see something that defied all logic, that did not fit easily onto a prefabricated shelf in your mind. Your brain thrived on the routine, on the ordinary. When faced with something outside that scope, it froze because it didn't know which resources to devote to it. Rationally, as a scientist, she knew she should not be seeing this. It was a scientific impossibility. The conventional wisdom was that until humanity perfected faster-than-light travel, which would be sometime around never, direct contact with another civilization would be impossible.

There it was, brooding, monolithic, bending time around itself.

It was black, but that didn't do it justice. Not just black, but bearing such a profound absence of color, almost as if there was nothing there, just this rectangular void that had been carved out of time and space. Almost as if she could reach into it and fall into another dimension, another universe. In fact, she wasn't sure that wasn't the case.

A crunch of grass behind her broke her trance. Then she

felt a sharp crack, a massive exquisite tingling against the back of her head and the world went dark.

SHE SWAM BACK TO CONSCIOUSNESS.

Her head hung low, her chin touching her chest as her eyelids slowly worked their way apart. She was sitting up, her back pushed up against a tree. A length of rope lashed her to the trunk, and her hands were tied together, resting in her lap.

Her head ached. The slightest movement sent ripples of pain through her, made her stomach flip. As she lay still, choppy flashes of memory strobed their way through her mind. Movement behind her. Then a terrific wallop to the head. A shake of her legs confirmed that her feet were lashed together as well.

What the hell happened?

Maybe Berry had an accomplice they didn't know about.

Maybe indigenous residents of the island.

A lot of maybes.

One thing seemed certain. It was unlikely that extraterrestrials had jumped them from behind like schoolyard bullies. Little green men with bicycle chains. Socks full of pennies. Yeah, Claire, that made sense.

Her mouth was dry, but the headache suppressed any appetite she might have had. It was late in the evening, the light dim, barely enough for her to see her legs. She told herself to stay calm as her eyes adjusted. Slowly, her pupils widened to let in more light and she got a better look at her surroundings. The sounds of the island were present but muted.

A chill rippled through her.

There was no way to know how long she had been out. Hours? Days?

Long enough to be secreted away like a hidden love letter. Her thoughts snapped to Hugo and Miranda. How old were they now? Ten? Twelve? Did they still remember their mother or had their memories of her begun to fade? Had Jack remarried, moved, on, followed the same formula she once had? Perhaps he had become a father again.

Sometime later, she heard the sound of someone approaching, and her body tensed up. There was something familiar about the ambient noise, and dread poured into her. It was Peter.

*Peter.*

Peter had done this.

Her Peter. The man she had once promised her life to.

Just the thought of it made her heart hurt. This wasn't the Peter of twelve years ago. This wasn't even the Peter of two weeks ago. Or perhaps he had never been the Peter of twelve years ago. Perhaps this was who he had been all along and absent the niceties of modern society, the mask he'd been wearing had been stripped away.

Maybe he had just snapped.

Everyone had their breaking point.

He had lost everything that mattered to him.

Had she expected another outcome? That he was going to shrug his shoulders about the whole thing? Guilt coursed through her. Yes, that was what she had expected from her Peter. To be the rock. To help her get home. To be the supporting character in her story. And she hadn't stopped to consider his well-being, had she? Not one time.

That hadn't been fair.

But there was no other way, was there?

They were at loggerheads when you got right down to it,

two immovable forces. She had to leave. He wanted her to stay.

"Good, you're awake."

Words failed her.

"How are you feeling?" he asked. There was a troubling chill to his voice. Like it had been stripped of its humanity, reduced to some basic functioning, following a prime directive.

"What?"

He approached her, knelt down on his haunches. He reached out and gently touched the side of her head; she jerked her head to the side, away from his touch.

"How are you feeling?" he asked again. "I'm sorry for that."

"Untie me."

"I can't. Not right now."

"Why?"

"I have to protect you."

"From what?"

"From this place. From you getting hurt again. From yourself."

"I don't need protecting."

"You say that, but you don't know what you're talking about."

"Peter!"

"Claire, there is no going back. This is it for us. I know that's hard to understand right now. But you'll see."

"How long was I out?

"Not long," he replied. "Couple of days."

"A couple of days! Jesus, Peter."

"Sorry."

"There's still a chance," she said. "The object. There might still be a way."

"What way?"

"They'll be back," she said. "You know they'll be back. They're not going to let this go. They could be here today or tomorrow. A week from now. They will be back."

Even as she said the words, she could not help but wonder whether they would be back. In fact, at the rate time was passing off the island, they should have been back already. Perhaps Murphy and Berry and their co-conspirators had succeeded in their plot. There had been no end to the lengths they would go to cover all this up. She wanted to believe that secrets like this rarely stayed hidden for long. Truth was like a seed, pushing its way through the loamy darkness toward the light. That was what she told herself. Perhaps they had snipped all the loose threads. Maybe they had closed all the doors, turned out all the lights, made sure that this island remained a secret for all time. To think such a thing was not possible was to believe in the fallacy of the happy ending. The kind of optimism that storytelling baked into you, the idea that ultimately, it all worked out, that the star-crossed couple would find their way back to each other, that the grizzled detective would get his man.

Sometimes, though, the bad guys got away.

"What then?"

"It doesn't matter," she said. "But you need to untie me."

He was shaking his head as she was saying it; it had been one of his more irritating habits. When they argued, which hadn't been often, he would do this little head shake, almost imperceptibly, a good sign that he had already stopped listening to her.

"Don't shake your head at me when I'm still talking," she snapped. "You need to let me go."

"Honey," he said, "we can't both have what we want."

"What do you mean?"

"You know what I mean," he snapped in an angry whisper.

She recoiled. Of course she knew what he meant. There was never going to be a way for them both to have a happy ending.

"Why are you doing this?"

"Because the only thing we have left is each other," he said. "Do you really want to go back and see your kids as adults? Do you really want to have that awkward reunion, where they give you tense hugs and they look at each other and they sort of wish deep down that you had never come back at all? Look at you like you're a freak? You might be younger than them, you know. What do you think that would do to them?"

Her eyes welled with tears.

"You know I'm right," he said, and she looked away because she could not bear to look at him. She did not want him to see the agreement in her face, that to love Hugo and Miranda now meant not disrupting their lives with this emotional car bomb. She could only hope that, despite their mother's selfishness and pride, her disappearance had darkened their lives for only a little while and that the years since had been filled with light and love and laughter. Jack would have seen to that. He had promised her the twins would know how much she had loved them. Not for her but them. They deserved to know their mother had loved them above all else.

The tears fell in earnest now.

It was true, she did love them above all else, more than Peter and Jack and herself. Her love for them bent her own existence, her love so broad and wide and deep that it rushed them along through life and away from her. She would give anything to have all that time back, from the

moment the nurses had laid them on her chest in the operating room to the last time she had kissed their heads.
Anything to see them bloom into adolescence and adulthood, the lives they would carve out for themselves, the love
they would give and receive into their own lives. Her time
with them had been a mere flash, just the blink of an eye, no
different than the fifteen days Peter had been here before
her arrival. Love, the one thing that made it worthwhile,
blinked away life like it was nothing at all. Love bent time,
pushing the beginning and end points together until they
were one.

Now she stood on the dark side of that. Claire's time
with the twins was over, she saw that now. As hard as it was
to accept, as unfair as it was, it was their time to find love
and perhaps find the kind of love she had felt for them. But
life wasn't fair. Eventually, you said goodbye to all the things
you loved, one way or another. Whether it was seven days or
seven months or seven decades, it all ended, and when you
looked back, it would seem like no time had passed at all.

Just like that lawyer had said.

Eventually, it all went bad.

To force her way into that would be cruel. It would break
their lives and add to their misery, because what was a
happy life but one that you could not believe how quickly it
had run its course?

"Claire," Peter was saying, "we can be happy here. I
promise we can be happy here."

She tried ignoring him as his words seeped in.

"Look how beautiful this place is," he said.

She tilted her head.

All she had to do was say yes, but she hesitated. To say
yes meant crossing some invisible line, to cleave her future
to this place. To say yes, even if she weren't being honest,

meant making a final decision, one that she would later have to talk herself into. The truth was that she was well on her way to *yes* for real, her seatback and tray table were in the upright position, the ding-dong of the seatbelt light.

"Claire?"

"Yes."

## 31

There had been a plan. When she had said yes, there had been a plan. A plan to secure her freedom and then get back to the work of finding a way off this accursed pile of rocks. Peter would understand eventually. You didn't get between a mama bear and her cubs. He would get it. He would understand that she might be there in body but that her spirit was elsewhere, far away from the both of them.

*Yes.*

As soon as she had said the word, relief burst through her like water from an open hydrant, blasting away the worries, the stress that had burrowed inside her. The relief that accompanied seeing your worries melt away. Worry sat on you, weighed you down, enveloped you. Enough time went by, you took on the shape of that worry until it defined you. It became you and destroyed you. She had been closer to yes than she had realized. But that was over now.

She didn't have to worry about the twins anymore. They would be fine. They were already fine. Somewhere far from here, they had already mourned her, already said goodbye to her. It would be their thing, that their mother had died when they were kids. It would be a story they would tell a romantic partner, a friend, a therapist. It would always be this scar on them that never quite healed, but hey, everyone bore scars that never healed. They would know she loved them. Again and again, she circled back to that promise Jack had made her.

They spent those first days of the rest of their lives hunting for the two crash sites they knew about and from that, extrapolating possible locations of the remaining two. It was an easy thing to focus on, working to consolidate the remaining supplies at a home base that they settled on. Using a rudimentary map of the island from one of the choppers, she made an X at the site of the crashes they knew about. From there, they made educated guesses where the others might be, likely in areas of the island to which neither of them had ventured yet. As each day wore on, she found herself not executing her plan. It seemed too big, too complicated, too hard, to doomed to fail. Sturdy tree trunks and long thick vines drew her attention, the raw materials she would need to construct a raft seaworthy enough to clear the breakers and catch the currents, move her along into the Pacific shipping lanes where she would cross paths with a cargo ship.

Impossible.

The craft would founder within sight of the island and she wouldn't drown; no, it was much worse than that. She would swim back to the island and know once and for all that she was doomed to live out her days here. But as long as she never tried, the future was always colored with the prospect of a successful mission. If you never tried, you would never fail.

So they worked to gather supplies and collect water and

fortify their shelter and the days drifted by in a haze. In the evenings, she would regale him with tales of the things he had missed. She told him about the two Presidents they had elected, about Hurricane Beatrix, the Category 5 monster that had turned downtown Miami into a swamp, about the proliferation of self-driving cars, another ground war, this one in Iran that the American populace had soured on long before the death toll hit ten thousand. They slept hard and woke early each morning.

He attempted to initiate sex one night not long after he had let her go, but she asked him to let her adjust to their new lives for a bit. She just wasn't ready yet, she told him. Then one night, a few weeks into their new life, it happened again. After an MRE dinner of spaghetti and meat sauce, Peter sat next to her by the fire and kissed her, but it wasn't the same as when they had made love on the hillside. She kissed him back, but it felt cold and dead. Her mouth stayed closed, even as she felt his tongue probing her lips. When she didn't reciprocate the deep kiss, he moved to her ear; the sensation of lifelessness did not go away.

This Peter, the one now stroking her arm, burying his face in her neck, had nearly killed her with a piece of drift-wood. Peter had attacked her. She tried picturing Jack hitting her and she had to stifle a chuckle. Jack transplanted bugs he found inside to the yard. Ladybugs, spiders, stinkbugs, all of them. Outside they went, even when the kids demanded that he smush them under his boot. She wondered if Jack had found someone to share his bed with. She hoped he had. He had done all that was asked of him and then some. She hadn't deserved Jack. She hadn't deserved any of them. She had been a walking lie from the beginning of it all, just a shell, an avatar of a woman rooted in the past. She hadn't meant for it to turn out this way.

That was when it hit her. There was no coming back from what Peter had done. From his lies, from him attacking her. If she had needed a good wallop to the head to make her see the utter insanity of all this, well, she owed Peter her thanks. What she did not owe him, what she would not give him, was herself. He held her chin and leaned in for another kiss, but she turned her cheek at the last second, an evasion he immediately took note of.

"What's wrong?"

"Not tonight," she said.

*Not ever, actually. But you don't need to know that right now.*

"Okay," he replied, a hint of disappointment in his voice.

"Why did you lie to me?" she asked.

"What?"

"About the object," she said. "You said you hadn't seen it before I got here. But you had, right?"

He leaned back on his haunches and smiled.

"I think you misunderstood me," he said. "I didn't lie."

"But you did see it."

"I never said I didn't see it at all."

"No?" she replied, fully awake, fully aware, knowing that she and Peter were taking their last trip together now.

He stood up.

"I said I didn't see it closely," he said. "I was really focused on prepping for a rescue so I didn't have time to be exploring it. I did want to see it, of course. But I allowed myself a little peek."

Claire was shaking her head slowly.

"Don't shake your head at me," he said.

"That's not what you said," Claire replied, ignoring his command. "You said you hadn't seen it."

"Claire, honey, why would I lie about that?"

Doubt crept into her mind. Was she misremembering

their conversation? As Peter said, there would be no reason to lie about it. But that would be a pretty big miss on her part, about a pretty big thing.

"I don't know."

"That's a heck of a thing to accuse me of," he said harshly.

A flash of memory electrified her as the significant moment of their conversation came back to her.

"Wait," she said. "You didn't say that you hadn't seen it. You said you'd never found it. You said you didn't want to violate the contact protocol."

He spread his arms in surrender, a smile spreading across his face.

"Claire, I don't know what to tell you. I did see it."

Her stomach tightened with anger. He was gaslighting her now, making her think she was the one in the wrong. But the specific words he'd used had been the clue. He had said he never found it. That was not a statement you misinterpreted. If he'd never found it, then he could not have seen it, not even for a second.

She was done arguing. Peter would keep moving the goalposts, never concede defeat. For whatever reason, he had decided it was critical that she believe he had not seen the object; for the life of her, she did not know why. Her skin prickled with heat and her heart was racing.

"I'm gonna get some sleep," she said finally. "We've got a lot of work to do tomorrow."

~

CLAIRE SLEPT.

She dreamed of her again.

It was always a girl in her dreams.

The dream always started the same way, Claire shuffling down a dim hallway, the gauzy yellow of a nightlight spilling around her feet. A baby was crying, her baby, in her crib, this one sounding like a *my diaper is wet* cry as opposed to *I'm hungry* or *I just feel like crying Momma.* Then she would enter the room, a square nursery, the crib in one corner, the chest of drawers under the window. In another corner was the nursing glider, which she rarely used because it was far more comfortable to nurse her in her own bed. The walls were indigo blue, decorated with gold stars and planets, blue and red and yellow. That's what you got when your mother was an astrobiologist. She gently rubbed the baby's chest, soothing her. The baby was dressed in a yellow sleeper that she was starting to outgrow, and her diaper was swollen and heavy.

"Mommy's here."

Then Claire turned to the changing table to prepare the supplies; as she did so, the crying suddenly ceased. Just *bam*, like someone had pulled the plug, and now Claire wondered if she should let the baby sleep and why did she keep calling her the baby? She had a name, it was a beautiful name, it was right there on the tip of her tongue, but her brain had seized up on her, what kind of mother forgot her baby's name? An exhausted, sleep-deprived mother, that's what kind of mother.

She decided to change the baby (*Emma? Mia? Emily? Lisa?*) now because if she didn't, she would wake up again in a few minutes, just as Claire had dropped off to sleep. But when she turned back to pick up the baby, the crib was empty. A tickle of panic as she realized she must have already put the baby on the changing table, so she spun back toward it quickly before the baby rolled onto the floor.

*See what happens when you don't get enough sleep.*

The changing table was empty as well and the crib was still empty and there was no baby in the room at all; panic crept up her throat like a newly-awakened serpent. She was alone in the room, she was alone in the house, a fact of which she was certain, although she didn't know how she was certain. Then she was screaming, even though she couldn't hear the scream, she could feel herself screaming, and that seemed weird too.

Then she woke up, bolting upright.

Her heart was racing and her cheeks were wet with tears.

She had lost the pregnancy two weeks after Peter's disappearance. The cramping began at work, followed by a bit of spotting. On the way to the hospital, the bleeding had intensified. A quick exam in the emergency room confirmed her fears; the baby was lost. Late in the first trimester, a bit unusual, the doctor had said, but these things do happen, unfortunately.

*You've been under a lot of stress, and sometimes that can be too much. It's nothing you did, of course, no, Ms. Hamilton, there's nothing you could have done.*

She glanced over at Peter, who was fast asleep. She had never told him. She took a pregnancy test the first weekend he was gone, having experienced a handful of unusual symptoms that she knew were consistent with pregnancy – heightened sense of smell, a metallic taste in her mouth, sore boobs. Sure enough, the test had come back positive, a big old plus sign glowing in the window like the Bat signal. A doctor's visit that week confirmed it, but she decided not to tell Peter until he got back. It wouldn't have been fair to saddle him with the news while he was away. He would worry, and he would fret. They wouldn't be able to enjoy it together. No, it was better to wait until he got back.

She'd stayed in bed for a week. Her friend Amy stayed with her, brought her takeout, sat next to her in bed and watched movies with her, cried with her. Claire hadn't felt any sadder; infinity times infinity was still infinity, after all. The miscarriage was just another thing to fold into the universe of grief expanding around her. Sometimes one tragedy made the other worse, creating a feedback loop of misery. Other times, thinking about one helped her forget about the other for a little while. And sometimes, they ganged up on her and just whooped her ass until she felt like she could not go on living one more second.

Every now and again, a glimmer of what might have been flashed through her mind; it was like thinking you'd seen an old friend in a crowd but losing them before you had a chance to confirm it. Tonight, though, the miscarriage loomed large in her mind. What might have been. If she'd had the baby, would she have had Hugo and Miranda? Would that baby's existence have altered her fate, pushed her destiny in a different direction? Any one of a million things breaks differently, she doesn't meet Jack, and she's a mother to a teenager. It was enough to turn your mind into putty.

She wondered if Peter had a right to know. Part of her did not want to tell him because Peter had lied to her and he had lied to her about something very important and this bothered her a great deal. For years she had beaten herself up for not telling him, for stealing that knowledge from him, for stealing that joy. Now she wasn't sure he deserved to know.

She lay quietly on her bedroll.

Time drew out like stretching taffy. The pieces of the puzzle were not fitting together. The sex and his lies and the

kids and Jack and the object and all of it. Two separate
pictures. Which one did she belong in? She did not know.

In that moment, she understood what Murphy had been
saying.

She did not agree with the means to justify those ends,
but right then, she understood the fallacy of wanting to
make contact. They weren't anywhere close to being ready.
They were too primitive, too immature to handle whatever
this was. She doubted very strongly that the various powers
would put aside their differences and work together on the
island. War would be a virtual certainty; there was a good
chance they would wipe themselves out in a struggle to
control it. It wouldn't even matter if they didn't know what
they were doing; the only thing that mattered was controlling it.

Whoever had sent this here had made a terrible mistake.

They might as well have vaporized Earth.

"Claire?"

His voice startled her. She didn't realize he was awake.

"I have to get out of here."

"What?"

"I'm sorry," she said. "I have to get off this island."

## 32

P eter was shaking his head at her. She didn't know if it was out of disappointment or anger or if he did not understand what she was saying.

"Claire," he said. "We've been through this. There's nothing for you back there."

"You're wrong," she said. "I've been telling myself that it wouldn't be fair for me to go back and disrupt their lives. And on the surface, that makes sense. But it doesn't. Not really. It should be their decision. If I make it back, they can decide whether to invite me into their lives. This way, I steal that from them. I don't even give them that chance. I've already taken so much from them. They deserve my trying to give them that choice. If I get back, I don't know, I'll contact them through an intermediary. Then they can decide for themselves."

"It won't work."

"Don't you get it?" she snapped angrily. "It doesn't matter if it works. What matters is that I try."

"Claire."

"Peter, I don't know why you lied to me, but you need to come too."

"I can't," he said. "I won't!"

The ferocity of his response startled her.

"Even if we got back, you think they're just going to let us walk free?" he said. "They'll stick us in some CIA black site and run tests on us for the rest of our natural lives. Even if they do let us go, what then? What am I supposed to do?"

"We'll figure something out."

"No," he said. "We have to stay here."

Her heart was breaking now, understanding that the rupture between them was permanent. There was never going to be a reconciliation; they could never undo what had been done. This was how it had turned out, no matter how badly she wished things had gone differently. In his voice was a twang of desperation, a final grab at the life that had been taken from him. Forget starting over with a new life. He saw only her. He had convinced himself that his happiness lay here with her.

"You do what you need to do, Peter," she said. "I'm leaving."

"Now?"

"It'll be light soon," she said. "I remember the way there."

This wasn't entirely true, but once the sun was up, she'd figure it out.

"You're shit with directions."

She didn't like the tone in his voice, its cutting edge that made her feel small. As Peter stood there, digesting his former wife's change of heart, she felt a prickle of discomfort. He was good at that, she remembered now, he was good at making her feel small when an argument was not going his way. He never had warmed up to her intelligence; it wasn't even that she was smarter than him, after all, how did you measure a thing like that in people with Ph.Ds in astrobiology? They were both damn smart, and that was what he hadn't ever been entirely comfortable with. It was a thing you didn't want to admit about the man you had settled on as the love of your life.

A few months before he vanished, she had shown him a journal article she'd written about planetary protection protocols, the plans to prevent the spread of Earth's microbes to other moons and planets during human space exploration. It was a piece of scholarship of which she had been immensely proud. He'd read it one snowy evening while she enjoyed a glass of wine and watched a home improvement show, doing her level best to leave him alone while he reviewed it.

"It's fine," he had said after finishing it.

"Anything else?"

"I said it's fine."

"That's it?"

"I mean, it's a bit derivative, but it's fine."

His words were hot knives to her chest. It hadn't been derivative. She had spent weeks researching this particular subject, ensuring that there were no other articles like it. Three other colleagues had read it and agreed with her; two told that they wished they had written it. She just wanted to share with Peter something she had been really happy with, and he had taken a big old dump on it. It was one of those moments she had never quite forgotten; even after he disappeared, sometimes the memory would slink in like a thief and she would hate herself for thinking it. What kind of grieving widow churned up her late husband's flaws? Wasn't he square with the house, all debts paid?

"I'm going," she said. "I don't know what else to tell you."

Maybe she hadn't known him as well as she thought she had. The old saying was that adversity did not make character; it revealed it. Adversity was peeling back layers of this man more quickly than she could keep up. No, maybe she hadn't known him well at all.

"No, you're not."

Everything had slowed down around her. The leaves fluttering in the trees, the gentle breeze brushing against her skin. Data was flowing in now, data that she needed to analyze quickly before it was rendered irrelevant. Peter was standing about ten feet away from her. The terrain sloped downward toward him slightly, giving her the high ground. To her left was a clearing of tall grasses, wispy and ghostly in the rising dawn.

Now.

She bolted.

"Hey!"

She cut hard through the grass, the fine blades susurrating against her legs as she powered away from Peter. At that moment, she had no idea if she would ever see him again because there was no way to know how this gambit was going to play out. Peter gave chase, but he was never much of a runner. His knees had always given him grief, and he was just one of these guys who wasn't made to run unless something was chasing him. Even then, it was a good bet he wouldn't make it far.

This plain continued for another mile or so, about eight minutes of hard running. She was thankful for the time she had spent in the pool over these last years, shaping her body and hardening her lungs. As her legs burned, crying out for a break, she came to the river. She hazarded a look over her shoulder; visibility wasn't great in the pre-dawn gloom, but she didn't see Peter. She followed the cut of the river east for a bit, back toward the general vicinity of the object, as best as she could remember. Still no sign of Peter, but she couldn't let her guard down. He was as smart as anyone as she'd ever known, which made his resentment toward her all the more baffling.

She was committed now, whether she liked it or not. Peter had forced her hand, and so she had chosen this path, the success of which was anything but guaranteed. For all she knew to the contrary, she was tilting at windmills. The odds were excellent that she would be dead soon. But that was fine, that was okay because she could not live with the knowledge that she hadn't even tried.

Dying would be better than giving up one more second away from Hugo and Miranda, away from Jack. Jack, sweet Jack, this good and decent man who had wanted her to pass on this trip not because he was afraid she was his intellectual superior but because he loved his wife and did not want anything to happen to her.

After a quick rest, she set out again. Dawn was breaking now, which was a double-edged sword. It would be easier for her to spot Peter, but the reverse would be true as well. She would have to be clever, stay out of sight. By mid-day, she had reached the center of the island. A stone bridge connecting two cliffsides lay ahead, above a series of jagged rocks awaiting anyone who missed a step on the bridge, shiny with spray from a fast-moving river below. The bridge itself was wide, about four feet across, although it did narrow in the middle, like an hourglass. It was there she would need to take extra care. But she had to get across this canyon, and there appeared to be no other way for miles in either direction.

The wind was blowing in toward her (*another thing to keep mind of, missy*), bringing with it the sound of the waves crashing on the beach to her east. Rising above her was a short cliff face; vines clung to it like a desperate lover. It was a lovely sight, one in which you could easily get lost. But there would never be happiness here. There would never be peace. Always, her thoughts would unspool across the ocean to the kids. That was why she could never stay. That was why she would have to die trying to get home.

Claire Hamilton was in no rush to die. She had always hoped people facing their own mortality were okay with dying. It bothered her to think about people being afraid of death. She had hoped that if and when she faced a moment like that, she would be okay with it. But she wasn't. Not by a long shot. She understood that those people probably were not okay with the end of their lives; it had been a stupid thing to think, a selfish thing to think, to protect herself from the truth. She would be afraid. She did not want to die.

A noise startled her.

Peter was at the edge of the bridge, holding a large stick. His eyes were wide and his skin was ashen. He did not look right in the head; he looked very much like a man who had nothing left to lose, nothing left at all, period. She didn't know how he had been able to track her down, but that point was moot. He was here.

"Peter, it's time to let this go."

"Do you remember when we went to that bed and breakfast on Catalina?" he asked.

She didn't reply right away.

"Do you remember?"

She recoiled at the anger in his voice. He was scaring her in a way that she hadn't thought possible.

"Yes."

"What did you say to me there?"

"I said lots of things," she said. "I'm a talker, as you liked to point out to everyone."

Her default attitude toward Peter had morphed into contempt. He didn't have the right to treat her this way. He didn't have the right to treat anyone this way, but especially her. She was in the same boat he was. The least he could do was afford her a little goddamn respect.

"Our last night there," he said. "Just before we went to sleep."

She racked her brain for the memory. It had been a lovely trip, a few months into the relationship, a game changer for them both. Funny that he had focused on a memory of another trip to an island. Catalina, about twenty miles southwest of Los Angeles, was smaller than the island on which she now stood but offered better amenities. They flew in Friday afternoon and left Sunday morning. That first night, they'd had dinner, taken cocktails on the patio, and enjoyed a roll in the hay before calling it a night. Saturday morning was spent exploring the island; they went zip lining and took a glass-bottom boat tour. The rest of the day was devoted to more bare-skinned extracurricular activities. They took room service for dinner; they ate in the plush resort robes.

It was on the flight home she realized she wanted to marry him, a revelation that hit her all at once. As the airplane leaped into the sky, Peter, a nervous flyer, gripped the armrests so hard his knuckles turned white. He didn't say anything or look at her; he just stared right at the seat in front of him, off to wherever he went to deal with the stress of air travel. She gently placed her hand over his, and she just knew. She didn't know how she knew, she just knew. A sense of peace washed over her, and for the first time in as long as she could remember she felt like she was where she was supposed to be. That was a big part of growing up, of becoming an adult. Figuring things out until you were where you were supposed to be.

"I don't remember," she said, and if she had, she wasn't sure she would have told him. She didn't want him to have the satisfaction.

"Sorry."

He shook his head disapprovingly even though she did not remember what she had said to him. That was a dumb thing people expected other people to know. People watched too many movies. Movies artificially inflated everyone's expectations about everything.

*Oh, this was how love is supposed to go with everyone remembering every little detail of every goddamn thing.*

*Oh, that's how cops are supposed to work, with the grizzled detective unable to follow the rules and having to turn in his badge and gun because he's a loose cannon.*

*And oh, this is how aliens make contact with humanity with massive spaceships and little gray men with big silvery reflective eyes and no mouths who communicate with humming or whatever.*

It was all bullshit.

"You're sorry," he said.

He unfurled his arms and shouted it to the heavens.

"She's sorry!" he bellowed. "Do you hear that, universe? Claire Hamilton is sorry!"

That estate lawyer had been right. Eventually, it all goes bad. Things deteriorated, things broke down, and if you didn't keep on top of them, if you didn't keep caulking and duct taping and taking out the trash, it would all go bad. That's what was happening here; it had all gone bad. It wasn't anyone's fault, not really. Bad luck. But it was the outcome that mattered, not the reasons for the outcome. It had all gone bad, here at the edge of the world.

"I am sorry, Peter," she said. "For so many things."

He was nodding his head, his lips were scrunched up and he was blinking rapidly. If he'd heard her or taken what she'd said to heart, there was no indication of it.

"You're coming back with me."

"No, honey," she said. "I'm not."

"I said you're coming back with me," he said, almost in a growl. He was breathing now, almost huffing, reminding her of the three little pigs. Peter's shoulders hitched up and down, and his fists clenched and unfurled over and over. There was a certain symmetry to his rage. They were in uncharted waters now. This was a side of him she had never seen, never even knew existed. Maybe she should have seen it.

"Yes, you goddamn well are," he said, taking a step toward her.

*Go, girl, you've got to go now.*

She turned and took a step onto the bridge. It was slick and much narrower than it had looked from afar. One step at a time. A stiff wind forced her to crouch down low. She gripped the edges of the bridge as she moved across it, reminding herself not to look down. Peter followed, negotiating the drop down. He was twenty feet behind her now, maybe fifteen.

Not only was it slick, it was longer than she thought. Sweat coated her body, making her feel even less secure. It narrowed significantly at the midpoint, until it was no wider than the distance between her shoulders, forcing her to her hands and knees. A quick peek over the side made her dizzy; it was a long way down to the rocks below.

Peter was on the bridge now, a look of rage in his eyes. Caution, meet wind, he was hauling ass now, quickly eating up the distance between them. She picked up the pace, her heart hammering away at her ribcage. Peter's heavy breathing grew louder behind her. At the three-quarter mark, her hand slipped, and her body listed to the left. She gasped as her weight shifted, the sudden momentum change threatening to roll her off; she clipped her right ankle to the far side to steady herself.

She let out a sigh of relief, but the slip had cost her valuable time. Peter had narrowed the gap even further and was just a few feet behind her. He was going to catch her; what he planned to do when he did was a question she did not want to learn the answer to. The idea he would hurt her was beyond everything, but he'd already assaulted her once, and who was to say he wasn't ready to escalate the conflict? He wasn't getting what he wanted, after all. That's whom he was – a little boy throwing a tantrum. They were going to die here on this stupid island because Peter was a child.

His hand grabbed her ankle tightly; she bucked hard against him, kicking herself free. She managed another few yards before he caught up to her once again. This time he reared up before bringing down his upper body on the backs of her legs. Pain ripped through her, but she ignored that, fighting to maintain purchase on the bridge.

"You can't go, you can't go, you can't go," he was saying over and over.

"Peter, stop, we're gonna fall."

He had worked his hands under her hips and was trying to pull her backward. She bucked her legs again, but this time he had leverage on her and she couldn't wriggle free. He got up on his knees and pulled her again; she lost her balance, and her chin banged against the stone. Her hands came loose and he pulled her back another stretch, back to the bridge's narrow midpoint. They were going to die.

Peter was crying and laughing now, the strange foreign sound of his sobs and giggles punctuating their struggle. The dam holding back all the emotions of preeminent scientist and world-renowned thinker Peter Abbott had broken and it was all coming loose.

"Happy, so happy," he said. "Happy, so happy."

Her arms were tiring and Peter seemed oblivious to the imminent danger they were in. Each time he popped up, she felt him lose his balance for a moment before steadying himself. It gave her an idea.

She let her body go slack for a moment, making it easier for him to pull her. He yanked hard, anticipating her resistance, but when she slid easily, he lost his grip on her, his momentum carrying him backward. Now a look of shock swept across his face as he seemed to become aware of what he had done. It unfolded in slow motion, his body rising up, his arms windmilling, looking for purchase.

He landed half on the bridge, half off, but he kept sliding, his weight pulling him off the edge. She swung around and grabbed his legs before he went over, but he was past the point of no return. He reached out and grabbed her hand in a desperate attempt to stop what could not be stopped.

He went over the edge, his hand still locked with Claire's, and she felt herself going as well. Death was now on the scene, this was really happening, Peter was going to fall and she was going to fall too. For a flash of a second, she had a vision of pulling him back up like you saw in the movies, but gravity was having none of it.

Their hands broke apart and Peter fell.

## 33

Claire was alone on the bridge, clinging to it with every muscle fiber, her body screaming and tearing and burning. The left side of her body hung over the edge, her legs clamped against either side of the slab of rock. The leg underneath the bridge began to weaken and her body slid as gravity demanded its penance. She slammed her arms down across the bridge's narrow throat and held on with all her might, hanging by a thread. The muscles in her biceps and shoulders burned; she was running out of time. She swung back and forth like a pendulum, once, then twice, enough to get her left leg back up onto the bridge. The relief was huge and immediate. Slowly, she swung her second leg up, and she was safe once more.

She held the bridge tightly, her eyes shut, gasping and struggling to catch her breath. Peter had fallen. He was gone. The whole reason she had come here. The thing she had hoped for all those years. She risked a look over the edge. She did not want to see, but she needed to. Peter lay flat on his back against the rocks, his right leg folded awkwardly underneath him. His arms were spread out on either side of him. Blood darkened the rocks and ground around him. Her mind went blank, empty. She stared down at what was left of her husband, of her old life. It wasn't supposed to go like this. It was supposed to be a good thing that he was still alive; it was supposed to be a good thing that she was here, that she could help him and unlock the mysteries of the object and be a hero and have funding for the rest of her natural life and have an elementary school named after her.

But there Peter lay, broken and quiet. His clock had stopped forever, and it didn't matter if that clock was here or back in the world. He was dead here and he would be dead there. He had deserved better than this. Now all he had ever been or would ever be was settled, there on those rocks below. It wasn't fair. It wasn't fair, the suffering that he'd had to endure, that she'd had to endure, and for what? For nothing. Nothing at all. That extraterrestrial object? It might as well have not even landed.

There were no tears on her face, to her surprise. Why wasn't she crying? Her husband had just died in front of her, and she didn't feel sad. She knew sad, she had a fucking Ph.D. in sad. Maybe you could only grieve someone once. Once you went through that door, there was no going back. After all, part of her was still grieving the initial loss; where was she going to fit a new layer of grief for the same loss?

Her skin prickled with heat as she lay there, staring down at Peter's body, recalling the lies they had been fed, by Murphy, Berry, Special Projects. Peter had been disposable, an object to be used in this game of theirs, from the initial plan to storm these beaches and control the narrative, to weaponize this discovery (of course, that's what they were going to do, that's what America did, that's what any country would have done given the opportunity), and then to abandon it, to play a little game of *If I Can't Have it, No One Can*, because that was something America did too. Of course he had snapped.

Now she would die here as well, alone, a victim of her own pride. Her children would be victims of their mother's pride. The sins of the mother visited upon the child. For a terrifyingly long moment, she considered how it would feel, to just hitch herself over the side, plunge to the rocks and end it right now. What difference did it make anymore? She was never getting off this island.

If hell was other people, as Sartre had once said, was the inverse also true? Was the absence of people also a hell? If she fell to her death and no one was around, would her body make a sound splattering against the rocks? See? She was already losing it. Five minutes of isolation and she was unraveling like a cheap sweater.

She could just let it all go, right here, and that would be that. No more suffering, no more worrying, no slow boat to insanity. She could fulfill the destiny that had been set in motion by Murphy; after all, she should have died in the explosion or when the sharks came for her or at Berry's hands, but she hadn't. Maybe she was supposed to die here, a good death that would keep them all safe from whatever was on this island.

*Record screech.*

*You dummy.*

*You're not that important.*

They would still come. They would come in canoes or on rafts, hell, they might hang-glide here because there would be no stopping the march of time, of progress, of discovery. How else did man measure time but through his accomplishments? Out there right now, advances were being made in every discipline, in mathematics, medicine, engineering, the sciences, weapons. That was how they measured time. Hell, they might already be here.

She was rationalizing now, justifying. It would be easy to let it go. Hard would be pulling herself to the far side of this stupid bridge and finding the object and seeing what there was to see; even harder would be realizing there was nothing to see and that all she could do was take her chances out on the water.

But she did not want to work hard. She was tired. This was more than she was capable of. Her willpower, her energy, her desire, these were finite resources, and she had expended all of them. She was a human being, and she had fought so hard to get this far, and *this far* wasn't far at all. Those other things, building a raft or figuring out the object, those lay beyond the sphere of her abilities. It was neither good nor bad. It simply was.

She needed time to think.

She climbed up onto her hands and knees and finished crossing the bridge, collapsing on the soft ground on its far side. Here she broke down and the tears did flow. She wept for the loss of all that she'd had. It was all gone now. Peter, Jack, the kids. The island had taken it all from her. NASA had taken it all from her. She wouldn't even be a footnote in history. Just some woman who had died during a research trip. The world had already forgotten her, had already moved on. That was the penalty for being here. The island held you down, chained you down while the world moved on.

Did Hugo still like his sandwiches with the crusts cut off, sliced diagonally? Did he still sleep with the stuffed Yoda? Just thinking about these things made her laugh while she cried because that was insanity talking, pride talking, vanity talking. Hugo was a grown man now, his mother long dead. Miranda. Did Miranda still think about her mother at all? Was she somber and morose, even more so than she had been before? Hugo would seek love to fill the hole in his heart; Miranda would go the other way, she feared. She would cap it off like a dead well because if nothing ever went into it, then nothing could be ripped out of it. A pragmatist, that child.

The weight of her isolation was crushing. It had been one thing to arrive here knowing that Peter was alive. Now she was alone. The solitude was almost sentient, talking to her, whispering to her.

The day was breaking hot and clear, the sunshine cooking her bare arms, red and tight with sunburn. She was tired and did not know when she would get another decent night's sleep, assuming she ever got another one at all. All she could do was keep moving. The quickest route to the object would be northwest, through dense jungle. She set off, dropping down into a valley before the terrain leveled off. Here the rainforest thickened rapidly, vines and branches weaving together to form a curtain of green. She pressed onward, focusing on the task at hand. Perhaps there would be time to grieve and reflect later, perhaps not. Getting lost in the jungle of her own mind would do nothing to help her negotiate the literal jungle before her. There was nothing she could do about Peter or time or the kids or Jack or Murphy right now. One step at a time.

An hour passed, then two. The jungle rose up and scratched and tore at her legs and arms and face with its branches and rocks and fallen logs, this morass of lush green and brown life everywhere around her. When she stopped at a spring to drink, she noticed she was bleeding from a dozen spots. Thin scratches and thick ones, some resembling small mouths leaking blood. Dirt and mud caked her arms, making her look more like she was part of the jungle itself than an interloper.

Several hours later, the trees thinned out, giving her a trail of sunlight to follow through the jungle, a solar carpet for her to traverse. As she came through, the tang of salt air tickled her nose; the wind had shifted, washing the island with an ocean breeze. On it, a strange sound caught her ears, freezing her. She held her breath, holding ramrod still as she tried to isolate the sound amid the island's ambient noise. Murmurs at first, her ears adjusting and sifting through the possibilities and permutations. Then she hit on a match.

Voices. Human voices. They appeared to be coming from the west, riding the wind, but it was difficult to tell how far away they were. From her vantage point, on a high ridge just beyond the river, she had a good look at the island's northeastern bulge. A mile or so away, she recognized a rock formation from her previous trip here, before Peter had coldcocked her. It took her a moment to orient herself; she was on the back side of the rocks, whereas before she had been in front of them. As she had told Peter, they would never stop trying to come here. The problem was that she didn't know where they were, and she could spend days trying to track them down. It was unlikely that they would leave their vessels unguarded. She could just turn herself over to them. They would take her back home, right? Even if they stuck her in some cell, that would be better than rotting away alone here.

A snap of a twig.

She turned and saw a machine gun pointed at her face.

## 34

The soldier was young. Claire wondered if he'd even been born when she arrived on the island. He was average height, fair-skinned, his red hair cropped close to his head. A thick strawberry beard cloaked the lower half of his face. He wore dark military fatigues.

"Who the hell are you?" he asked.

She didn't respond, still stunned by the man's presence.

"Hands on your head."

As she complied with his request, he placed two fingers in his mouth and whistled sharply. Moments later, three more soldiers joined him, two men and a woman, all dressed similarly, all armed. The woman stepped forward; she appeared to be the leader of this squad. A patch over her left breast identified her as Miller.

"She say anything?" Miller asked, glancing back toward the red-headed soldier.

"Negative."

"What's your name?" Miller asked, giving Claire a quick patdown for weapons.

"Claire Hamilton."

Miller's eyes widened briefly and then narrowed again.

"Let's get her back to camp."

The squad escorted Claire across the ridge, behind the rocks, toward the landing site. The soldiers did not engage with her. They had not restrained her, which was nice. It wasn't like she was going to try anything. At the next bend, a flurry of activity greeted them. A score of soldiers milled about, some standing guard, others taking samples from the soil and flora, others doing God knew what. As Claire passed through the hubbub, the other soldiers fell silent, stopped what they were doing, stared. She gathered that her presence on the island was a surprise. Half a dozen camouflage green tents sat in a large clearing. On the far side of the camp sat a larger tent, this one white in color.

Miller led Claire to the second biggest tent and pulled the flap aside, motioning for Claire to enter. A woman about Claire's age was seated at a plastic table, flipping through a thick binder. She looked up and did a double take when she saw Claire.

"Colonel Weiland, we just found this woman. Says her name is Claire Hamilton."

Weiland's eyebrows jumped at this.

"Thank you. If you'll excuse us, Captain Miller," the woman said.

"Ma'am," said Miller. After an exchange of salutes, Miller left, leaving Claire alone with the colonel.

Weiland closed the binder and got up from her seat. She was shorter than Claire by a good bit. Her black hair, streaked with gray, was pulled behind her head in a ponytail. She eyed Claire for a moment and then sighed loudly.

"Jesus, this place is fucking weird," Weiland said, rubbing her eyes with the thumb and forefinger of her left hand.

Claire nodded. It was weird.

"You're supposed to be dead," Weiland said gently.

"So you know who I am."

"I do," she replied. "Claire Hamilton. Born October 28, 1994, missing and presumed dead following the sinking of the *Kingsman*, November 6, 2039."

They stood silently for a while. Weiland crossed her arms across her chest and tapped a finger against her bicep.

"So I guess we should start from the beginning," Weiland said.

"Okay."

"Were you, in fact, on the *Kingsman*?"

"Yes."

"How did you make it here?"

"Dumb luck," she said. "The explosion threw me clear of the ship before it sank. I swam to shore."

Weiland's eyes widened.

"That ship was a mile out."

"I swam in college," she said. "It helped."

"Hmm," she said, her tone decidedly chilly. "Did you blow up the boat?"

"What?"

"Did you blow up the boat?"

Claire laughed out loud.

"Are you serious?"

"Very."

"No, I did not blow up the damn boat."

"Were you involved?"

"No," Clare said. "I came to find Peter."

"Right," she said. "Peter Abbott. Did you find him?"

"I did."

"Where is he?"

"Dead."

"Dead?"

"There was an accident," she said. "He fell from one of the cliffs."

"Is that right?"

"Yes."

"When did he die?"

"It happened this morning."

"This morning?"

"Yes."

"And you had nothing to do with the attack on the *Kingsman*?"

"I honestly had no idea."

"When did you find out?"

"Murphy - you know who Murphy is, right - he told me as it was happening."

"I see," Weiland said. "Ms. Hamilton, more than fifty people went down with *Kingsman*. Another forty died back at Ames."

Claire's stomach flipped. Her heart broke at the news of so many victims.

"Well, I guess we should cut to the chase," Weiland said.

"Meaning what?"

"How long do you think you've been here?"

"A few weeks. But I know it's been longer."

Weiland's eyes narrowed as she considered Claire's answer.

"So you know about the time issue?" Weiland asked.

"Yes."

"You know," Weiland said, "they told us about it, but seeing you here, it's hard to wrap your head around."

"What did they tell you about it?" Claire asked, curious about how much they knew.

"Scientists way smarter than me figured it out," she said.

"Something about the object bending time, affecting the island's place in the space-time continuum and whatnot."

"You don't seem terribly upset," Claire said.

"I'm here to do the job I was sent to do."

"You realize that every day here is almost a year back home."

Weiland shrugged her shoulders.

"It is what it is. All of us are single. No children, no immediate family. It was a mission requirement."

Just hearing the word *children* made her heart ache. She wanted to ask what year it was, but she was too afraid to. The temporal anomaly did not seem to faze the colonel. Just another fact to be cataloged for analysts to look at later.

"So how long has it been?"

Weiland scrunched up her mouth, considering Claire's question. It was going to be bad, Claire understood, she just wanted to know how bad.

"How long?" Claire asked. A strange calm had come over her. She wasn't nervous and she wasn't afraid. The time for that had come and gone. It was time to be a scientist. And what was the purpose of a scientist, after all, but to help humanity? She could do that. Maybe she would never make it home. She would never see her kids again. She could, however, make their lives and their kids' lives and their grandkids' lives better.

"You sure you're ready?"

"As ready as I will ever be."

"Forty-four years."

There it was. Four decades since the *Kingsman* had gone down. She was the freak now, the outcast. She remembered the sense of pity she had felt for Peter, the thought that his whole life had been thrown away on his island without his even realizing it. She supposed that was true for many people anyway, people who blinked and they were middle-aged and they had never started that business or written that book or taken that trip to Italy. She supposed it was true for everyone. Time just got away from you. If it got away from you and it felt like it had only been a minute, what difference did it make if it had been a minute or a month or a millennium?

"Why did it take so long?" she asked.

"Claire, did you hear what I said?" Weiland replied. "I wasn't even born when you got here."

"Yes, I heard."

"Are you okay?"

"No," she replied. "But losing my cool isn't going to help. I knew the clock was running. I knew my only chance was to make it to the object."

Weiland nodded sympathetically.

"Do you know what happened to my kids?"

"I'm sorry," she replied. "I don't."

Miranda and Hugo would be in their fifties now, past middle age, on the back side of their careers, parents of young adults, perhaps even grandparents. Claire would be nothing more than a memory to them. All she had feared from the moment that she'd discovered the anomaly's existence had come to pass. Had they lived happy lives? Had they found their passion, found their soulmates, traveled to beautiful places, seen magnificent works of art, tasted delicious foods? Or had it gone the other way, had things not worked out for them? Were there dreams still unfulfilled, left behind in the light of youth, not carried into the shadowy world of adulthood? Were their lives pockmarked with regret and pain and suffering like a cratered moon?

She hoped not.

She wondered if she would recognize them, if she would

see in their wizened faces the babies they had once been, now wrinkled with time. Would they recognize their mother, who would look exactly the same as the day she had kissed their heads, saw them off to the school bus and then exited their lives forever?

And Jack. Was he still alive? If so, he would be nearly ninety.

"And you're okay with being here?" Claire asked. "The instant you set foot on this island, you became what I am. You're no longer a passive observer."

"Like I said. That's why they sent us."

"I don't understand."

"Look, Claire, I'm just the tip of the spear," Weiland replied. She lit a cigarette with a match, took a long drag, exhaled a stream of smoke. "I'm not even sure I understand what I just told you. We're career soldiers. They told us the odds of us making it home were basically zero."

"I'm sorry," Claire said.

"Don't be sorry," she said. "This is the shit we live for. And if I do I make it back, I'll be a time traveler. I get to see the future. How fucking cool is that?"

Claire couldn't help but smile. It was true. When you were unburdened, you could do anything. She was a bit envious of Weiland, she had to admit. It all changed when you had kids; you stepped into a deprivation tank for half a decade, at least, where it went by quickly and slowly all at once and the world continued moving around you and you missed out on everything, on the news, on new movies and books and music and the world filled up with new and exciting things while you were distracted by the hundredth *why* of the day but then it stopped and you couldn't believe it had gone by so fast. It wasn't that different than being here on the island.

"So what do you know about the object?" Weiland asked.

"Very little."

"Is it hostile?"

"I don't know."

"Have you seen it?"

"Briefly."

"Any ideas?"

"Not many," Claire replied. "Could be a drone. A portal, some kind of doorway. I don't know. Why is it affecting time? Why only here? What's the point of it? Is it intentional or just a byproduct of the object being here? I have a ton of questions and precisely zero answers."

Weiland looked disappointed.

"Why did it take so long to get back here?" Claire asked again.

"The attack set the project back years," Weiland said. "Decades. Very few people knew about this place and all of them were killed in the attacks."

"All of them?"

"These were serious men, Claire," Weiland said. "They were hellbent on putting an end to this. They had a list of every single person who knew about the project and they killed every last one of them. Except you. The conspirators all killed themselves. Most of the records were lost as well. Just about all of them, in fact."

"So how did you find out about this place?"

"Dumb luck," Weiland said. "Dumb fucking luck. Few years ago, this lady finds an old diary written by her grand-father, a Jerome Layton. He died in the bombing."

Jerome had been there the day they told her.

"It sat in a drawer in his house for forty years," he said. "He confessed to everything. It was handwritten. Contained dates and events. From there, we were able to reconstruct the timeline, up until the moment the craft was detected on radar. It took years."

"What's your mandate here?" Claire asked.

"Simple. To get it off the island so we can study it. Whatever it takes. They're sending a team every day until we figure it out. Believe me, there are some motivated folks out there who want to get this thing back to the U.S. Hell, if we have to use ball bearings to roll it off the island, we will."

"Is it public yet?"

"Not yet, but you and I both know that won't last."

"You sure this is a good idea?"

"I'm not paid to think about whether something is a good idea," Weiland said.

It sure didn't seem like a good idea. This thing would wreak utter havoc on humanity. It literally broke time. It would transform the real estate within its reach into a fountain of youth. Who would get to go inside it? Why? The implications of the object being in a populated area were staggering. And that was assuming it behaved in the same way it did here. What if moving it changed it in some way?

The thought of a bunch of politicians and military commanders getting their hands on the object suddenly filled her with dread.

∽

SHE SLEPT ALONE IN A TENT.

Somewhere in that sliver of the night where good things rarely happened but bad things often did, she awoke to a warm shimmering light. She opened her eyes to a disc of light floating just above her midsection. There was something strangely familiar about it, opening a channel in her mind, deep in its recesses, but she could not quite connect it to any specific memory. It was like catching a scent of home, undeniably home, without exactly knowing why it was home. A combination of things, her mother's perfume combined with the tang of her father's pipe smoke that swirled together to forge an entirely new aroma.

The urge to touch it was strong, but she resisted for the moment. She wanted to understand it as a scientist, free of any emotional entanglement that might come from direct interaction with these kaleidoscopic contrails. Spoor of the anomaly, a byproduct that it generated. Did it have a specific purpose or was it more akin to a car's exhaust? Was it dangerous, either intentionally or otherwise? She held a hand up inches from the light but felt nothing. No heat or cold or any energy of any kind.

Part of her did not want to see. Even if it weren't real, seeing your fears in three dimensions made it feel real. Like you were bringing them about via a million different decisions, even by those decisions you believed were orchestrated to prevent that future. But she had to see. She had failed in her role as a mother and wife; she could not fail in her role as a scientist. She would have to endure whatever horrors this discovery saw fit to show her.

She got up and poked her head outside the tent, curious if the light had drawn any interest from the soldiers. The camp was quiet. In the distance, she spotted a soldier in front of the object standing guard, smoking a cigarette, the orange tip glowing in the darkness. Her tent remained dark from the outside. There was no indication of the light glowing inside. She ducked back inside the tent.

Her attention returned to the floating disc of light before her.

Frustration bubbled up inside her. Again, she was

working without a safety net here, deep in the realm of the unknown unknowns. There was no science on which she could hang her hat, this was more like magic, and it frightened her to her core. She didn't like things that could not be explained. And if she didn't like it, she could only imagine how the world at large might take it. America could barely handle its first black President without coming apart at the seams in the subsequent decade.

The disc measured about four feet across and hovered silently above the floor. It bore a deep orange-yellow color, the hues swirling together in a tone that reminded her of a frozen Creamsicle, a favorite treat from her youth. The Judge was not big on treats; he liked steak and he liked potatoes. Desserts were for weak-willed people. But once in a while, she would come home from school and there would be a box of Creamsicles in the freezer. The agreement was that if she finished her dinner and did all her homework, she could sit in his study and eat one while he worked, handwriting his opinions.

The disc's color gave her pause. Was it this same orange-yellow for everyone or just for her? Could the object read her thoughts and adjust its appearance accordingly, perhaps to make it more inviting? The extraterrestrial equivalent of a beat-up old van with the words *Free Candy* painted on the side. Another observation – the disc appeared to have no front or back or sides. It looked the same regardless of the angle at which she looked at it.

Actual contact.

She was ready to see now. She held a palm up to the disc, bringing it ever closer, her mind clear, her heart rate normal. Her hand touched the disc and everything went dark.

## 35

There was a falling sensation, like she was on a roller coaster through a darkened tunnel where up was down and inside was out. Then it stopped just as suddenly as it had started and when she opened her eyes, she was in a small crowded room. It was hazy, like an old pool hall, a permanent cloud of cigarette smoke hugging the ceiling.

There were a lot of other people in the room, actually, at least twenty, as many as thirty. Men, women, children, old and young, huddled together. Some had their eyes cast upward toward the ceiling while others huddled, crouched down, their hands covering their heads. Murmurs rippled across the room in a quiet wave. Under those, the sounds of whimpering and tears. It was warm and dank, the air ripe with the metallic stink of unwashed bodies, bad breath, stress, and fear. A single track of fluorescent lighting bathed the room in a strange blue hue.

A television mounted in the corner flickered to life; a chyron on the screen simply read *Please Stand By*. A crawl at the top of the screen read *Emergency Broadcast System*.

"How long since the last one?" someone asked.

"Forty minutes?"

"Forty-two minutes," a third voice, a woman, said.

"Is it safe to go out?"

"No."

"It could be."

"I'm going up," another woman said. "We need water."

This triggered an angry argument, voices climbing on top of one another until it was a messy cacophony of noise in which everyone was getting in their two cents but no one could hear a goddamn thing. Water was important, it was hard to dispute that. Yeah, water sounded like a good idea.

She wanted to see.

She had to see.

*Come on, Me.*

"I'll go," Claire was saying, but it wasn't Claire saying it. It was the Claire inside the room saying it.

"Follow me," a young woman was saying. She was tall and thin, her graying hair cropped close to her head.

Claire and six others fell in line behind the young woman as she carved a path through the room.

"I'm Frannie," the woman said.

"Claire."

"You hurt?"

"I don't think so."

The door on the far side of the room opened up into a dark stairwell. The air was thick with dust and floating detritus. Claire and the others exchanged glances before they started the climb up the steep stairs. She pressed her body against the wall, carefully negotiating each step. At the first landing, they came across a pile of rubble partially blocking their path. The air was thick with dust.

"Oh no," Frannie said.

"What?"

She pointed, drawing Claire's gaze to an arm protruding from a heavy pile of rubble. The arm was streaked with grime and blood and looked utterly pathetic.

"What happened?" Claire asked.

"Not sure," Frannie replied. "Good thing this place had a bomb shelter. It couldn't have been ten minutes from the time the alarms sounded?"

Claire did not reply.

There was an opening in the rubble just big enough for them to crawl through. Frannie went first; Claire and the others followed. It was a very tight fit, her hips snug against the edges of the gap in the rock. It was tight enough that for a moment she believed she was stuck. A twist of the hips set her free and she tumbled forward onto the far side of the landing.

Here the wall of the building had been sheared away, leaving behind a cross-section of the building's innards. Bits and pieces of concrete crumbled away from exposed rebar; wiring and cables fluttered in a warm breeze blowing across her skin. They were at ground level now, a parking lot stretched out before them. The cars lay scattered across the asphalt like a child's forgotten toys. The sky was a strange purple color, the clouds rushing from west to east, as though something was shoving them along.

She scanned the area, looking for a familiar landmark but coming up short. Virtually every structure had been damaged; most had been leveled. There were some familiar marquees. A Philips 76 globe. The remains of McDonald's golden arches. If the Claire she was hitching a ride on knew where they were, she wasn't letting on.

War.

She was looking at the ravages of war. War in the homeland. The one thing that no one ever imagined could happen here with the two protective oceans and the military and the undying belief in its own invincibility.

"Let's try that gas station," Frannie said.

They ventured clear of the building's remains, snaking around the cars and debris in a line. The area was deathly silent but for the sound of their footsteps crunching along the gravel and bits of glass that had been sprayed across the lot. A single string of stoplights hung limply from its post at the intersection, the light blinking green. The group paused at the intersection, looking both ways before crossing because some habits were ingrained in you, almost impossible to break.

As Claire stepped out onto the street, a siren began to sound again, that grating howl signifying an approaching maelstrom of death and misery. They froze where they stood, scanning the skies. Claire saw nothing at first but then in the distance, a flash of light, so bright it took her breath away. The light, which was everywhere and for an instant made everything seem alive, receded to a point far away; what looked like a bubble emerging from the ground narrowed as it climbed before widening at its throat into the scalloped edges of a mushroom cloud.

Then everything went dark.

When she opened her eyes again, she was back in the tent again. The disc was gone. She was breathing heavily, her body damp with sweat.

She lay back down on her bedroll.

What if it wasn't a dream?

What if it was a vision?

What if that was their fate?

The end. She had just gotten a little sneak peek at the end of all things. A metaphor for the miniature Claire-sized apocalypse she was currently living through. This was what Murphy and his cohorts had been afraid of. When word got out, it would change everything, back everyone into a corner while they jockeyed for the upper hand that would come with control of the object. It didn't even matter if anyone knew what to do with it. In the land of the blind, the one-eyed man would be king. She did not want to believe that the monolith would drive them to such a fate, but she was all too aware of the allure of ultimate power.

It never changed. From the days of scratching images of one tribe massacring another into cave walls through possessing the ability to end all life on earth at the touch of a few buttons, the quest for power had been the red thread tying thousands of generations together. That was how things would play out with the object. There was no doubt. It was embedded in their DNA to be this way, to lie, cheat, steal, obfuscate, commandeer, inveigle, hell, when the government did it, they even gave it a fancy name. Eminent domain. Any benevolence associated with the object would be subsumed at the altar of American exceptionalism. It was their nature.

She began to understand Murphy's state of mind when he had the gun in her face and *Kingsman* was listing in the waters of the Pacific. For twelve years, he had struggled to unlock the mystery while simultaneously trying to keep it quiet. He knew, as she now did, that if the secret ever got out, all bets would be off. The world's great fleets would steam here with their guns armed and their torpedo bays at the ready. Total nationalistic mayhem. It wouldn't take long before one captain miscalculated another's intention, and then the missiles would fly and before anyone had had time to take a breath, the things she had seen would become all too real.

Somewhere far from here were her grandchildren or perhaps her great-grandchildren, or maybe Hugo and Miranda had never had kids, but still there would be other children and grandchildren and they would want to grow up and live lives and fall in love and find their passions, and the very presence of this thing made it virtually impossible.

Incontrovertible proof of extraterrestrial life would upend human civilization. Just that one tiny detail would change everything; it would be like jamming a stick into the spokes of humanity's bicycle. People couldn't even agree on universal healthcare without coming unglued. This would push people over the edge. They would go to war, not because of any ideology or cause or even for oil, but because they would not know what else to do. They would go to war because they would be afraid.

Maybe if they, whoever they were, had landed here and brought offerings of peace and an *Encyclopedia Galactica* or maybe a blueprint on how to build a faster-than-light warp drive or perhaps a really good chili recipe, something perfectly spicy but not too spicy, then it would be different. But this was scary, the not knowing. And this wasn't the good kind of not knowing. As she'd gotten older, Claire had come to believe that whatever you wanted was often on the other side of fear. You quit that job and started your own business or you went and got that mole checked and removed or you told that person you loved them before it was too late. If your little diner went belly up or if the mole was malignant or if that woman replied "okay," in response to your declaration of love, well, the unknown instantly became known.

This was the bad kind of not knowing because it opened doorways that were incomprehensible.

That was when she understood what she had to do.

SHE POKED her head out of her tent and took a quick look around the camp. A soldier had taken a position across the way, sitting on a rock and smoking a cigarette. He wasn't guarding her so much as he was keeping an eye on her. After all, she wasn't going anywhere. She was unarmed, hungry, thirsty. She wouldn't dare jeopardize her seat on one of the pilot boats leaving this rock in a few days. He spotted her and acknowledged her with a nod of his chin. She gave him a wave.

She stepped out of the tent and approached the soldier. It was the redhead who'd found her.

"Bum one of those?" she asked, pointing toward his cigarette.

"Sure," he said, fishing one from his breast pocket.

"Not the healthiest habit," she said, as she leaned in for him to light her cigarette.

"We all have our vices."

"That we do."

"Ask you something?"

"Sure."

He took a long drag and then dropped the cigarette to the ground, crushing it with his boot, which annoyed her. This pristine land, now contaminated with their presence. Wrecked aircraft, discarded packaging from MREs, half-smoked cigarettes. It was what they did. Everywhere people went, they made everything a little worse. That's how it would go with the object. Whatever its purpose, whatever its function, they would find a way to make things worse with it. Of this she had no doubt.

"You really been here forty years?"

"It hasn't been forty years for me."

The soldier gave his head a hard shake and laughed.

"Makes no sense."

"You're right about that. And you're part of it now too, you know."

"Yeah," he said. "Yeah."

They smoked in silence for a bit; the nicotine made her head swim, left her feeling amped up.

"I need to use the bathroom," she said.

He shrugged.

"You gotta go, you gotta go," he replied. "You know where?"

Claire nodded.

"Don't get lost," he said. He winked at her in the moonlight spilling across the clearing.

"I'll do my best."

He opened a granola bar from his pocket and began to eat. She left him behind, a bit surprised he didn't hear her heart beating in her chest. The tents were quiet as she passed by them. A bit farther north, clear of the main camp, chatter peppered the night air.

Weiland's team had set up a curtain around the object, leaving one end open for access. A small spotlight illuminated the work area; it wasn't terribly bright, but it was enough to work by. Clearly, NASA had learned from its previous failures in delivering men and materiel to the island. Claire took cover behind a trio of boulders on the far end of the crash site, which gave her some cover and a half-lidded view behind the curtain.

There it was.

Black. The opposite of color. Just the very edge of it, a small cut from reality.

She glanced over her shoulder, an irrational bolt of terror that Peter had risen from the dead suddenly shooting through her. She crept to the center rock and found a gap that gave her a better vantage point. Weiland was inside the tent, her arms crossed against her chest, her hand covering her mouth. She leaned over and said something to the soldier next to her; the soldier shook his head.

Claire held her crouch, her mind empty. This was now her lengthiest view of the object. The lack of color was hypnotizing, demanding her constant attention. She just wanted to sit there and look at it. She wondered if the soldiers had made any progress. The look of puzzlement on Weiland's face suggested they had not. She stole another glance around her; she was still alone, but she was probably pushing her luck. A patrol would probably be along soon.

As she chewed on her options, the decision was made for her.

"Ms. Hamilton!"

She froze at the sound of her name.

"Why don't you join us down here?"

## 36

Sheepishly, Claire emerged from her hiding place and shuffled down toward the tent. Weiland didn't look angry; she appeared more bemused. Four other soldiers stood behind her, glancing at one another, smiles on their faces.

"Ms. Hamilton," she said, "my soldiers are the very best in the world. You're not going to be able to sneak up on anyone."

Claire flushed with embarrassment.

"I didn't mean to-"

"Don't sweat it," she said, turning back toward the tent. "So you wanna see it?"

Claire nodded, and Weiland motioned for her to follow. She took a deep breath as she ducked inside the tent. The object took up most of the tent's square footage, leaving only enough room to loop around its perimeter. She was close enough to touch it. It was unnerving to be this close to something that had been constructed by non-human hands. Claire did a lap around the object, slowly, drinking it in, committing every detail to memory. It absorbed the glow of the spotlight illuminating it; it was smooth and glassy but returned no reflection. The corners were seamless.

"No engines," Claire commented. "No doors, no hatches."

"None that we could find. Any thoughts on that?"

"They can generate thrust without combustion," she said. "Something we haven't even dreamed up yet."

"Like a warp drive."

"I guess," Claire replied, "but I wouldn't have the first clue how they built it. Can I touch it?"

Weiland motioned toward another soldier, who handed Claire a pair of heavy gloves.

"These are lead-lined gloves," Weiland said. "We didn't think it would be wise to make actual contact with the object."

Claire nodded and slipped on the gloves. She stepped forward, raising her palm to the surface of the object. Her mouth was dry and her hands trembled. Then she was touching it, she was actually touching it; she had made physical contact with an extraterrestrial civilization. Tears streamed down her cheeks as she pressed her hand against it. A warmth spread through her, like that third glass of wine hitting her just right.

Despite the danger the object posed, Claire could not help but feel a lightness, a joy that it had all been worth it, generations of study, of looking to the heavens, aiming directly at this moment. How badly she wanted it to be perfect, this union of humanity with all that lay beyond. How badly she wanted to know everything there was to know about it – who had built it, who had sent it, what it was made of, what it could do, where it had come from, why was it here, a million questions ripping through her like falling stars.

She struggled to shepherd her thoughts into a coherent group, but it wasn't easy.

*Focus.*

*Breathe.*

*Live in this moment.*

She zeroed in on the sensation of her palm against the object. It felt like nothing at all. If she wasn't looking at it with her own eyes, she wouldn't have believed she was touching anything at all, even when she pressed harder on it. She raised her other hand to the object and leaned into it like she was stretching after a workout.

"What the hell is this made of?" she asked, more rhetorically than anything.

"You're the scientist," replied Weiland.

"Have you tried moving it?"

"We can't even get it to budge."

Claire considered this. Why here? They were in one of the most remote places on Earth, one of the few places that the object's arrival would have drawn little attention, where it would have caused the least interruption of human activity. If they had picked this spot intentionally, that meant the sender had known enough about life on Earth to make that call. This was heartening. It meant they understood at some level the impact its arrival would have. If they had gone to all that trouble, that made it less likely that they had hostile intentions. For God's sake, if they had the power to build an object that could bend space-time and catapult it light-years across the universe, they certainly had the power to wipe out humanity.

She leaned in her face and took a hard sniff. Nothing. The object didn't smell like anything in particular. Just the fragrant humidity of the jungle around them. She glanced back at Weiland, who watched her curiously, with a bit of detached amusement.

"Any thoughts?"

"Not really," Claire replied.

"We have to get inside," Weiland said.

"I don't see any entry points."

"Then we're gonna have to make one."

Claire's stomach flipped.

"I'm not sure that's the best approach."

"Why not?"

That was the difference between civilians and the military. As Jack, an Army vet, had explained it, you negotiated until you couldn't, and then you went to war. Violence got you the answer where diplomacy could not. It might not be the answer you wanted, but it ended the status quo, which had been unacceptable because why else would you have entered negotiations otherwise? That was where Weiland was. The current state of affairs could not stand. She thought about Murphy again, about how haunted he looked at the end. He seemed relieved that it was over.

"We don't know what will happen," Claire said. "There is no precedent for this. For all we know, the object will defend itself."

"Defend itself? How? It's been here for years."

"I don't know, but do you really want to find out? What if the object itself is sentient? An artificial intelligence. Maybe the craft itself is the life form."

"I've got my orders," she said. "We're busting in at daybreak. The next team will be here soon."

"Wait a minute," Claire said. "Let's take a little time to think on it."

"Time is a commodity we do not have."

Claire's face tightened with frustration and her head

began to hurt. She detested these kinds of arguments, where the two sides weren't even arguing the same issue let alone two sides of the same issue. To Weiland, the possibility of a hostile response was simply a variable to prepare for, not something to avoid. To be sure, it was an obstacle in the path to the objective. Nothing more.

"That doesn't even make any goddamn sense," Claire said. "Even if it doesn't retaliate, we might destroy it. We might lose the most important discovery in human history."

"We've lost dozens of people here," Weiland replied angrily. "It's been here for years and we don't know a goddamn thing about it. Maybe it's time to think outside the box, if you will pardon the pun."

Just then the jungle night was peppered by the sound of gunfire, cutting the conversation short. A series of screams and a second round of gunfire followed. Weiland and her troops shifted into battle mode, immediately bringing their weapons to the ready.

"Miller, report!" Weiland barked into a communicator affixed to her shoulder.

"Under attack," came a reply over a heavy report of automatic weapons. "Unknown subjects, coming from the east."

"Fuck," Weiland said. "Set up a perimeter."

"Already on it."

"What's happening?" Claire asked.

"Shut up," Weiland snapped.

"Tell me what's happening," Claire shouted.

"Chinese or Russians, probably."

"So it's out," Claire said.

"It would appear that way."

A boom echoed across the island.

"Mortar fire," Weiland said.

She raised a clenched fist, then motioned with two

fingers to her left and to her right. The quartet of soldiers exited the tent at her direction and disappeared into the night.

"Shit," Weiland muttered. "I really thought we'd have a little more time."

Once again, the fragile status quo of Claire's life had shattered, changed in a manner that defied comprehension. She was at the mercy of mysterious forces that would determine the course of whatever life she had left. This bothered her at a deep level, down in the place where her gut lived with her intuition and her instinct.

"What are we gonna do?"

"You're not gonna do anything," Weiland said. "We're gonna take care of these fuckers and blow this thing open."

Claire pressed a hand against the object, ruminating on the ruin this relic had brought all of them. That the senders may not have intended to generate so much chaos was irrelevant. When someone built a house, they didn't necessarily mean to obliterate the anthills dotting the site.

"Miller!" Weiland was back on her communicator. "Send me six guys to cover the object."

Seconds ticked by with no reply from Miller.

"Miller! Anyone?"

Claire glanced at Weiland as she listened to static on the open channel. A second boom rocked the island, drawing Claire's eyes upward, but the night sky was empty.

"Dammit!" Weiland barked at Claire. "You stay here!"

Weiland disappeared into the night to join the fray, the colonel's warning fresh in Claire's ears. To stay here was not who Claire Hamilton was; Claire didn't get this far in life by staying behind. She made her way outside the tent and darted quickly to the three rocks she'd hidden behind, giving her a look down at the camp. The gunfire had not

abated. Tongues of flame erupting from the soldiers' automatic weapons licked the night air. In the spill of moonlight,
she could see a number of bodies dotting the campsite. It
was utter chaos. The pitched battle reached a crescendo, an
overwhelming symphony of staccato gunfire, pain, misery,
screaming. Then just as quickly as it reached its peak, the
battle began to die, as all things did. Even a dance of death
was a dance, one with an endpoint. A large group of soldiers
swarmed the camp; they weren't speaking English, but they
were too far away for Claire to identify their language.

A flicker of movement on the edge of the camp caught
her eye. A small squad was moving her way. It was about
twenty yards back to the tent. She could make it if she ran,
use the object for cover. She considered just making a break
for the woods, but there was too much open ground. If they
spotted her, there was a good chance they would cut her
down before she made it. Too risky.

She broke for the tent, sprinting as fast as her exhausted
legs would carry her, and took cover behind the object.
Gasping from her run, she struggled to catch her breath.
Weiland was probably dead. Her whole team was probably
dead.

Outside, the sound of footsteps crunching on the dry
grass and gravel.

"We have you surrounded," a voice said in heavily
accented English. Maybe Russian. Possibly German. "Lower
your weapons and step outside."

Claire's heart sank. It was over. She placed her hand against
the object and closed her eyes. If they were lucky, the fallout
from humanity's intersection with another civilization would
be minimal. She wanted to believe that, she really did. She
wanted to believe that it would unite them in a way nothing

else had because they would know that they were not alone in the universe. All their petty differences, blah, blah, blah, and she was not buying it at all. For all their progress, for all their advancement, they were still the same flawed species, scared of their own shadows. Humanity's biggest weakness had always been fear of the Other. Fear of blacks, of Muslims, of Asians, of women, of gays, of children, of the elderly. Of everyone.

Eventually, it all went bad.

"I'm coming out," she said. "I'm unarmed."

She stepped outside, squinting in the harsh glow of the spotlight. A dozen soldiers arrayed in a semi-circle surrounded the opening of the tent.

"You are not a soldier," the leader said. He wore a black uniform. A small German flag patch was sewn on the breast pocket of his shirt.

"I'm a scientist."

"Excellent!" the soldier said. "What is it?"

"I have no idea," Claire replied. "That's the truth."

The soldier glanced back at his troops.

"Not a very good scientist then, are you?"

"No," Claire replied. "I guess not."

"That is unfortunate," the soldier said.

Something in the tone of his voice chilled Claire to her core; she turned and bolted for the tent as he drew a pistol from a hidden holster. She did not know if she had moved quickly enough, and hell, maybe death would be better than being trapped in this temporal netherworld, living as a ghost in the machine. She ran to the back corner of the tent and pressed her body up against the object, suddenly realizing the comical futility of her escape attempt. They would be on her in within a few seconds, and the soldier would finish her off.

Instead of years or even months, her life could now be measured in seconds.

She closed her eyes and pictured Hugo and Miranda as she had last seen them, asleep in their beds, protected by the innocence of childhood and an army of stuffed animals, not yet burdened and traumatized by the disappearance of their mother, everything in their lives in perfect order. This made her happy, even here at the end.

As the first soldier rounded the corner, she felt a warmth at her back. There was something odd about the man's movement, something precise and languid, that confused her. He fired his pistol directly at her, but it was like she was in a dream. The gun hitched slowly in the soldier's hands like a wave. Even stranger: she could see the bullets exiting the barrel of the gun; one at a time, the Glock spit them into being. She leaned forward, amazed by the phenomenon, but when she did, the effect disappeared and everything was fast again. Terrified that she might catch a stray round, she slammed back up against the object, which brought everything back to a near standstill. That's when it hit her; her proximity to the object affected her perception of time beyond it. She watched raptly as the soldier moved toward her. He saw her, but he did not appear to understand that they were perceiving time in two different ways. He fired directly at her; it unfolded in slow motion, the rounds from his weapon all but floating toward her.

The warmth at her back intensified to the point of being uncomfortable, almost painful.Just as she was about to cry out, the heat dissipated and then she was falling, falling, falling.

## 37

Claire's eyes opened.

It was so deathly quiet that she could hear her eyelids separating, like a piece of paper tearing slowly. She could not see anything. She waited a minute and then two, hoping her eyes would adjust and draw in some light. But there was no light to be had, not even the tiniest flicker. She did not know where she was, to the extent that she was anywhere at all. She assumed she was now inside the craft – *first person ever, Claire, not bad*, an achievement that might draw an approving nod from her father – but she wasn't entirely sure about that.

A voice in her head startled her, repeating a sound over and over again. Usually one syllable, sometimes two, always unintelligible. The voice was pleasant enough, perhaps female, but she wasn't certain. She pressed a hand against her chest, which reassured her that she was indeed here, wherever *here* was. It felt like she was standing up but there was no way to know; she crouched down to touch the ground, but there was nothing to touch. The voice continued cycling, gibberish mostly, although every now and again, a hint of familiarity bled into the metronomic oratory.

"Hello?" she finally said aloud.

Her own voice echoed back toward her.

*Hello, hello, hello, hello, hello, hello*

The echo continued, but her voice was replaced by the one she had heard previously, which turned her *hello* into a mantra.

*Hello, hello, hello, hello, hello, hello*

Claire was finding it hard to breathe. They were communicating with her, and she didn't have the first damn clue what to say to them. She froze, afraid that any movement she made might be interpreted as hostile. Just her luck to be the final nail in humanity's coffin.

"I'm Claire," she said hesitantly.

*Claire Claire Claire Claire Claire Claire*

She sighed with relief. It was unclear if they understood what she was saying or if they were simply repeating the sounds she was making. In fact, this could be nothing more than a sound studio of some kind. Her name repeated on a loop; after a few minutes, she began to hate the sound of her name. It was a dumb name, the worst name in the history of names, how had she navigated the world for nearly half a century with such a dumb name?

Anything to stop it.

"What do you want?"

It was such a silly question, but she could not think of another one to ask. It seemed so pedestrian, something straight out of a straight-to-cable science-fiction movie premiering at two in the morning. Now she understood why it felt silly. Because they didn't know. They didn't know anything about anything and so they wrote stupid movies and silly books to help ground themselves regarding a truth that was beyond their comprehension.

The cliched stories weren't silly.

They were.

*Want want want want want want*

To make it worse, her question was not acknowledged. The word *want* continued repeating on a loop. She worried his was how she would spend the rest of her life, trapped in this pitch-black netherworld listening to random words *ad nauseam* until she experienced a psychotic break and forgot who she was, where she was or that she simply *was*.

"Why are you here?"

*Here here here here here here here here*

She chuckled softly. At least it was predictable.

She decided to move. A hesitant step, and then another, and then a third. Slowly, she extended her arms outward, futilely looking for purchase. The scientist in her took over, collecting data, storing it, waiting for an opportunity to apply it in some way. The more information she could collect, the better the odds of figuring out where she was and what she could do.

It was possible that she was, in fact, dead, but she didn't think so. Her heart was still beating and she was afraid, hell, she was sweating and her deodorant had long since failed. As she picked her way through the darkness, it occurred to her that she had already covered more ground than should have been possible, given the exterior dimensions of the object. That was instructive, certainly, but of what, she was not sure. Was she still on the island, or was she somewhere else?

It was maddening.

Never had she felt so dumb, so powerless, so insignificant. At the doorstep of a sea change in their comprehension of the universe, and she didn't even know what the door looked like let alone how to open it. The temporal price she was paying for it was almost more than she could bear. If time was moving even more slowly in here than on the island, how much more had been lost off the island? Centuries? Millennia? Murphy had been right, even if the means had not justified the end. They were not ready. They'd been better off before this thing had landed. They hadn't earned it yet. At least her generation had not.

She walked for a long time in the dark, the voice repeating the word *here* over and over; at some point, it had become white noise.

*Here here here here here here here here*

The edges of a plan began to form like a casserole starting to set. The object's most profound impact on Earth had been its effect on time. It could slow down time, as though time was a tangible thing. But scientists had always treated it as the backdrop against which everything else operated rather than as its own tangible dimension. Time was the canvas, not the paint in the artist's palette. It was treated as a constant because, as best as they understood, it was a constant.

"Time," she said.

*Time time time time time time time time*

A sudden flash blinded her; she did not know if the light was particularly bright or if it was because she'd been in the dark so long. Her pupils constricted like frightened turtles withdrawing into their shells and when she could see again, she was surrounded by a veritable sea of doorways, stretching away as far as the eye could see. Each blink of her eyelids brought more doorways, more and more stretching away to forever.

*Door door door door door door door door door*

Had she said the word door?

No. No, she had not. Her pulse quickened and her heart was in her throat. They were communicating with her now. There were so many doorways that they blurred together, left her feeling queasy. She directed her attention to the one closest to her. It was red and wooden and a large brass knocker adorned its center; there was something strangely familiar about it. Then it hit her. It was the door to her home back in Seattle, with Jack and the kids. It was identical, down to the worn-down knob on the knocker.

Then she remembered. She had merely *thought* the word "door."

This was for her.

And it terrified her.

She checked either side of the Seattle door; those doors were identical to each other, but not to the Seattle one. Then a second flash of recognition illuminated her mind like a bolt of lightning. It was the door to her childhood home in El Paso. A wider view confirmed the same for the other doors. One Seattle door and countless doors to her childhood home. A memory of the day she left for college began to play, walking through those hallways and rooms for the last time, her little white Toyota packed and ready to go. Her father had hugged her in his study but had not come outside to see her off. All the doors save one matched the door she had exited on her way to her life as a scientist, on her way to this island.

Her body trembled as she drew near the Seattle door. She twisted the knob and gently shoved it open, fairly certain what she would see behind it. It opened on the island, right where she had entered the object. A group of soldiers, milling about, looking for her. Only a few seconds of island time had elapsed since she had entered the craft.

She could step through it and be right back where she started. Whether she could get back on this side of the doorway was another matter.

She left the door open and stepped over to the one on its left. When she twisted the knob, the door held fast. She jiggled it a few times, turning the knob one way and then the other, but the door would not budge. Then she understood.

She had to choose.

The Seattle door was the way out, the way back to the world as it was. These other doors? Who the hell knew? But before she could open them, the Seattle door had to be closed, and she feared that once she closed it, it would not open again. This was their offer. She had to choose without even knowing what was behind the other doors.

But the other doors. What lay behind them? What were they trying to show her? Clearly, they were presenting themselves in a manner that she alone could understand. Why so many El Paso doors? Why only one Seattle door? Frustration bubbled up inside her as she stood there with this impossible choice. What was this? First contact with an alien civilization and they had turned it into a parlor game. Why? To what end? Why not just show them everything? They could handle it. She could handle it.

She needed to see what was behind the other doors. Perhaps it was a puzzle for her to solve. Her heart racing, she pushed the Seattle door closed. Then she stepped up to the El Paso door on the left, gingerly placing her hand on the knob. It was worn and warm, the way it felt at the end of a Texas summer day. She turned the knob, barely able to breathe. The latch disengaged and the door opened slowly.

On the other side of the door was her street in Seattle. It looked to be an ordinary day in the neighborhood, but there was something strangely familiar about this particular scene. Then it hit her. A black Suburban sat at the curb. It was the day Murphy and Berry had come to tell her that Peter was still alive. A chill ran through her as she remembered the very profound sense of déjà vu that had washed through her that morning. She did not know what that meant, and quite frankly, she was too frightened to find out. Did she have déjà vu that morning because she had already gone through this once before? If she had, what had she chosen?

These beings had mastered time. They had made it a tangible thing they could touch and manipulate like a carpenter whittling a piece of wood. The full spread, discrete moments of her life that she could drop in on and redo. Time had stopped moving here, inside the object. When that happened, you could put your hands on it, shape it to your liking. She slammed the door as hard as she could, the sound echoing through the alien parlor.

It was even worse than Murphy had feared. They would go to war over a technology they would never be able to understand or use responsibly. She did not want to see what lay behind the other doors. Little slices of pie, served up for her amusement. She did not want to go through this again. But she would. Perhaps this time she would feel déjà vu when Murphy told her that Peter was still alive, but it wouldn't matter. The allure of the trip to the island would be too great, and once again, she would kiss those sleeping kids on their sweaty sweet-smelling foreheads and leave them again.

She had to destroy it.

"No," she said.

*No no no no no no no no no no*

Look, she just wasn't interested, and she couldn't accept

such extravagant gifts from someone she just met. She really wasn't that kind of girl. And you know what?

*It's not me, it's you.*

*You you you you you you you you*

They can't be like a normal extraterrestrial species, maybe land in a cornfield in Iowa, bring a translator or something? No, no, they have to send down this space-time blender that put all of them in danger. Maybe that was what they wanted. They didn't even know why it was here. They had the right to say no.

*That just wasn't going to work, no sir, no ma'am, thank you and goodnight.*

*Night night night night night night night night night night night night night*

Bet they never imagined a puny Earthling rejecting their little gift. It filled her with pride, standing here for the rest of the planet, for Hugo and Miranda and their children and their children's children.

*Kiss my ass!*

*Ass ass ass ass ass ass ass ass ass ass ass ass ass ass ass ass*

But how? How could she destroy something she didn't even understand? She knew nothing about its makeup, about its composition, about its weaknesses (assuming it had any that she could exploit), or even where the hell they were.

She couldn't.

That was the answer.

She couldn't destroy this object any more than that mole could stop the bulldozer from tearing up its home. Trying to do so might invite even more ruin.

"What happens if I go through that one?" she asked aloud, pointing at the Seattle door.

*One one one one one one one one one one one one*

She started to fire off a snarky reply but thought better of it.

Madness. Humanity was stuck with this thing, and there was nothing she could do about it. Of course, some would insist that this was their future, their manifest destiny, just the first step in humanity's march to the edges of the universe. They would call her a coward, a fool, a bitch, how dare she speak for the rest of them, how dare she turn her back on this stunning discovery. The thing was, they hadn't earned it. It had literally fallen in their lap. Compare that to every one of their scientific discoveries. Each built on the previous one, like bricks in a wall that they themselves had built with their own understanding and comprehension.

"We're not ready," she said.

*Ready ready ready ready ready ready*

*Shut up, you stupid aliens. Shut up, shut up, shut up.*

*Up up up up up up up up up up up*

*Claire, it's just a damn simulation.*

There was no door to the home she shared with Jack and the twins, there was no door to her childhood home. This was merely the manifestation of whatever it was they wanted to show her. Great, super, the problem was that she didn't understand the why any more than the proverbial mole understood.

Her hand drifted to the locket still laying flat against her skin. She unhooked the clasp and opened it to the thumbnail photograph of Peter. The picture was taken on a day hike on Mount Rainier, a lovely summer day not long after they were married. She'd snapped it when he wasn't looking, a profile shot of him looking out over a valley. His face was smooth and still in the grips of a smile; she did not know if she had just said something funny or if he had thought of something that tickled his fancy.

For more than a decade, this locket had hung from her neck like a talisman. A benign connection to her past. A reminder not to take anything or anyone for granted. That was what she had told herself. But it had been so much more than that. It was an anthem to a time in her life that was gone forever. Even now, surrounded by the twins and Jack, she would catch herself thinking about how much easier life might have been if Peter hadn't disappeared. Excused from years of grief and suffering. Sure, they said that loss made you stronger, the way lifting weights tore muscle and it grew back stronger. But it wasn't like that, not really. When something broke you, you were never quite the same again. You could put the pieces back in the same order, but there would always be scars. Always. And for what? What good did they do you if you didn't change, if you let the scars rather than the pieces define you? It made her angry to think about it, about the pain, the grief, the loss that had defined her life.

A hard tug broke the chain free from her neck for the first time since she had put it on twelve years ago. She tightly squeezed the pendant in her hand, the ends of the chain dangling free like broken veins, hard enough she could feel its edges digging into the flesh of her palm. It was a cheap throwaway piece she'd bought at a mall kiosk, using a digital photo to set in this twenty-dollar locket. She didn't even know why she'd been at the mall that day, during one of those spasms of grief in the weeks after Peter vanished that was capable of landing her anywhere. The little placard mounted to the kiosk had drawn her interest and just like that, she was sharing the digital photograph with the teenaged kid with the pentagram tattoo peeking out from his undershirt. She'd never shown the locket to anyone, and as the years rolled by, she only grew more embarrassed by and protective of it, which fueled her resolve to keep it secret; neither Jack nor the kids had ever seen the inside of it.

She opened the Seattle door once more, the necklace still clenched in her fist. Then she flung it through the door, toward the soldiers, watching as it spun its way across the extraterrestrial plane, the ends fluttering like long hair caught in a breeze. As it crossed the threshold, she realized she had not given any thought to the ramifications of such a maneuver, but before she had time to consider it further, everything blinked out.

SHE HIT THE GROUND HARD, her shoulder breaking her fall. The force of the impact took her breath away but filled her with a shot of adrenaline. Instantly, she was up, her legs bent in a defensive crouch, her fists up and ready to go. The tent had collapsed, crumpled up like the bedcovers of a seventh-grade boy who'd woken up late and was running to the bus stop. All four posts had been ripped out of their holes.

The object was gone.

"Jesus," she muttered, craning her neck toward an empty sky above her.

A group of soldiers stood before her dumbfounded. The leader's head darted around like a dog's whose master had hidden a tennis ball. There was no sign of the object. If it had taken off, it had done so silently and instantly, without any combustible thrust. Just like that, it was over. A rejection of their offer.

"What have you done?" he asked, his face tilted upward, scanning the skies. Then he barked at his subordinates in

German; the soldiers broke off into squadrons of four and scampered away.

"I don't know."

But she did know. She had kept them safe. She was disappointed that it had come to this. Never in a million years did she ever think she would make such a decision. Once upon a time, Claire Hamilton would have walked into a black hole just because she could. She would not have stopped to consider the wisdom of such a decision because the wisdom was in the decision itself.

It was, however, a necessary decision. Granted, she may have just signed her own death warrant, and at best, would probably spend the rest of her life in a prison or laboratory, just as Peter had warned her. That would be just fine. It may even have been the wrong decision. Who was she to speak for all of them?

Ask Eugene Murphy.

He'd been the one to send her.

Someone had to speak for them. Someone had to say that they were not ready. And she had been the one to speak. There was a reason you didn't let a first-year medical student perform open-heart surgery. He hadn't earned that right yet; humanity hadn't earned the right to commune with these visitors. Ironic that she had spoken with the voice of Eugene and his fellow saboteurs. It didn't make what they had done right. Maybe their alien benefactors were equally unprepared. Shouldn't they have done their due diligence? Wasn't it their responsibility to make sure that they were ready for this gift?

Indeed. This was the right call.

It had to be.

They escorted Claire back down to the American campsite, dotted with the bodies of Weiland's team. A search of the camp evolved into a salvage operation as the soldiers secured all the provisions, water, MREs, desalinization pills, weapons, medications. The solar-powered lights illuminating the camp continued shining, bathing the tents and the dead alike in a strange salty white glow.

It was time to go.

They hiked through the predawn gloom. As the night wore on, the smell of the salt air intensified, growing stronger until it tickled Claire's nose. She tried not to think about the object or where it had gone or why it had disappeared. Perhaps it was that simple. They had made an offer, and she had rejected it. She had rejected it by disposing of the locket. If they could read her thoughts, then they would understand the power the locket held over her. By letting it go, she was rejecting the gift of time, the gift of time as a physical construct to be shaped and manipulated.

Dawn was breaking as they made it to the beach. The landing team's pilot boats lay where they had beached them. There would be another ship along shortly as they continued their assembly line of recovery efforts. They would not stop. They were like children in a way, all of them, insisting on that which they could not have. And the crew aboard the next ship would be very disappointed with what they found.

She would tell them what she had done. They could do whatever they wanted to her; it wouldn't matter. She had kept them all safe.

The ocean was calm on this cloudless day.

She didn't have to wait long.

≈

≈

## ABOUT THE AUTHOR

David lives in Richmond, Virginia, where he works as a novelist and attorney. His first novel, *The Jackpot*, was a No. 1 Legal Thriller on Amazon in 2012 and was later published in Bulgaria. His second book, *The Immune*, was published in 2015 in serial format and made it to the top of Amazon's bestseller list for post-apocalyptic novels. *The Living*, a sequel to *The Immune*, followed in 2017.

He is the writer and creator of a series of popular animated films, including *So You Want to Go to Law School*, which were featured in the *Washington Post*, the *Wall Street Journal*, and on CNN. They have been viewed nearly 3 million times and are always available on YouTube.

Email him at dwkazzie@gmail.com

Made in the USA
Coppell, TX
06 October 2020